He closed his eyes, leaned his head against the wall. "It's—Oliver—the name on my birth certificate. Oliver Shaw."

"Oliver." She repeated it again, softer, her voice caressing his name. "Thank you for telling me."

He shrugged. "Yeah, well..."

Why had he told her? What happened to keeping it impersonal? To not getting involved? Too late for that. He'd let her get under his skin in the space of a few short minutes and there was no turning back.

He was linked with her. If The Father found out...

Oliver shuddered, drawing the worn fabric of his shirt closer around him. "We shouldn't be talking."

She didn't say anything for a long time and he figured she'd gotten his not-so-subtle hint. He crouched to his feet, flattened his palms on the wall and prepared to move back to the shadowy corner of his cell where he could write in his journal and visit his beachfront home in his head.

"Oliver?"

He leaned his forehead against the pitted metal, drinking in the lovely cadence of her voice. "Yeah?"

"I need you to help me find a way out of here."

**Available from Cynthia Justlin
and Carina Press**

Edge of Light

CYNTHIA JUSTLIN

EDGE OF LIGHT

CARINA
PRESS™

CARINA PRESS™

ISBN-13: 978-0-373-00226-9

EDGE OF LIGHT

Recycling programs
for this product may
not exist in your area.

Dear Reader,

When Oliver Shaw, the hero in *Edge of Light,* first burst from my imagination and onto the page in the form of a dark and gritty prologue, I became consumed with the need to tell his story. He was so raw and broken in that moment, a man on the verge of completely giving up. Enter Jocelyn Hewitt, a woman who'd built her entire life on a sliver of hope that she'd one day uncover the truth in her dad's mysterious disappearance. Jocelyn doesn't know the definition of defeat, and as she slowly coaxes Oliver back into the light, she shows him that life isn't just something to survive. It's meant to be *lived.*

Three-quarters of the way into the writing of this book I was diagnosed with stage IV colon cancer. Without a doubt, it was the darkest moment of my life. I was an extremely healthy thirty-six-year-old mother of two, and my body had decided to turn against me. I felt imprisoned—by circumstances, by fear, by the complete unfairness of a six-inch tumor suddenly taking control of my life. In short, I felt an awful lot like Oliver. And I finally understood my desperate compulsion to write his book had come from the deep, dark place inside me that knew I'd soon need to learn how to fight for my own life.

The thing is, life isn't always sunshine and roses. Sometimes it's downright painful and scary. But there's always beauty to be found if we choose to look for it as Jocelyn does. The day I typed *the end* on *Edge of Light* was the day I realized that while my future may have been uncertain, I could not let cancer rob me of all my joy and optimism. Instead, I chose to cling fiercely to that little sliver of light. I leaned on God and said a whole lot of prayer through six months of chemo and a second surgery. Now, as I write this, I am approaching an amazing milestone—three years completely cancer-free.

For those of you battling your own darkness, no matter what form that may take, this one's for you. Know that the light is never too far out of reach.

I love hearing from readers! Please visit me at www.cynthiajustlin.com, where you can drop me a note, subscribe to my newsletter and connect with me via Facebook and Twitter.

Cynthia Justlin

EDGE OF LIGHT

PROLOGUE

YOU'RE STILL ALIVE.

The taunt hissed across Oliver Shaw's foggy brain, bringing with it an unwanted sense of awareness. Cold concrete pressed against his cheek. A bead of moisture leaked out from under his eyelids, loosening the dried blood that had crusted there. His stomach heaved. He sucked in a breath and choked on bile and the stench of excrement and putrid food.

Open your eyes, you gutless coward.

He gritted his teeth and dragged his eyelids open. A sliver of light speared into his retina, blinding him with a sharp ache to the back of his skull.

The light bulb.

That single fucking bulb. Always on. Always grounding him in its glaring reality. He couldn't take another day in this hellhole.

He shifted, biting down on his lip and letting the metallic taste of his blood fill his mouth. Cement scraped his bruised stomach. The movement set fire to the hundreds of cuts across his back. He stiffened and pulled a hiss through his teeth, concentrating on the tracks of dirt and dried blood covering his arms while he waited for the burning to dial down to an acute throb.

His kidneys throbbed from dehydration and repeated kicks to his lower back. A chunk of his long, matted black hair fell into his eyes. He tried to brush it aside, but his tingling hands refused to work properly.

He flexed his fingers against the tattered fabric of his cast-aside shirt until the digits cooperated in an awkward dance that pulled at his joints. Sliding his palms against the pitted concrete, he combed the crevices hoping for a sharp piece of metal, a rusty nail, anything he could use to pierce the thick artery pulsing in his neck.

His fingers closed around a jagged rock. Relief spilled into his gut and diluted the gnawing hunger there. He inched over onto his back. Fresh blood oozed down his arm. He blinked the nasty laceration into focus, and a new clarity edged into his vision.

This wasn't his cell.

The wall was rough cement where it should have been scarred metal, the floor more heavily pitted. Memories assaulted him, of his last caning, more brutal than the others, the ropes that had dug into his raw wrists and ankles, angry voices that jarred his skull—then nothing. How long had he lain here, unconscious?

Irrational fear squeezed at his heart, making it race. He dug his knuckles into his coarse, tangled beard. How many days since his capture? They'd made him lose track. How could he—if he didn't know—oh, Jesus, he'd been holding onto his sanity by a thin thread and now those bastards had cut his only life line.

How many days? Five hundred? More? Less?

His breath choked past his lips, the garbled sound knocking some sense into him. Who cared? One day was the same as any other. His reasons for counting the days were long gone. He didn't exist. Not to the Central Intelligence Agency which would deny his very existence, nor to his family, of whom he had none. And Catrina—

His throat tightened. Flashes exploded in his head, voices and faces of those he'd failed. He was the only one left. His captors delighted in reminding him of that fact, rubbing his nose in his own judgmental stupidity. He had nothing but his own self-righteous integrity to blame for his predicament. If he'd only broken, like his teammates were willing to do, and let himself be used as propaganda against his own government, maybe they'd have allowed his friends a respectful death without suffering.

Their brutal butchering played through his mind twenty-four hours a day in a continuous reel until he was compelled to imagine a different outcome. One where he'd found a way to save them, rather than ending up helplessly chained to the wall.

Now he glanced around the humid cell, where the crumbling floor was saturated with large rotting leaves and God knew what other kinds of fetid waste. Everything in this place had been left to die, including him.

He tightened his grip on the stone and called upon every ounce of strength he still possessed to drag the sharpest point across his jugular. His breath huffed from his mouth. Warm, sticky moisture welled against his fingers in a trickle. He dug into his neck and waited for the rush of blood to wash over his hand.

Nothing.

"No." The denial sprang past his lips in a rusty warble he no longer recognized as his own voice.

He squeezed his eyes shut, but the salty sting of tears still managed to leak onto his cheeks. He chucked the rock across the cell and heard its ping against the wall before it kissed concrete. He needed something better. Sharper.

He collapsed back against the nearest wall. His left hand slipped along the groove where wall met floor and his fingers plowed into soft mush. He lifted them into his line of vision. Red. Staining their tips. He rolled his thumb across the substance, caught a whiff of the pungent smell.

Rotting fruit. A pomegranate. But the texture transported him. Took him back to another time when he'd swirled his fingers in brightly colored paints, his father silently working on a canvas at his elbow.

There was hope in art, his father used to say. Hope and beauty and life…

Oliver pushed himself to his feet and stumbled over to a pile of mottled fruit and vegetables near the door. The guards must've continued to throw his daily rations inside despite his condition. Flies swarmed around the fermenting pulp, but scattered when his toes plowed into a pile of mango. The juice stung the open gashes along his tender soles. He pushed the pain aside with a wince.

He bent and scooped a handful of red mush into his palm. Shuffling to the nearest wall, he dipped his fingers into the fruit then smeared them across the bumpy concrete in a wide arc. He slashed at the wall again. And again.

When his palm was empty, he returned to the make-shift palette and scooped up more of the sticky goop. He squeezed guava between his fingers, scooped up eggplant, yams, okra and wet jungle leaves, his frantic movements creating a wash of color. Oranges, reds, browns, greens. Black. A landscape slowly took shape before his eyes.

He stepped back to observe what he had done. Sweat coated his face in a clammy film and several of the scabbed-over wounds on his body had reopened. But he ignored the blood trickling down his arms and legs and the shaking in every weak muscle, keeping his focus on the mural in front of him, desperate to remain rooted in an alternate reality.

Here, at last, was a place he could survive, a place where freedom didn't scare him every bit as much as captivity.

His eyes fluttered closed.

Hope and beauty and life…

Knees buckling, he collapsed to the ground.

PHEAKDEI JANGLED THE heavy key ring in his gnarled hand as he approached the iron door. Apprehension tingled in his hunched spine. What would he see when he opened that door? He'd learned never to underestimate the prisoner, but a man could only take so much.

The American had already survived endless beatings and mind games that would have cut down a lesser man. A cowboy, that's what he was, like John Wayne or—or Clint Eastwood in *The Good, The Bad and The Ugly*. Someone who managed to rise up again and again despite the odds.

And every time it happened, it made Pheakdei feel like a wide-eyed kid again instead of the downtrodden puppet he'd become. But he kept his mouth shut, never once voicing support or objection, never summoning the gumption to protest that he preferred Pheakdei, his given name, to Petey, the cheap Americanized slang version.

He rolled his shoulders and pushed the key into the crusty lock, forcing it open. The door swung back with a discordant creak and he nudged it the rest of the way with the toe of his boot. His gaze narrowed on the lifeless body in the middle of the floor. He stared hard for a minute, but could detect no telltale rise and fall from the prisoner's chest. Had he finally given all he had to give?

Pheakdei shuffled over to check the man's pulse. A

swatch of color caught the corner of his eye. A large setting sun seemed to shimmer against the back wall. Streaks of orange, red and pink spread out from the large orb in thick, vibrant fingers. Brown earth swirled below the sun, a hint of frothy gray waves peeking between the two stark lines.

What—? He stepped around the man's body, his hand reaching out of its own accord and touching the large black bird taking flight at the edge of the mural.

"Beautiful." The murmur rolled off his tongue in his native Khmer.

Where had the breathtaking scene come from? Surely the prisoner hadn't—

A faint groan jarred him away from the wall.

He stumbled into the man's bare feet. The prisoner's hand flexed. A long flinch started at the man's dark head and rippled through to his toes, squeezing out another low groan.

The prisoner lived.

Pheakdei bolted for the door, unclipping the two-way radio from his belt as he went. He lifted the radio to his mouth, but before he depressed the button and shouted in to it, he paused to take one last look at the mural on the cell wall.

ONE

Cambodia. Six Months Later.

"NO ONE WOULD fault you for letting someone else take the lead here, you know. It's not every day a daughter digs up her dad's remains."

"I have to do this." Jocelyn Hewitt didn't bother to hide the waver in her voice. Matt understood her, better than anyone. "I owe it to my dad."

She pressed her lips together and thought of the letters tucked safely in her backpack. She no longer needed to touch the pages to recall their soft, worn texture, nor re-read the passages to conjure up the exact shade of the faded ink bearing her father's trademark scrawl. The bold crisp lines of his detailed doodles, each one of his carefully weighed words—they were written on her heart.

Matt shoved a hand through his hair with a curse. "How could Commander Norris be so insensitive? He never should've put you on the team."

Her heart hiccupped around a rush of guilt and heat flooded her cheeks. She turned her back on Matt before he could pick up on the unease that slithered through her. Maybe she should've told him, but really, how did one go about admitting that Norris *hadn't* put her on the team?

Everything she did as an anthropologist was supposed to be done in the blind—without knowing the suspected identity of the remains or the details surrounding the loss. Norris wanted an objective scientist, not someone who'd spent every moment since her eighth birthday trying to make sense of her father's disappearance.

When the tip had first come into the offices of the Joint POW-MIA Accounting Command (JPAC), she'd hoped Norris would at least appoint her to the discovery team in an unofficial capacity. But no amount of begging, pleading or reasoning changed his mind.

In her desperation, she'd resorted to downright lying while Norris was out in the field. He'd urged her to take a vacation. She'd taken him up on the offer.

No one had thought to question her when she'd shown up at the airport as a last minute addition to the team. Forensic anthropologists were frequently juggled between assignments. By the time he returned and discovered her deception, she'd be up to her knees in Cambodia's fertile jungle soil.

"This is what I do. It doesn't matter whether it's my dad or someone else." Jocelyn shifted and caught Matt's gaze. "'Until they're home.' That's always been JPAC's motto, right? Well I'm here to bring him home," her voice cracked, "where he belongs."

Matt studied her for a long moment, his eyes as brown as the muddy river they'd crossed several miles back. Finally, his mouth flattened into a grim slash. "We'll have to go on foot from here." He hopped down from the massive truck bed and lobbed a canvas rucksack in her direction. "The jungle's so dense up ahead we'll never get a vehicle through to the site."

The site. It seemed such an impersonal way to describe her father's final burial place. How could he rest in peace amongst the rusted and twisted shrapnel of his OV-10 Bronco? She swallowed the huge lump in her throat.

Objectivity, Josie. Find it.

Donald Hewitt was just another case to close over at JPAC, one more step toward their goal of achieving the fullest possible accounting of Americans missing in action as a result of past wars. This one shouldn't be any different.

Except it was, and no amount of telling herself she was a professional had prepared her for the pain.

A warm hand settled on her shoulder and she glanced up from untying a knot in her pack to meet Matt's frown. "Are you sure you're okay?"

She forced a ragged smile. "Right as rain."

He narrowed his eyes at her, far too perceptive for his own good. Damn him, she didn't want a friend—not now. She wanted a detached Team Sergeant who failed to see the conflict roiling in the pit of her stomach. And if he didn't stop looking at her that way she'd give in to the temptation to sink into his embrace and take the comfort he was offering.

Not the time or the place.

Jocelyn ducked away from Matt's gaze and climbed into the bed of the truck, heading for the stack of crates at the back. They'd have to transfer the most essential supplies into their packs and abandon the rest. The vehicle's door opened with a squeak. Claire, the team's forensic photographer, stepped out into the mucky road, securing a bright green bandana around her blond hair.

"You know, you should be wearing a hat." Jocelyn winced, already forming an apology for the admonishment, but Claire only grinned, a dimple denting her cheek.

"I thought you were going to let me play mother this time."

"When you remember to bring a hat, it'll be your turn." She reached up, plucked the wide-brimmed straw hat from her own head and tossed it to Claire.

She caught it in one hand and tossed it right back. It fluttered to the floor of the truck. "Someone's got to look out for you while you're busy taking care of everyone else."

Josie tried to suppress her smile and failed. "Ah, but you see, I've got a spare." She reached into her back pocket, yanked out her father's old, faded blue AIR FORCE cap, unrolled it and snugged it down onto her head. She retrieved the abandoned straw hat and flicked it to Claire like a Frisbee. "Put it on."

Claire wrinkled her nose and tugged the hat down on her head. "Don't you ever get tired of being right?"

"Hmm." She tucked her tongue in her cheek, trying to suppress a smile. "Unfortunately, no."

"Dr. Hewitt thrives on being right and making the rest of us look like uneducated hicks."

Her mirth dissolved at the sound of Jason's acidic voice. The medic had taken an instant dislike to her and, no matter how polite she was to him, he always seemed to take pleasure in cutting her down.

She clenched her teeth and vowed to say nothing, but her emotions were running too close to the surface. She couldn't stop her frustration from bubbling over. "Why would I try to make you look bad? You do a good enough job of it on your own."

He scowled and his cool blue eyes turned frigid. "Then since you're all-knowing, maybe you can tell me where Rithi went."

Rithisak, a local they'd met in Siem Riep, had agreed

to guide them through the jungle. Jocelyn's team had learned to rely on the steadfast, quiet young man over the last several days.

She frowned. "I thought you two were scouting out a suitable path."

"One minute he was beside me and the next..." He shrugged.

"Maybe he slipped away to take a leak," Matt suggested with a wink in her direction as he hoisted a crate filled with MREs from the truck.

Jocelyn smiled and tried to shake off her worry. For Rithi to up and disappear...it seemed highly unlike him. He probably needed a break from Jason's constant griping and would pop back up by the time they were ready to move out. She turned her attention to the division and packing of their gear.

However, two hours later, Rithi still hadn't returned. A fine mist molded her linen shirt against her hot skin and clung to her sweaty face. She batted away a mosquito, squinting into a red sun that had already started its downward slink toward the horizon.

"Do you think we should look for him?"

"No, that's not wise. The sun's getting ready to set in—what?—forty minutes or so." Matt rubbed at his brow, his frown directed at the thicket of leaves that started high in the orange streaked sky and draped their way down to the dirt floor. "It's better to camp here for the night. If Rithi doesn't show by morning, we'll set up the sat phone and try to touch base with the command center, let 'em know what's going on."

"I've got dibs on a dry patch of grass." Claire sighed and wiggled her pack from her shoulders. "If there is any dry grass to be had in this place."

Jason hoisted Claire's bag in one hand, using his

other to guide the small of her back. "Come on, I'll help you find a spot."

His boot slipped in the mud and he stumbled, barely managing to right himself before he kissed the ground. He tossed a glare at Jocelyn, as if she were to blame for the soggy May conditions.

"Damn monsoon season." With that parting shot, he hunched his shoulders, and walked off with Claire.

Jocelyn caught the roll of Matt's eyes and snorted. She tried to choke it back before anyone heard, but Matt's you're-so-busted grin widened.

He cocked his head at her and lifted his brows. "Care for some help setting up your tent, Ms. Hewitt?"

"As long as it's nowhere near Jason's—"

A short burst of noise—like the crack of a thick branch—cut her off. She froze, her gaze straying to Matt's automatic rifle as he unhooked it from his pack and settled the gun firmly between his hands. What—? Another thwack disturbed the hush of the jungle, then the whoosh of a machete slicing across leaves.

A shiver ran up her spine. She located Jason and Claire some twenty yards away, their heads bowed together in conversation, then turned back to Matt.

"Rithi?" she mouthed.

Before Matt had a chance to respond, three men materialized from the dense foliage. Two held assault rifles in their grip, the third brandished a pistol and a machete, the setting sun glinting off its sharp curved blade. Rapid-fire Khmer shot from their lips in a threatening jumble of consonants and vowels.

What were they saying? Stop…something. Stop what? God, she couldn't—why didn't they speak slower? Her understanding of Khmer was limited to common tourist phrases, making Rithi all the more valuable to their small team.

Who were these men? Bandits? Military? Could they possibly be friends of Rithi's? Their guide didn't carry ammo strapped to him, nor did he wear guerilla-style paint across his cheeks. Had Rithi accidentally led them on to someone's private turf?

She honed in on the short man at the front of the pack, hoping to catch his eye and convey her apologies. Maybe if she showed them her team's papers—

Matt moved in front of her, blocking her view. "Get Claire and Jason. Run for the truck."

Matt wasn't messing around. He believed these men meant them harm, and had appointed himself team guardian, even though he was outgunned three to one. How could she abandon him to face down these—these—who the hell were these people?

"Go. Now." Matt's terse command succeeded in turning her quaking legs to steel.

She swallowed her objections and inched backward. The man at the center of the trio stared at her with flat, dark eyes, his mouth hiked in a snarl that showed off his blunt teeth and wide jaw.

Goose bumps rose on her flesh despite the humidity. Why was he studying her as if she were a target? Her heart pumped hard in an erratic rhythm against her ribs.

No longer caring whether she kept the man in her sights, she spun. Her legs carried her over ground faster than her feet could gain traction. She slammed into a hard body and lost her balance. Her palms plowed into the mud to break her fall. The brunt of her heavy backpack butted into the base of her skull.

"What's going on here?" Jason's strained voice wobbled as he stuck his hand out to help her to her feet.

Her earth-caked fingers connected with his immaculate ones and curled together. A rifle cracked. The bullet whistled through the air above her and slammed into Jason's chest with a sickening thud.

Blood splattered across her face and clothes. A scream ripped from her. She tried to shut her mouth to cut off the high-pitched keening, but her lips wouldn't cooperate. Her head swam, a series of blue-black spots sparked along her vision. *Jason.* Oh, God. What had they done to him? She scrambled into the damp grass—green blades awash with red—and stopped in front of his body. Her crimson-stained hands shook when she tried to reach for him.

Couldn't do it.

A blur of color zipped into her line of sight. Claire dropped to the ground beside her. Where had she come from? Without hesitation, she did what Jocelyn couldn't, pressing her palms to the gaping hole in Jason's chest.

"No, he's—we need—the truck." Jocelyn tripped over each one of the words, her thoughts a twisted mass of urgency and dread. She curled her fingers into Claire's shirt and tugged.

She'd expected the other woman to come willingly, but Claire jerked out of Jocelyn's grasp, leaving a smear of blood across the fabric of her faded yellow shirt. "Jason—"

"Is gone." The raw truth croaked from Jocelyn's lips.

Another shot echoed in the muggy air, this one shorter, less explosive. She whipped her head in the direction of the sound and watched Matt crumple to his knees. The wake of a thin wisp of smoke curved from the barrel of the machete-wielder's pistol.

She shot to her feet on wobbly legs. Her heart folded in on itself. Where was he hit? She couldn't tell—

couldn't see. Claire's hand clapped on her arm, wrenching her toward the truck.

Jocelyn flicked one more glance over her shoulder
and her gaze collided with the black eyes of the man
who'd studied her so intently moments earlier. He broke
away from the group and stalked toward her. The barrel
of his machine gun swept back and forth between her
and Claire, like a sick game of *eeny, meeny, miny, moe*
that no one wanted to win.

"Jocelyn. Hewitt."

His heavily accented voice leeched the breath from
her body. She froze. How did he know her name? Sweat
drenched her palms. Claire wasn't slowing down, and
neither should she. But her legs wouldn't support one
more step.

He was in front of her. Close enough to see the
yellowish-whites of his eyes. She sucked in a gulp of
air. Her stomach roiled against it and she clenched her
muscles hard, bracing for the impact of the bullet to
her chest.

But it never came.

Claire's scream pierced Josie's ears, its ragged edge
growing sharper as the other two mercenaries somehow caught up with Claire and shoved her down into a
patch of sodden grass.

"Claire!" Jocelyn lurched forward.

"Josie. Josie, help me!" Her muffled plea sliced Josie
to ribbons.

"Claire!"

A vicious tug on Jocelyn's rucksack sent her sprawling to the ground. The weight of a man's knee settled
across her back. She bucked, unsuccessfully, against
her captor and reached a hand out to Claire, who did the
same, her wide-eyed gaze clouded with despair.

Jocelyn's shaky fingertips almost managed to graze Claire's. If she could just—

A flash exploded from the muzzle of one mercenary's AK-47. She squeezed her eyes shut. Droplets splashed against her skin, and she knew, without even opening her eyes, that it was Claire's blood. Her stomach rebelled, acid shot up her throat and she retched the meager contents of her stomach into the grass. Hot moisture slipped from the corners of her eyes and coursed down her cheeks, her own tears washing away the physical evidence of her friends' suffering.

Hands clutched at her and dragged her backward. She screamed, kicked, twisted. Tried to break free. Two of the men tore at her clothes, their mouths moved— shouts, by the way their taut muscles bulged in their necks—but the ringing in her ears swallowed the sound.

"I don't—leave me alone—I don't understand!"

They pressed her face into the ground and the sharp point of a pebble scraped across her cheek. Her cap fell off her head and tumbled beside her. Someone grabbed a hunk of her hair and yanked her head up. Searing pain shot through her neck.

Rithi suddenly pressed through the trees at the edge of the clearing. He stood there, directly in her line of vision, watching. Just watching. Neither surprise nor fear lined his expression, and after a minute, he slipped back into the trees and disappeared.

She gasped, coughing up outrage. He'd done this. He'd brought these men down on their heads.

"Why?" Her mouth strained to form the question.

The weight of her pack scraped over her, chafing and pulling the skin on her arms as one of the men wrestled it from her. He tossed it to another who ripped it open and rifled through the contents until he hoisted her dad's letters in his grip. His thumb fanned the pages with contempt, defiling that last precious link to her father.

"No!" The ringing in her ears finally subsided enough for her to hear her own voice.

Her hands were bound behind her back, the rope biting into her wrists. She was hauled to her feet and shoved forward. She recoiled, licking the sting of perspiration from her lips. Where were they taking her? A flash of movement caught the edge of her vision. A man with smears of crimson staining his fatigues. A coarse blindfold slammed over her eyes, but recognition rumbled through her.

Matt! He was alive!

"Josie!" Matt's splintered rasp came from her left.

She dug her heels into the ground. She had to fight, had to get to Matt. Maybe by some miracle they could both find a way out of this alive.

She threw her body to the side, hoping to dislodge herself from the bastard who held her captive, but he outweighed her and all she received from the effort was an elbow to her temple. He pushed her forward again and she stumbled. Her knees struck the ground. Pain jarred into both hips, but she focused desperately on the rustle of movement around her.

Cold metal dug into her back. Her muscles seized. From somewhere off to her left, Matt grunted. Feet scuffled.

"No. God, no, don't—Josie, run! Run, Josie!" His breath grew choked, his voice more distant, the footsteps even more harrowed.

He was trying to fight them off.

"What are you doing to him?"

"Jos—" She could barely hear him anymore, but somehow her name caught the wind and drifted to her.

A gun blasted through the current.

Matt.

Her throat closed, she doubled over and tried to suck in a breath, but the effort only made the lack of oxygen worse. Before the gunshot stopped echoing around her, the bastards yanked her to her feet once more, one man on each side, digging their fingers into her arms. Leaves slapped at her face as they dragged her into the jungle.

How would anyone know where to find her?

She'd never had the chance to tell Matt the truth. And now, the horror of her omission settled in the very marrow of her bones, chilling her from the inside out.

No one would come for her.

She wasn't even supposed to be in Cambodia.

TWO

CLANG.

The metallic knell broke the endless silence.

It was a sound Oliver hadn't heard for more than six months. He jerked his head up. His stubby pencil fell from his numb fingertips. He froze.

They'd placed someone in the cell next to him.

He shoved aside the ragged copy of *The Count of Monte Cristo* he'd been scribbling in and covered his ears, his attention riveted on the opposite wall. Enough ghosts already inhabited that cell. The room didn't need another, more corporeal occupant.

The new prisoner wasn't his concern. He couldn't make them matter. Not this time. But he somehow found himself on his feet, scrambling across the floor. He snatched up his metal cup with shaky hands, poured the stagnant water onto the concrete and shrugged out of his linen shirt. Sinking onto his haunches, he wrapped the thin material around the cup and set the bottom against the wall. He pressed his ear to the cup's rim and waited.

The tin carried vibrations from even the smallest of sounds. Knowing he wasn't alone could give him the strength to endure another day—or it could drive him further into hell. He didn't want to witness another man's fear, didn't want to hear haunting screams magnified by the room's flat echo.

Please, God, let him have imagined that iron door slamming.

His palms grew clammy and slipped against the cup. He righted it in time to hear the vibration of a feminine sob. His heart accelerated in an erratic dance—as if caught on Ozzy Osbourne's "Crazy Train"—causing him to teeter for a moment before falling back on his butt.

Another hostage was bad enough, but a woman…

His fingers tightened around the cup. He hurled it at the door where it bounced against iron with a clash before it hit the floor and rolled to a stop in front of his feet. Eyes squeezed tight, he tried to block out the impulse to listen in further.

Ignore her. Ignore that room.

Knowledge was not power. Caring about anything outside his cell was a mistake he wouldn't be foolish enough to repeat. He turned to retrieve his discarded book, but his fingers snagged the edge of the damn cup instead.

Don't do it. Do not listen in on her again.

He wound the shirt around the metal circumference once more and set the cup against the wall.

Silence.

He held his breath. Maybe he had just imagined—

"Hello?"

No, she was real. He drank in the vibration that lingered inside his cup, as if that single word were a drop of cool, clean water he could reach out and caress.

He flattened his palm against the wall. God, he craved the contact.

"Is—is anyone there?"

He bit the inside of his cheek to keep from responding. It would be so easy to call out. After six long months of slow and painful rehabilitation from the brink of death, he desperately wanted to remember what conversation felt like, but he wouldn't give the woman false hopes just to indulge in a single moment of selfishness.

A sob tore from her. "God, help me."

Her whisper clawed at his battered heart. He lowered the cup into his lap, squeezed his eyes shut and tipped his head back against the wall, listening to his pulse rush in his ears.

God.

How long would it take her to realize that He didn't exist in such a place?

JOCELYN HUNCHED HER shoulders, choking down another sob. She'd heard something. A scrape of metal on metal…a clatter. It couldn't have been her imagination.

Friend or foe?

She strained to listen for the sound, but her pulse thundered too loudly in her ears. Where had the noise come from?

After a full night of trekking through the jungle blindfolded, of tripping, stumbling and being dragged through the dirt, her captors had shoved her in this room and left.

Jocelyn tilted her head and tried to catch a glimmer of light from beneath her blindfold. Nothing. She wiggled her wrists, ignoring the chafe of the rope against her raw skin, and touched the floor. Concrete crumbled under her fingers. She scooted backward on her butt. Something plopped on her head, skittered across her hair.

She screamed and vaulted off the floor. Her bound hands hit metal first, catapulting the back of her head against the wall. She slid back to the ground, dazed. Debris fell from the ceiling, over her hair and down her shirt. Her stomach clenched on a wave of nausea. Oh, God what was that stuff?

She pressed her cheek to the barrier and tried to slow her choppy breaths. Perspiration seeped into her hair. Panic crammed down her throat. She had to get this blindfold off. Had to see what was on her, around her. She dragged her face against the surface, abrading herself from jaw to brow.

Please, God. Please get it off. The blindfold slipped enough to let a sliver of dull light in. She renewed her efforts. The material moved higher, the bottom edge clearing her eyes and coming to rest against her forehead.

She blinked hard. Her breath whooshed. A cell. She was in some kind of prison cell. Only a heavy iron door broke up the monotony. A dim light bulb hung from the ceiling. The corners of the room crawled with shadows. Dark stains marred the cement under her feet. She scrambled into the middle of the room, hugging her knees to her chest.

Oh, God, was that blood? How many others had been held here? Had they died in this very room?

Her gaze slid across gouges in the rusty wall. Claw marks? She shivered and shifted her attention to her khaki pants. The poor lighting couldn't hide the smatters of dried crimson. Claire. Jason. Oh, Lord. Matt. He'd never again argue with her over Chai Tea, or take up half her sofa and hog all the popcorn while watching a movie. He was her rock. Her anchor. Her best friend.

She closed her eyes, which only served to sharpen the violence imprinted on her brain. They'd all had so much to live for—why had they died and not her? She angled her head back and let the light from the dingy bulb spear her eyes. Her fingernails dug into her palms until they stung, but her guilt only intensified. Who would find them? Who would bring their bodies home to their family and friends? Would they become nothing more than another unsolved case in JPAC's massive database?

Had she stayed back home in Hawaii instead of deceiving her way onto the team, would her friends still be alive? A shudder wracked through her. The cell was far too quiet.

Don't think about the silence. Don't think about how alone—

"Come on," her voice cracked, but she pushed the words from her tight throat, "if you're there, please, say something."

A muffled shushing sound—something dragged across concrete?—answered her plea. She scrambled to the wall and pressed her ear tight against the metal.

"I know you're there." Tears burned a path down each of her cheeks and pooled in the hollow of her collarbone. She splayed her hand against the cool metal. "Why won't you speak to me?"

She counted off the seconds of silence, focusing on her ragged breathing as a way of stalling the inevitable time when she'd be forced to sit alone with her thoughts. But the tight, dim space surrounded her—suffocated her. All she *had* were those thoughts.

Why did her captors single her out? Would they let her go when they realized she was of no use to them? Or would they…get rid of her the way they'd done with her friends?

She shuddered and shot away from the wall. "Let me out of here!" Her scream reverberated, piercing her own ears, but she continued to add to the din, pounding her fists against the door. "Damn, you! You can't keep me here."

She pressed her throbbing palm against her raw throat. A soft fall of rain started to pitter-pat against the metal roof and when she tilted her head back, her gaze snagged on a rivulet of water running along the seam in the roof. She followed the trail to the back corner where it dripped onto the concrete. Opening her mouth, she let several inadequate drips gather in the back of her throat and swallowed.

Something scraped at the door. She flinched against the wall and held her breath as a key turned in the lock. The door swung open and the two men who'd captured her barged into the cell, their harsh faces shadowed.

The taller of the two motioned her forward. "You. Come with us."

"Wh—what do you want?" The chattering of her teeth prevented the words from leaving her lips in a tone stronger than a whisper.

"No questions. Just come." This from the shorter, flat-nosed, square-jawed man.

She swallowed hard, and though her knees shook, she pushed herself from the wall, straightened her spine, and bluffed. "Look, I don't know what you want with me, but if I don't show up back in Stung Treng tonight, people will come looking for me. This jungle will be crawling with search parties and—"

The taller one lunged forward and struck her. Pain raced up her cheek. She reared back, hunching her shoulders.

"Wh—why are you doing this? I'm just a forensic anthropologist on assignment. I—I study bones for a living." Her voice broke. "Bones. I have nothing you could possibly want."

He shoved her against the wall. She yelped, tasting the tang of blood on her lips.

"Okay." She whimpered and the small act sent a shard of pain through the cut on her mouth. "Okay. I'll come. Please…just…"

Don't rape me? Kill me? Hurt me? What plea could possibly soften the hearts of monsters?

One of the men yanked the blindfold back over her eyes. The sudden bleak darkness illuminated the truth in a way the paltry light had failed. She was alone. No one could help her. The mercenaries jerked her toward the door. She wanted to fight, wanted to force them to kill her now rather than later, but fear had drained her strength.

Her feet dragged against the concrete. She resisted. No use. She couldn't hold her ground. They were dragging her farther and farther out of the room—

A series of short, staccato taps pattered against the wall off to her left.

Shave and a haircut.

She dove toward the sound, wrenching at her captors. "I hear you!" She found the remnants of her voice to rasp a response. "I—I'm here."

She lost her footing and fell. Her knees smacked the concrete, but a rush of adrenaline flooded her veins and she barely felt the pain. Someone was behind that wall. Someone who wanted her to know she wasn't alone.

THEY CALLED THEMSELVES "The Trinity," three men united under a common goal. Anarchy. Neither God nor Government had the authority to limit their desires. If it felt good, they did it. If they wanted it, they took it. But for the past three years, the one thing Jude Larkin most wanted had remained out of reach.

Kala's Ashes, a cache of rare red diamonds hidden away for centuries in their limestone cave in the Cambodian jungle. His fingers yearned to caress the cool, smooth stones, to hold them up to the light and bask in their refracting crimson sunburst. He could almost taste the diamonds' purity on his tongue and feel their fire in his belly.

Jude stared hard at the precise symbols inked across the paper until his eyes stung, forcing him to squeeze them shut. With only half the map in his possession, all attempts to decipher the cryptic markings had led to a dead end. So he'd bided his time, mining sapphires that went for a fraction of the price red diamonds would bring, but now—today—his hope for his kingdom was reborn. Anarchists everywhere would have no choice but to exalt him. He'd sit on high and mete out justice as he saw fit. The world was his to destroy. No one could stop him. No one would have the balls to try.

A sharp rap on the door jarred his concentration. He blinked the cipher's jumbled impressions from his brain. "Come in."

The heavy door swung open and Leo Burney slunk inside. His ghostly pale skin and colorless eyes were almost translucent in the faint beam of sun that filtered through the high narrow window to strike him full in the face.

He lobbed a bundle of papers at Jude. "We've got her."

Jude caught the stack in his left hand and dropped the pages neatly in the center of the table. He pumped out a squirt of sanitizer into his palm and massaged the liquid into his skin, frowning down at the twisted scar tissue that fused the fingers of his right hand.

"I trust Thom and Veha left her in good condition."

The two head mercenaries on his security payroll weren't known for their restraint, but with their reputation well publicized on the Philippines' most wanted list, Jude had known exactly what he was getting.

Leo snorted. "I haven't seen her, yet. But I'm sure they followed your instructions to the letter."

Of course they did. They wouldn't want to risk him pulling funding for the New People's Army, their terrorist group of choice. Jude plucked a tissue from the nearby box and used it to slip a folded letter from beneath the strap that held the bundle together.

"Where's Chann? He hasn't checked in since last week."

Chann was the glue that held them together, the peacemaker who brought out the best in them all. It was odd that he was suddenly avoiding Jude.

He shook the piece of paper open, revealing even lines of slanted handwriting.

"I hesitate to even bring it up—"

His head snapped to meet Leo's shuttered gaze. "Please do."

"It's been weeks since we've hauled anything other than trace sapphires out of the mine. I'm afraid there's nothing left."

His suspicions were right. The mine's resources were all but depleted. If they didn't find Kala's Ashes soon they stood to lose millions of dollars in arms trades.

"As for Chann, he's out looking for some new…recruits. We've lost three of our best miners. Dengue fever."

Miners. Leo and his proclivity for tact. Why didn't he just call a spade a spade? "Dengue fever weeds out the weak and the imperfect. The unworthy. Double the rest of the children's shifts until Chann returns with more."

Leo's complexion went even whiter. "The others are too young to keep up that pace."

"Give them incentive to do so." He sharpened his voice; the hard edge lashed out with enough force to make Leo stumble.

Didn't the children understand how special they were? Jude took them under his wing and gave them the chance to rise to greatness as The Trinity's righteous instruments. He'd saved them from an obscure and superfluous life, provided for them and showed them the way, the truth, the light. But sometimes even his chosen ones needed to be punished accordingly to bring them to their full potential. "Cast out those who still don't measure up."

"But—"

"You know what to do."

He shouldn't have to remind Leo. Or ask after Chann, for that matter. They'd been together more than half their lives, protected each other, and learned how to survive on next to nothing. They were his brothers. Not just of the heart, but of the cause. But something was changing both Leo and Chann of late, eroding their taste for glory.

Only Kala's Ashes could reunite them.

He scanned the first few lines of the letter, one finger absently rubbing the twisted fissures of the melted flesh on his right cheek.

His body tingled with anticipation. The rest of the map was finally in his grasp. Better still, he had the key to interpret the cryptogram. If anyone knew Donald Hewitt's secrets, it was his daughter—and she'd been so easy to lure with one false tip planted to JPAC. Paying Rithi to lead her and her team into the jungle had ensured she'd be where his mercenaries could snatch her.

Leo's tall form cast a sudden shadow across the

paper. Jude pinned Leo with a hard stare. "Go. Tell Thom and Veha to bring me the woman. Now."

A TUG ON Jocelyn's bound wrists brought her up short. The strong smell of lye hit her full in the face. She stiffened her spine, blinking rapidly behind the blindfold.

"Where am I?" Her voice quavered.

The guards' silence cranked up her pulse until her heart slammed against her ribs. Sweat blanketed her palms.

"Where have you taken me?"

A loud creak abraded her nerves. One of the guards shoved her forward, ripped the blindfold from her eyes. Jocelyn blinked against the fluorescent lights.

A shower. They'd brought her to shower.

Her shoulders relaxed, heart rate slowing to a normal rhythm. An open stall took shape in front of her. Rust ran down the pitted and chipped metal in a dark streak that extended from corroded showerhead to floor. The erosion smattered to a halt as it reached the scuffed drain in the middle of the concrete. The rhythmic drip tempted her to get under the spray and wash the blood from her skin.

She pulled in a relieved breath that crystallized in her lungs when one of the guards shoved her. "Hey—"

"You take shower."

"Yes." She spun to face the leering bastards. "As soon as you leave."

The taller guard snickered, taking a step in her direction. "She funny, eh?"

Her heart knocked against her ribs and she shuffled backward until her shoulders pressed against the cool metal. "Wh—what are you doing?"

He flicked the blade open on his knife. She stared at

the serrated edge. The saliva fled her mouth. Her stomach clenched, but she lifted her chin. If he planned to hurt her, he'd do so without her cowering in the corner.

The sharp tip of the blade poked the skin of her neck. She held in a breath, but then the pressure let up as the man slid the knife along the collar of her shirt. She wanted to look away but forced herself to meet the guard's flat black eyes. When his hand reached the slight vee of her t-shirt, he jerked the knife downward and rent the fabric in two. He moved to slash at the sleeves. The gesture ripped a scream from her. She reached for the torn edges of the shirt, but her hands were still restrained behind her back.

"Untie me!" She tugged against the rope, its cords chafing her wrists.

The other guard crowded in on her. He yanked the ruined fabric away from her body and ground the frayed pieces beneath the heel of his boot. Goosebumps rose on her skin, her thin cotton bra failed to provide coverage. She curled her fingers into tight, chilled fists, and when the larger guard reached for the button on her pants, she lashed out with a kick.

Her foot connected with his shin. "Get the hell away from me!"

He muttered something unintelligible. Rough hands grabbed at her from both sides and threw her to the ground. The back of her head struck concrete. Bright spots shifted in front of her vision. She blinked them out of the way, bucking and twisting beneath the guards.

Stay strong. Don't let them win.

Her shoes and socks were yanked from her feet. Pants dragged down her legs. When they reached for her bra and panties, she doubled her efforts with a swift kick to the shorter one's groin. He caught her ankle and bent it, while the taller guard used his knife to slice the last scraps of dignity from her body.

A sob convulsed through her. She'd promised herself she wouldn't let them get to her. Wouldn't let them have the satisfaction of seeing her fall apart. But she could no longer hold her emotions in. She squeezed her eyes shut. A spray of tepid water hit her in the face. Its steady stream ran in her mouth and up her nose, filling her throat with the slight taste of rust. She choked—sputtered—flailed her head side to side.

Were they trying to drown her?

They hauled her to her feet and shoved her directly beneath the showerhead. The water started to warm to a more agreeable temperature, but it didn't stop there. It kept growing hotter, ready to boil the flesh from her body.

She grit her teeth against the urge to scream, the muscles in her neck pulling taut. Her breath wouldn't flow properly, her limbs quivered and her nose and throat stung.

One of the guards raised her bound arms, straining them at an awkward angle behind her, while the other guard took a coarse soapy brush to her back. She arched her spine and cried out, but the bastards just dug in tighter.

Hot steam rose around her and half shrouded the guards, but she didn't need to see them clearly to feel every poke and prod to her body. The hard bristles of the brush rubbed her skin raw—down her arms, buttocks and legs, around to her stomach and up her breasts—each vicious stroke more humiliating than the last. She blinked a stream of wetness from her eyes and tasted salt mingled with the bite of iron-tainted water.

Jocelyn retched. She coughed, choking, and before

she could regain her breath, the guard's brush slashed at her face, scrubbing her mouth and cheeks with bitter soap. They tugged her head back by her hair until the water hit her square in the face and washed the lather away. Her chest hurt with suppressed sobs and her knees started to buckle. Rough hands caught her. The brush hit the cement with a loud clank, and the pipes squealed until the shower spray decreased to nothing more than a slow drip.

She shivered from the sudden rush of cool air. Her skin prickled and roared into a full flame when the guards started rubbing her down with stiff towels.

"Stop. God, please, stop." Her ragged voice sounded like a stranger's.

The shorter guard forced her legs into some sort of lightweight hemp pants. "We take you to see The Father."

"W—who?" The other guard cut her wrists free and wrapped her in an oversized white tunic.

She flexed her fingers to coax feeling back into her hands. She should make her move—attack them, run, something—but her sluggish limbs refused to cooperate. *Do something!* She couldn't just go quietly.

"Let's go."

"No." She curled her bare toes into the concrete, forced her spine stiff, and stared them down.

The beady-eyed guard narrowed his eyelids into slits. "Move it."

Jocelyn hauled in a shaky breath and tried to find the courage to spit in his face. Her mouth was too dry. The sick bastards laughed, dragging her out of the shower.

She bowed her head and let them lead her out into the corridor.

THREE

THE GUARDS SHOVED Jocelyn into a windowless room.

Gray cracked tile buckled beneath her feet. The two caged bulbs dangling from the ceiling failed to completely chase the shadows from the murky corners. Cracks spidered across the plaster from floor to ceiling.

An absurd longing shuddered through her for the concrete and tin of her cell, for the person on the other side of that wall. The one that, without a word, had made her feel less alone.

"Please…" *Let me go. Take me back there.*

This room with its battered metal folding chair and rickety table—whatever reason they'd brought her here wouldn't be good.

And her cell was any better?

No…yes…at least maybe they'd lock her in and leave her alone.

Jocelyn took another step forward, her attention drawn to the papers on the table. Her eyes widened. "What—"

She squinted, recognizing her father's letters sitting next to some sort of leather-bound ledger and an issue of the *Journal of Anthropological Research.* Open to an interview they'd done on her sometime last year, complete with a black and white photo of her at the top left of the page.

Before she could get a closer look, the guard yanked on her bindings, sending her crashing into the chair behind her. Her butt struck the seat and wedged her hands between the metal. Pain shot through her arms. She tried to push out of the seat but a hard hand held her down. A rope wrapped tight around her.

"What is this?" She sputtered.

The guard cinched the rope tighter and the braiding dug into her arms, her ribs. She opened her mouth to hurl obscenities—or—or spit in his eye, but found the massive churning in her stomach wouldn't allow her to do it.

"What are you going to do?" She notched her chin, but the guard had already turned away.

The door behind her slammed shut. Footsteps faded. The taut silence goaded her into action and she wriggled in her seat, trying to loosen the rope. The legs of the chair scraped against the floor like fingernails on a chalkboard.

She clenched her teeth and froze. Too noisy. What if someone had heard?

A sudden click came from the right to chase across her spine. She flinched. Oh, God. The guards *had* heard. They were coming back for her. She swung her gaze in the direction of the sound. A section of the wall opened up to reveal a hidden door. A tall, dark-haired man stepped into the room and slipped out of the shadows.

Light from the overhead bulb caught the right side of his face, highlighting the twisted and scarred skin and graying strands of hair at his temples. His sable eyes pierced Jocelyn with a ruthless glint more frightening than his disfigured features. She reared back and pressed into her chair. Her arms strained behind her.

Without taking his gaze from hers, he brought up his right hand, a knotted, foot-long piece of bamboo clamped between his fused fingers. "I'm going to ask you some questions. If you cooperate, you will not be harmed. But if you decline…"

He slapped the bamboo across his palm. The hollow whack of wood against flesh sent a tremor rippling through her body.

She swallowed. "Who are you?"

The man's mouth tightened. "I am the one asking the questions here."

His voice held a distinctive accent, a meld of several different cultures, but his tall form and Roman nose told her he was not of Cambodian descent.

She sucked in a breath. "I don't know what you want with me, but—"

"Veha didn't explain? Shame on him." He towered above her, smelling faintly of spicy jasmine and burnt wood. "I've cautioned him about being such a brute with the prisoners."

"How many have you had?" The cloying scent tickled the back of her throat.

He tsked. "There you go again. Questioning me." He reached into the pocket of his shirt and drew out a silver case. His movements unhurried, he pulled out a cigarette and stuck it in the corner of his mouth. He shoved the case back into his shirt, then produced a lighter and lit the tobacco. "You don't mind if I smoke, do you?"

"Actually—"

"Good." He took a pull on the cigarette. A thin wisp of smoke curled into the air and he waited for the tendrils to dissipate. "Now, where were we? Oh. Yes. Donald Hewitt."

"My…father?" She hesitated. "Why are you asking—?"

"Quiet!" He snatched a piece of paper from the desk and she immediately recognized the creases that crisscrossed the stationery and the dog-eared top corner, folded from one too many reads. "I already know everything I need to know about your father." He shoved the letter under her nose. "I want to know about these symbols."

The symbols? She blinked the inked markings into focus—one looked like a primitive elephant, another, a skull—then the man yanked the letter from her view, tossing it back on the desk.

"His scribbles? This is what this is all about?" She lunged against her bonds. "You had my friends killed over those four measly doodles? You—you bastard."

Bamboo slapped fire across her cheek. Her head snapped sideways and her body followed the movement, toppling her, chair and all, to the floor. Her shoulder slammed into the tile followed by her hip. Pain jarred her teeth and she barely managed to keep her head from smashing against the hard surface.

She screamed. A trickle of blood ran down her jaw.

"The symbols," he snapped. "What do they mean?"

"Please. I—I don't know. I swear I don't know."

The bamboo stick came down across her shoulder. She whimpered, trying to shift herself out of his reach. Her toes fought for traction on the floor, but the leg of the chair caught in one of the cracks in the tile, pinning her in place.

"Try again."

"How the *hell* should I know? I was only eight when he wrote these. I never saw him—" The stick whacked across her shoulder once more. His foot nudged her ribs. "—again."

He circled around her, snatching the letter off the desk once more. "He said you would know."

"Who?" She choked on the question. "I don't know what you're talking about."

He stabbed the tip of the bamboo into her back, robbing her of breath and the ability to think.

"Please. Stop. I don't understand what you want—"

Out of the thin shadows, three paintings suddenly took shape. The canvases were neatly lined up on the floor, leaning against the wall instead of tacked to it, and when she narrowed her eyes, she could make out…. churches. Two were cathedral-like with their intricate spires jutting into the sky, and the third was small and primitive, set against a colorful meadow.

Jocelyn blinked hard, clearing the blur of pain from her eyes, but the images didn't disappear like some desperate, stress-induced hallucination. If anything, the paintings shifted into sharper focus. The lush brushstrokes swirled with hope, freedom, passion—and a gnawing angst that lurked at the edge of every canvas. She wanted nothing more than to lose herself in the paintings. To run her fingers along the vibrant textures—

Bamboo prodded her spine, plunging her back to the reality of the musty room.

"If you want to live, you will decipher this map."

Map? What map? Did he really think those silly pictures were some sort of a treasure map? The man was insane.

The stick whistled sharply against air and Jocelyn braced for impact. Wood sliced across her back, far more potent than she'd expected. She squeezed her eyes shut and bit down on her lip to unsuccessfully stifle a cry.

"My dad was always sketching or whittling on something. He hated idle hands. Those drawings mean nothing." An inferno raced up her back, and her cheek throbbed every time she moved her mouth, but she couldn't stop the flow of words. "Please. You've got the wrong person. I swear it. My dad didn't believe in chasing after hidden treasure. Not when there was so much he wanted to discover right on the surface. People. Cultures. Traditions. That's all he cared about."

No. That's what she thought he'd cared about. But how well did she really know him? Her memories had faded over time. Like a photograph left out in the sun too long, only the faintest outline of her dad still remained in her mind. She'd come to Cambodia full of hope, anxious to discover her dad's final resting place and finally reclaim that last elusive piece of herself. Her friends had died because she'd refused to stay home while someone else sifted through her dad's bones. She'd needed to connect with those lost memories, and now this— this asshole was making her doubt everything she knew about her dad.

If he wasn't the man she'd thought he was, then who did that make her?

ANOTHER NIGHT HAD fallen.

Oliver knew by the faint buzzing and chirping that filtered through his cell walls. He listened to the cadence of crickets, trying to remember the last time he'd sat outside and looked up at the stars. How had they changed since he'd last seen them? He swallowed and dropped his head back against the wall. How had *he* changed?

He'd become an empty drone, that's how. Going through the motions, doing the bare minimum to survive, challenging no one. Not even himself.

For what purpose? Why was it so important for him

to continue to exist? Like a dark King Midas he caused pain to everyone he touched. Oliver dug his fingers into his temples, trying to stem the memories, but he knew the tidal wave would come. He could never stop the jumbled onslaught, could never predict which horror would flash across his mind. But this time when the visions came, they were of a nameless, faceless woman—The Trinity's newest prisoner—crying out for help.

His help.

The guards had returned her to her cell long before Oliver's dinner of rice and overripe vegetables had slipped through the slot. And still she'd not made a sound. Was she asleep? Not likely. He'd been unable to sleep for days after his initial capture. Unconscious? Possibly. And if that was the case, she was better off.

He frowned. Better off?

Even though he knew it wasn't a good idea, he scooped his cup off the floor and slid over to the opposite wall, pressing his cup to the metal. Nothing. Just as he was about to pull away, the woman on the other side let out a painful moan. The first was followed by another, even stronger in intensity. Her sobs started coming faster and faster until she was gulping for breath.

God, what had they done to her? His throat squeezed. Like he had to wonder what the bastards had done. They'd beaten her. No going easy on her just because she was a woman.

What did they want from her?

None of your business, Shaw. Put the cup down. Like you can help.

But her cries wrenched a place in his heart he'd believed no longer existed, and he couldn't bring himself to let her suffer alone.

He opened his mouth to say something, but…where

did he begin? It had been over a year since he'd held an actual conversation—and even then he'd never been good at it. He flattened his palm against the wall and tapped on the metal in a short rhythm.

Her crying hitched. "Wh—who's there?"

Oliver waited, listening to the rustles of her movement, and when he was sure she'd put her ear against the wall he put his mouth close.

"St—" He cleared his throat and tried again. "Steady strain."

"I'm sorry?"

"Steady strain. Don't let your emotions control you."

She didn't answer and silence stretched between them. Had his raspy voice scared her off?

She let out a gasp that ended on a groan—no, she'd just been trying to do as he'd said. Hold in her emotions. *Nice going, asshole.* The first thing out of his mouth, and he makes her feel like she's not allowed to cry.

He pressed his lips together, trying to formulate a softer response, to let her know that if crying helped her deal, it was more than okay to do so. But, if he did that, she might start sobbing again and he didn't think he could handle listening to the gut-wrenching sound.

"I hurt…everywhere," she said after another minute of silence. "Why did he—?"

"Beat you? Because he can. Questioning isn't going to stop it." The anger in his voice surprised him. He'd been numb for so long, and now this woman was stirring up a turmoil he'd long ago put to rest.

He shifted away from the wall. He'd thought he could offer…what? Comfort? Hell, this woman would be much better off without any contact from him.

Better off? There went his twisted reasoning again. No one was better off in this hellhole, and whether he talked to her or ignored her, nothing was going to alter that fact.

"They killed my friends." Her aching whisper tugged him close again.

He touched his forehead to the wall. "Don't."

"Don't what? Talk about it?" Her voice took on an edge. "Keep my emotions in check? They're dead because I brought them here."

The self-recriminations echoed within him, but unlike her, he'd had plenty of time to understand their destruction. "You'd do well to forget about them."

"If I don't remember them, who will?"

He closed his eyes, letting the powerful inflection in her faint voice roll around in his mind, over and over. She wanted to remember. He needed to forget. Dwelling on anything more than basic survival needs served no purpose.

"How badly are you hurt?" He hadn't known he'd intended to ask until the question left his lips.

"My face feels on fire. Back too."

What had they done to her? He scrambled over to the corner of his cell and sifted through the small stack of leaves he'd discarded from his dinner plate earlier. Sometimes the guards amused themselves by adding inedible garbage to his food to see if he would eat them.

He found a large, flat leaf, crammed it into his mouth and started chewing, grimacing at the bitter taste that flooded his mouth. Tucking the mushy bits into his cheek, he returned to the wall, and felt his way over to the three-inch hole in the metal. He'd forgotten it was there—conveniently—and now, as he touched the jagged edges, a shard of memory dug into his heart.

Catrina.

She'd used a rock to wear down the corroded metal

until they could both poke their fingers through the wall. In the early days of his capture he'd desperately needed that connection, but somewhere along the way, before Catrina had—

He bit his tongue. *No. Do not think about her.* He had the desire to do something good for the first time in a long time. If he thought about Cat now, he'd never go through with it. He tapped on the wall near the hole and bent to press his mouth against it.

"Here."

The woman's harsh breathing grew louder as she moved closer to the hole. A weak sliver of light flickered across the jagged opening then disappeared altogether when she knelt in front of it.

"Yes?"

Oliver spit the chewed leaves into his hand and pushed the bulk of the paste onto his fingertips. He stuck his fingers through the hole. "Take this."

"What…is that?"

"Broadleaf. *Plantago major.* It's…soldier's herb. Slather the mush on your cuts. It will take the sting away and help with healing."

Her fingers connected with his, the tentative touch so powerful he almost snatched his hand away. He clenched his teeth, enduring the light friction of her fingers against his as she scooped up the pulpy leaves.

"Got it?" He had to put some distance between them.

"Yeah…thanks."

Oliver yanked his hand away from the hole and sank back to the floor. He held his breath, listening for her retreat. Sweat popped out on his brow. He'd done what he could, why didn't she move away?

"My name's Jocelyn." The sound of her name sent

his heart plunging into his gut. "Jocelyn Hewitt. But my friends call me Josie."

Friends?

He curled his fingers into the hem of his shirt and clenched the worn-out fabric in his fists until the muscles in his hands ached.

Friends.

Oh, hell, no. He should've kept his mouth shut, his hands to himself.

To befriend him was to sign her death warrant.

FOUR

CHANN HOVERED AT the edge of the tiny village. He retreated into the cover of the tall banyan tree and watched Leo creep toward the thatched hut without a sound. The late afternoon downpour had left the night air heavy. Suffocating. The oppressive moisture rattled in Chann's lungs. He swallowed, tugged at his damp collar.

How many similar abductions had he and Leo done over the years?

He'd long since lost count. Why should one more make a difference? He clenched his fists. One more. He could almost hear Jude whispering in his ear. *We're so close. Just one more.* One more month, one more year, one more life.

How had they strayed so far? Or maybe they hadn't strayed far at all. Maybe this was always Jude's intent. Even at fifteen he'd had a way of bending both Chann and Leo to his will. Not that it had been hard. From the moment Jude's family set foot in the small village, he'd emerged as the natural leader of the ragtag bunch of missionary boys.

They'd lost everything—parents, community, home—in the fire that swallowed the newly built church and took out the entire village. Everything except each other. Chann had his suspicions about how the fire started, but he'd never once voiced them. As the youngest at only eleven, he hadn't wanted to alienate Jude. Not when Jude had so readily slipped into the role of caretaker for both Chann and Leo.

Closer than brothers, they'd become almost one in their effort to survive. The Trinity. Father, son and unholy ghost.

Chann, as the only native Khmer in the group, developed into the go-between. While other tribes would have looked warily at Jude and Leo tramping through the jungle, no one thought twice of him mingling with the villagers. They welcomed him into their huts, their lives, and never suspected his deception allowed Leo to slip into their villages and rob them blind.

The plan was perfect in its simplicity. They needed to eat, and they weren't hurting anyone. For ten years, it had been enough. But then Jude had stumbled upon the sapphire mine...

Within months they'd seized control of the village's lifeblood. Jude brought in mercenaries to maintain order and paid pennies for ownership of starving children brought in from far away farming villages hit hard by floods. And when Jude got even more greedy and stopped paying for the children altogether, Chann could no longer justify their acts as not hurting anyone.

His own father had worked hard to teach him not to forget his roots, to treat others with respect and compassion. As a part of The Trinity, he'd done worse than forget. He'd abused the very people who had put their trust in him. They cried in his arms, wailing about the mysterious force that snatched their children in the night.

And what did he do? He comforted them, feigning confusion and pretending to share their distress.

Chann swallowed back a lump of shameful bile. The constant chir-oop of insects buzzed in his ears. He felt their clicks and warbles in the marrow of his bones. A chill skated up his spine. What was taking Leo so long? Chann inched forward, his boots sinking in the mud as he crossed to the steps of the hut.

No wood or fabric obstructed the doorway. The darkness did a good enough job of that on its own. He stepped onto the uneven porch. The worn wood creaked beneath his soles and he froze. Footsteps thumped inside the hut. A young girl's scream was cut short by Leo's growled curse.

Chann rushed inside. Duct tape rasped off to his left. To his right someone stirred, an oil lantern flared to life. He blinked the bright spots out of his eyes and swung in the direction of the light. An old man sat up on his pallet. His dark eyes widened on Chann.

Recognition.

Chann's pulse spiked. Perspiration popped out across his brow. He lunged for the old man and hauled him to his feet, wrapping an arm around the man's frail neck. What was he doing? Was he really going to strangle this old grandfather to death?

He tightened his grip and weak fingers tugged at his arm.

Can't let him go. He's seen. He knows.

The old man jerked. Garbled keening choked from his lips. Chann's stomach twisted. He squeezed his eyes shut and increased the pressure against the man's windpipe until the body went limp. Silent.

Chann exhaled on an anguished breath. He carefully lowered the dead man to the pallet and reached up to close his vacant eyes. With shaking hands he made the sign of the cross, whispering a frantic prayer for the man's soul.

"Ready?" Leo's gruff voice pulled at Chann.

He stood and backed away from the body.

"Here. Take her." Leo shoved a child into his arms.

"Her?" He glanced down into the child's face, the wide slash of duct tape across her mouth making her features indistinguishable. "You were supposed to grab a boy."

"No boy. Beggars can't be choosers." Leo leaned over and extinguished the lantern. "I need to secure the area. That little bitch's scream might've woken the entire village. Go. I'll catch up."

Chann nodded, coiled his fingers around the girl's slender shoulders and ducked out of the hut. The girl whimpered. Her body bucked, arms flailed. He slapped at her cheek to quiet her, then juggled his hold, throwing her over his shoulder.

Winding his fingers around her legs, he forced himself to keep moving through the trees.

Don't stop. Don't think. Get to the truck.

Branches slapped at his face as he hurried farther away from the village. A narrow strip of strategically cleared foliage appeared at a break in the trees and he veered onto the path, following it until it widened into a road.

He paused at the Land Rover to take a strained breath. *Hurry, Leo.* He set the girl on her feet. Moonlight washed across her face, illuminating brown eyes that shimmered with terror. The sight punched him in the gut.

What would happen if he ripped the tape off her mouth and hands and let her go? Hopped into the truck and just…left her here. Left Cambodia. He pulled in another breath, letting the clean smell of rain fill his nostrils.

This jungle was his home. His blood. He could never leave.

Leo came crashing through the trees. "Let's get out of here."

Chann opened the Land Rover and shoved the girl into the backseat.

No, he couldn't leave. But he could start over. Disappear into the vast jungle and live a simple life, fueled by his love of the land.

He slid into the seat, glancing over his shoulder at the girl as he pulled the door shut. She couldn't have been more than eleven or twelve years old. Those big brown eyes of hers pleaded with him. Nostrils flaring, she breathed harshly through her nose.

And suddenly he was a boy again, watching as fire roared through the clapboard church. Watching as his sister pounded against the window, flames devouring her from behind. If his suspicions were right, Jude had robbed him of Jorani. The memory of her dark, desperate eyes tormented him from beyond the grave, accusing him of choosing The Trinity over her.

Eyes so very much like the girl in the backseat of the truck.

LEO PAUSED IN the hallway, narrowing his eyes on the short guard barreling toward him. Petey—*oh, excuse me, the man prefers Pheakdei*—normally went out of his way to avoid him. And when that didn't work, he'd throw in a sign of the cross for extra measure. The gesture made Leo's lip curl. Stupid Cambodian. Leo may have preferred to move about in the darkness, but he was a flesh and blood man, like any other.

His translucent skin and colorless eyes had earned him the name of The Ghost amongst The Trinity. The comparison was Jude's idea of a clever pun on the Holy Spirit, but Leo had never found the moniker amusing.

The nickname, along with his broad build, all six-foot-three inches of height, and his shock of white-blond hair, didn't command respect. Instead, it made people nervous. Disgusted. They'd bow their heads, hiding their revulsion, but Leo always knew.

He was the pathetic albino, the freak to fear or pity. No one ever understood he, too, had hopes and desires. They dismissed his humanity, preferring to think of him as a cold apparition, something without beliefs and feelings. And he let them, retreating into that role more and more even though the struggle to prove them wrong made his skin itch.

Someday soon. He had only to bide his time a while longer. The world would come to know the real him. Just like Jude and Chann did.

Jude. And Chann. And...Ruthie.

He burned at the thought of her. She'd seen his beauty. She'd loved him just as he was.

He scratched at a bothersome spot on the inside of his elbow, scrubbing away her memory. He waited for Petey to hustle past, but this time the guard slowed to a stop and looked Leo in the eye.

"Something's wrong with the woman," he said in his clumsy, broken English.

The woman.

Leo had yet to get a good look at her. Most days Jude relegated him to the dark, stuffy mine. Forced to spend his days with children too weak to pull their weight, and his nights with children too sick to sleep. He hated the chore.

"Show me." Leo pushed away from the wall and started down the corridor.

The old man's keys jangled as he fell into step behind Leo. The rhythmic jingle soothed his frayed nerves, like the miniature set of bells his sweet missionary mother used to carry with her from village to village.

Petey brushed against him. "In here." Petey withdrew his keys from his belt clip, selected one and unlocked the reinforced iron door, pushing it open and coaxing a grating squeak from the hinges that scratched up Leo's spine.

Hurry.

He battled the urge to shove Old Petey aside.

The woman lay curled on her side in the middle of the room, one hand gripped in her chestnut hair, her bare feet chafing against one another as she rocked back and forth. The white cotton tunic she wore was bunched under her breasts, revealing the smooth, pale skin of her stomach and the dark purple bruises on her back.

His fingers started twitching. He had to touch her. He knelt beside her and skimmed a palm up her back. Perspiration coated her hot skin, like damp velvet, and he couldn't resist gliding his palm over her bare stomach before reaching up and gripping her shoulders to turn her.

She moaned. Her hand fell away from her face, exposing her flushed cheeks and her full, chapped lips.

Ruthie?

He blinked hard.

No. The woman's dark hair was cut just like his Ruth's, but this couldn't be her. Ruth had gone away. After all he'd done to save her life when the fever had swept through the nearby village of Ban Pong where she'd taught English, she'd up and disappeared. Broken her promise to love him forever.

He swallowed the bitterness of treachery and focused on the woman. Bits of pasty green leaves clung to her skin. He brushed the stubborn pieces away, revealing a long, angry welt—the unmistakable brand of a bamboo rod. His hands fisted.

Jude.

He'd gone too far this time. Women should not be caned this way. And now she was sick. Burning up. Leo fingered a lock of her hair, brushing the dark strand away from her closed eyes.

What was she called again?

"Jocelyn," he whispered.

Her name rolled off his tongue in a boldness that elicited a shiver of longing through his body. He could help her. Make her well. She would love him. Just like Ruthie. Only this time, this woman would stay.

Her lips parted on a gasp and he couldn't resist lowering his head, ready to touch his mouth to hers, but her beautiful, fever-glazed hazel eyes fluttered open.

"No." The single syllable fell from her lips and gained volume. "No, no, no."

He covered her mouth with his palm. "Shh. They'll hear you."

No, not they. Jude. Just Jude.

Jude would hear her. He would come. And he would take her.

Not fair. Jude always took what he wanted. He said he loved Leo like a brother, but he never once asked what Leo desired. Jude's kingdom always came first.

Petey stepped into Leo's line of vision, intruding. The woman was his—he wouldn't tolerate interference from Petey or Jude, or Chann.

A smile turned Leo's lips. He didn't have to worry about Chann. The choirboy would look the other way like he always did, preferring to sit among the villagers and conveniently forget he was the man doing them the most harm.

Leo slipped his palm against Jocelyn's forehead. "We need to bring down her fever."

Petey shuffled his crooked feet, clucked his tongue. "I go get Jude."

"You'll do no such thing." Leo's voice vibrated with the command.

Petey shook his head, already moving toward the door. "Jude needs to know."

Jude. Always Jude. Leo barely managed to choke off a sour laugh. It was Leo who did all the dirty work to keep things running smoothly. Without him the sapphire mine would've stopped producing long before now.

No recognition. No reward.

He was long overdue.

He slid one hand beneath the woman's head, the other under her knees and gently lifted her into his arms. "Come. You will help me take care of her."

"But—Jude—he tell me—"

"Jude doesn't need to know about this." He narrowed his eyes at Petey until the man met his stare. "Understood?"

Petey tucked his chin to his chest. "I don't like this. No, I don't like it. If the woman dies, Jude will kill me."

"Then you'd better make sure she doesn't die. Right, Doctor?" Leo sneered at the lofty title. Even Petey commanded more respect from Jude. As if the old guy was more than just some village medicine man. Leo ground his teeth together and strode out the door, the woman cradled in his arms. "Don't forget. I know where Jude's hidden your family. He spared them once. Don't expect the courtesy again."

HALTING FOOTSTEPS ECHOED outside the corridor. Oliver tensed mid-pushup and listened for the turn of the lock.

His door swung open and a tired face came into view. The other guards referred to him as Petey, but Oliver always called him "old man."

"The Father wants to see you."

Oliver nodded and rolled to his feet, relaxing his muscles. He had no gripe with the old guard who kept him fed and left him alone. Unlike the other bloodthirsty mercenaries that worked for The Trinity, the man was neither friend nor foe. He just *was*.

The weathered wrinkles on the man's face spoke of a hard life. His eyes were weighty with all the harsh things he'd witnessed, and yet they weren't without compassion as he tracked Oliver's move across the cell.

Oliver struggled to maintain indifference under the scrutiny. The old man'd seen far too much—every flaw, every shame. Oliver wanted to hate him for that.

His gut burned. He curled his fingers into his palms and waited.

The old man inclined his head. "We go."

Oliver shrugged.

He'd been through this ritual hundreds of times in the past six months and knew what was expected. Petey shackled his hands in front of his body then bent to do the same to his feet before leading him out into the shadowy corridor. The open hallway eased the breath in Oliver's tight chest. Just for a moment. Once he was before The Father, the constriction would return tighter than before.

He straightened his shoulders, his focus drawn to the open door up ahead where the woman—Jocelyn— was being held.

His footsteps quickened. "Hey, Old Man." He jangled his shackles, trying to get the guard's attention, and peered into the cell. "Why is the door—" *Empty. The woman was gone.* "What have you done with her?"

The guard shook his head. "She's gone."

Gone?

"What happened?" Oliver ignored the tug on his chains. "Where is she?"

"They took her away."

Dread slammed against his ribs. Took her away. The Trinity never just took someone away. "What do you mean? Where did they take her?"

The guard hesitated. "Away."

Oliver jerked forward with the tug on his bindings. Rage crawled through his veins, rooting him to the spot. His vision hazed and he lunged, slamming the guard against the wall.

No, not away. Away meant dead.

God, help him, he'd touched her. He'd sealed her fate as surely as if he'd strangled her.

Blind panic took hold. He shook his head and tried to blink the corridor back into focus. His fingers tightened around something solid, something like…his gaze shot to Petey's wide eyes and open mouth. The man was choking.

Oliver flinched. *He* was choking him.

He tore his hands away from Petey's throat. What had he done? He hunched his body, curled his fingers around the chain at his wrist. "I…I'm sorry. I…"

The old man touched his hand to his throat and looked up at Oliver, anger etched into the lines on his face, disgust darkening his eyes. "Shower. And then to The Father."

Oliver drank in a breath, but his chest weighed a ton and he couldn't get enough air. He went about the motions of showering, letting the scalding water numb him from the outside in.

He had no recollection of walking to The Father's musty room, but when the smell of oil assaulted his nostrils, he found he was in front of a makeshift easel. A primed twenty-four inch canvas waited, along with tubes of paint, a palette and assorted brushes.

"You're late." The Father pushed away from the desk in the middle of the room and stood.

Oliver flicked a glance at him but said nothing. He knew the drill. Paint what was asked of him. Listen. Don't speak unless commanded to do so. He'd adhered to the routine for the last six months without complaint.

He turned to Petey who hovered in the doorway. "Aren't you going to unshackle me?"

"No." Petey's eyes narrowed to dark slits. "You try to kill me."

"I didn't—"

"You can paint shackled today," The Father ordered, dismissing Petey, and turning back to his desk.

The chain dangled between Oliver's wrists as he shuffled closer to the easel. He lifted one of the brushes off the ledge and contemplated shoving the wooden handle into The Father's eye.

Could he go through with it?

He ran the stiff bristles of the brush over his palm to quiet his shaking. The hesitant touch reminded him of Jocelyn. What if she was dead? What if they knew he'd tried to help her? Just a simple salve, nothing more…but they'd used less against him. No good deed went unpunished here, no wrongdoing escaped consequences.

If Jocelyn died because he didn't heed those warnings…

"You will paint me a church." The Father's sharp voice pushed its way into Oliver's thoughts.

He stiffened. "A church. What a surprise."

The Father swiveled around. Droplets of hand sanitizer clung to his cracked palms and he swiped them away, his mouth drawn into a scowl. "Tread very carefully, Shaw. This is the only reason you're still alive. So when I say paint, you paint." He bared his teeth like a predatory lion, the visual enhanced by the shock of brown hair that draped wildly against his forehead.

When Oliver still hesitated, The Father took a step forward and raised his fists. His face twisted, drawing attention to the red scars embedded in the damaged tissue of his right cheek. His knuckles leeched white. "I want a church. A nice, white-washed church secreted away in the jungle. You have fifteen minutes."

"Fifteen minutes isn't enough time to piss on your canvas, let alone paint on it."

The Father struck him on the side of the head. The sharp crack of the man's palm rang in Oliver's ear. "Paint."

Oliver forced his lips into a scowl. "And so I will."

He dropped his brush, picked up the palette in one hand and a tube of Raw Umber in the other. He uncapped the tube, squeezed a large blob of paint onto the palette and went to work thinning it with a few drops of linseed oil. With a small brush, he sketched the outline of a church on the canvas. But when he went for the tube of Titanium White to begin building up the layers of the church façade, he found himself holding Slate Black instead.

Oliver squeezed the paint onto the palette, crushing the tube in his fist, before tossing it onto the floor. He plunged his brush into the excessive glob and swept the color across the canvas. Again. Sharp, angry lines obliterating what he'd just sketched.

He couldn't stop. Didn't want to stop.

He snatched up the tube of Crimson, squeezed all the paint out of it in one massive pile and dropped it next to the black. He slashed that across the canvas as well. Raw Sienna came next, followed by Graphite, and Viridian, and Indigo. Tube after tube, until he'd exhausted them all.

Jocelyn. Her name pricked his heart. *Josie.*

He'd forsaken prayer long ago, but now, with his throat tight and his taut muscles working to eradicate the purity of the canvas, he bowed his head.

Please, God. Let the woman be alive.

He dropped his brush. It clattered to the floor, splattering more paint amidst the tubes littering the gray tiles.

"What have you done?" The Father yanked Oliver away from the canvas. "You—you insolent piece of— how could you? You—you've ruined everything!" With each screech he drove his fists into Oliver's face.

Oliver dropped to his knees, lifting his shackled hands to block the blows. Sucking in a ragged breath, he raised his eyes to the painting. Angry black and red lines formed a face, its mouth twisted in agony, the eyes sunken into nothing more than dark sockets.

He tensed every muscle in his body and waited without remorse for the sting of bamboo against his back.

PHEAKDEI RUBBED AT his neck. He bent over the woman's cot and squinted at her face, relaxed in sleep. His skin stung from the prisoner's attack two days ago. A dull ache still accompanied each swallow.

He'd never seen Oliver act that way before. Violent

and feral were words he reserved for The Trinity, not the prisoner he'd come to admire. What would possess him to break when nothing else had ever managed to rattle him?

The woman.

Pheakdei pressed his palm to her forehead. Her skin was cool to the touch. Her fever had finally broken.

Leo would be pleased. And when Leo was pleased, Pheakdei could breathe easier. Something about the albino always unnerved him. Not the hue of the man's skin, or the way he often appeared out of nowhere beside Pheakdei, but his profound silence, the anger that lurked beneath his cool features.

Pheakdei knew better than to rile him. He'd seen Leo wield a knife with sick, calculated precision.

And what about Jude? The Father could call for the woman at any moment. If he realized she wasn't in her cell, who would face his wrath? Not Leo. Not even Pheakdei. Jude would take the disobedience out on his family. His wife, his children, they were the reason he kept his mouth shut when he wanted to speak. Leo's reminder that Jude had spared them once weighed heavy on Pheakdei's mind. The others in his village weren't so lucky. The Trinity's butchers had slaughtered them and taken their children. If it weren't for the missionary doctors who'd taught Pheakdei all they knew, he'd have had nothing to offer The Trinity in exchange for his loved one's lives.

He touched his sore neck again. Couldn't he have at least broken his silence to ease the prisoner's conscience rather than letting him think the worst?

Pheakdei chewed on the inside of his cheek and turned to leave. No, he'd done the right thing. The woman would be returned to her cell, safe and healthy, soon enough. And he would no longer have to worry that Jude would discover his part in Leo's obsession.

A gasp halted his exit. He spun on his heel and found the woman's wary gaze on him.

"You're awake." He tried to smile, but dread sank like a stone in his stomach.

Leave. Get out of here before Leo discovers you talking to her. The albino had made it clear she was his. Even a polite hello could be misconstrued as horning in on his territory. Pheakdei backed up.

"Where—where am I?" The woman's raspy voice stopped him once more. She grabbed for her throat but the chains shackling her to the cot pulled taut and froze her attempt halfway. Her eyes widened. "Oh, God. What is this?"

He cringed at the pain in her voice and knew he couldn't leave without at least offering her water. Surely even Leo wouldn't begrudge her that one small comfort.

He crossed to the sink in the corner of the room and plucked the plastic cup from its rim.

"Where am I?" she repeated. "How long have I been here?"

What could he say? The less she knew the better— for the both of them. He turned the handle of the faucet. The neglected pipes squeaked and after a brief hesitation, tepid water spilled from the spigot. He filled the cup to the brim and shut off the water.

"You had a bad fever." He shuffled over to her, relenting in his silence just long enough to pass on vague information. "Two days, we keep you here until you are well."

She watched his approach, her brows knitted into a tight frown that stayed in place until he reached the cot and held the cup out to her. When she made no move to take it, he realized she couldn't, not with her wrists bound. He slid a hand beneath her head, tipped the cup to her lips and allowed her to sip at the lukewarm liquid until she'd downed most of the contents. He pulled away and took the cup back to the sink.

"What's your name?" Her voice was still raw, but the water had managed to smooth out most of the croak.

His name?

No one had asked him that before. No one ever chose to differentiate him from the rest of the men that roamed The Trinity's fortress.

He curved his fingers around the edge of the sink and bowed his head. "I...I am Pheakdei."

"Thank you, Pheakdei. For the water." She'd butchered the pronunciation of his name, but the sweet sound still brought moisture to his eyes.

Not Petey. Not Old Man. Pheakdei.

He straightened. "You are welcome."

Pheakdei waited for her to speak again, but a hush had fallen over the room. His curiosity got the better of him. He turned.

She had slipped back into sleep.

THE ACHES AND pains Jocelyn had been able to ignore in sleep returned with a vengeance once she awakened. She lay still for several long minutes, listening to the silence, but when her body started to tremble, she flattened her palms on the ground hoping to steady herself. Instead of the cold concrete she expected, her hands met the slight give of a thin mattress.

She jerked her eyes open, moonlight spearing into her pupils from a window set high in the wall.

A window? Where—?

Awareness seeped back in. She'd been moved. To the

gray and yellow room, with its sparse furnishings and peeling paint, and its old metal sink. What had Pheakdei told her? She'd been sick. Feverish. But why had they brought her here? Why hadn't they just left her in her cell to suffer?

She struggled to lift her head but it felt heavy—fuzzy—and she only got as far as tucking her chin to her chest. Enough to allow her to scan the shadowy room.

A man sat slumped in a metal folding chair.

Pheakdei.

She mouthed his name, but as soon as it soundlessly passed her lips she knew the figure couldn't be him. This man was much taller. Broader. He barely fit in the chair. And his skin…even in the faint light of the moon she could tell his skin was much paler than Pheakdei's, almost eerily translucent. His white hair was cropped close to his head, and his features had a washed out, colorless quality to them.

Who was he and what was he doing here? With her?

Uneasiness turned her stomach. She lifted her hand to press against her abdomen before remembering she was chained to the bed, but somehow her hand managed to complete the movement. The coarse weave of her shirt scratched at her palm. She bolted upright, every muscle screaming in protest. Her head swam and she froze, blinking the dizziness away.

Someone had unchained her.

Her pulse skittered. She was free. Unbound. How?

She smashed her lips together and glanced at the man snoring lightly in the chair. Still asleep. But for how long? Her gaze strayed to the door. Just a few feet separated her from freedom. Now was her chance. She might not get another one.

Jocelyn swung her shaky legs over the side of the

cot as quietly as possible. Her feet touched the cool tile, making her empty stomach lurch. She squeezed her eyes shut. *Ignore it. Get out of here now before he wakes up.*

She forced herself to stand despite her trembling muscles. Clenched her teeth to keep them from chattering. The door was no more than five feet in front of her. Surely she could make that distance. She inhaled and slid one foot forward. Then another. She kept her gaze pinned on the man slouched in the chair as she continued forward. The tile crackled audibly beneath her feet and she froze.

Oh, God.

The man shifted in the seat and let out a snort. His head lolled to the other side. If he woke up she couldn't outrun him. But she had to try.

She counted off another few seconds of silence. Keep moving. Just a few more steps.

And then what? She had no idea what was on the other side of the door. What if the guards lurked in the next room? What if their guns were trained on the door? What if she couldn't find her way out?

Jocelyn reached the door and glanced up at the window, the full moon infusing her with hope. Freedom was nearby. It had to be. She slowly turned the knob.

"Where do you think you're going?" A hand clamped on her shoulder like a vise and spun her around.

How had he come up behind her without so much as a creak of the chair or the thunk of footsteps on tile?

She clawed at his shirt, trying to dig her fingernails into his skin, but he twisted her in his arms and slammed her against the door. Her spine bounced off the knob, the sharp jab spearing an echoing pain behind her eyes.

He twined a hand in her hair and tugged, forcing

her to meet his gaze. Moonlight sifted across his face, illuminating his filmy eyes and the white of his skin.

"Jocelyn." He tightened his pallid lips. His white-blond eyebrows drew into a frown. He ran a palm down her face, stopping when he covered her mouth. "Were you going to leave me?"

She shook her head, sucking in air through her nose.

He invaded more of her space and thrust his forehead against hers. "No one else would've nursed you. They would've left you in your cell to rot, without food or water. But not me." His warm, musty breath blasted across her cheek. "I made you well. You can thank me."

Her denial got lost in his sweaty palm. She turned her face to the side, trying to dislodge his grip on her mouth, but he only increased the pressure and leaned in closer. Her heart thundered in her ears, her chest hurt and each breath grew shallower.

He touched his tongue to her jaw, licking a rough, wet path up her cheek. Her entire body started to tremble. Bile threatened to rise within her, but she concentrated on bucking against his hold, gnashing her teeth into his palm. He jerked his hand away and let out a chuckle.

She shoved at him. "Stay away from me, you freak!"

He lost his footing and stumbled backward. She found her opening and darted around him, but hadn't taken more than two steps when he grabbed a fistful of her shirt and yanked her into him.

They fell, crashing into the cot on their way down. She took the brunt of the impact to her side, dislodging the creep's hold on her. The sharp pain robbed her breath and blurred her vision, but she scrambled blindly to her feet.

Go! Run.

The door loomed ahead of her—a fuzzy portal to

freedom across the expanse of wavy tile. She ran. Her slick palm slipped on the brass doorknob, but she held on by sheer willpower and yanked open the door. The humid air hit her as she flew into the empty hallway. She careened left. No time to stop and get her bearings.

She only managed a handful of steps before the man caught up and slammed her to the ground, jabbing his knee into her back.

He yanked on her hair, tugging her head up. "You're not like Ruthie. Not even close. That mouth of yours speaks vile words, blind to what's right in front of you."

"Leave me alone," she wheezed.

His mouth brushed her ear. "Not to worry." He nipped at her earlobe with his teeth. "I'll make you appreciate my beauty in time. Beneath skin and bone, my heart beats same as yours. We're not so different, you and I. Look closer. See me."

Nausea overflowed in her stomach, spilling into her throat. She pressed her cheek harder against the cold floor to avoid his eyes. An acidic taste filled her mouth. Her ears buzzed, and it wasn't until he cursed that the hum registered as a ring tone.

He yanked her to her feet, squinting at the message in the glow of the emergency lighting. A text.

His mouth tightened. "The Father has requested your presence." Barely leashed resentment coiled his words. "We'll have to continue this later."

FIVE

THE PAINTINGS WERE gone.

Jocelyn yanked herself away from the pale man's bruising grip and wrapped her arms around herself. Chills edged over her body. She did a quick scan of the room. Same scarred table, same metal folding chair, but the paintings that had calmed her the first time in The Father's room had been removed.

She wanted out of this place.

Her breath quickened as she spun toward the door, but the albino's broad frame blocked the exit, forcing her to retreat. Her hip bumped the table and she reached back to grip the edge for balance, but her fingers closed over a thick leather-bound book instead. She picked it up, her gaze immediately drawn to the gold lettering engraved in the bottom right-hand corner.

DJH.

Donald James Hewitt.

She gasped. Her thumb fanned the pages. Dates and coordinates leapt out at her. Her dad's handwriting. She'd know it anywhere. This was his flight logbook, the one he carried with him whenever he flew. The one that never left his plane.

"Oh, my God." Her knees threatened to buckle, and she sank back against the table.

She flipped open to the middle of the book. A small photograph of a pig-tailed girl with a gap-toothed smile was tucked against the spine.

Her.

Jocelyn's heart banged against her chest, rattling a gasp from her. She touched the faded photo with trembling hands and moved it aside. Scribbled on the page in a precise square block was another one of those symbols—a sun. She flipped through the pages again and found more of the same. Two blocks containing weird lines across the center. Another with a serpent.

And then nothing.

The rest of the pages were blank.

"You can go now."

She lurched at the sound of The Father's voice. He shouldered into the room past the large ghostly pale man.

The albino straightened in the doorway. "She wants me to stay."

"Is that so?" The Father raised a brow at her. The gesture pulled at the naked skin above his other eye.

Jocelyn's fingers curled around leather. She clutched the logbook. "No."

He turned back to the albino. "You're not needed here."

The albino's nostrils flared and his translucent cheeks blanched white. "Don't you touch her."

The Father ignored the command. "Have you looked in on our little workers today?"

"I know my duties. You don't need to remind me."

"Good. Then I'll leave you to them. Fair enough?"

The albino grunted, shot Jocelyn one last lascivious stare and faded off down the hall. Her two sadistic guards appeared and took up their positions in the doorway.

The Father stomped over to her and ripped her dad's book out of her hands.

He might as well have been ripping out her heart. "How did you get my dad's flight log? Were you there, when his plane went down? Tell me where he is!"

The Father stared at her with a satisfied gleam lighting his eyes. "He's dead, of course. As for this," he waved the book in front of her face, "finders keepers, losers weepers and all that."

He tossed the journal on the table. The carelessness of the action burned in Jocelyn's gut. She lunged for the book, but The Father clamped down on her shoulders and yanked her back.

"I know he's dead," she whispered, pulling herself free. "But you know how he died, don't you? Did you… kill him?"

His mouth turned up into an uneven smirk, the scars on the right side of his face twitching. Everything she'd believed about her dad's death crumbled.

No. Don't let him fool you. Dad died from injuries sustained in the crash.

That had to be how it went down. To think otherwise was to crush twenty-four years of strongly held beliefs. And yet, under The Father's knowing sneer lurked a dark and dangerous truth. One she had to uncover.

She flew at him, raking her fingernails down his disfigured cheek. "What happened to my dad?"

He didn't flinch. In one smooth move, he reared back and smacked her against the mouth. She stumbled backward. Blood welled on her lip. She'd aimed for the wrong cheek. The burned flesh didn't have any feeling left in it.

The Father's hands came around her throat. He propelled her against the wall, got right in her face. "Forty-eight hours. The clock starts now. Decode your father's cipher and I just might let you live." He shoved her at the guards. "Take her back to her cell."

The guards dragged her through the maze of corridors. She tried to memorize each turn, but her thoughts crowded in on her, clouding her concentration. Elephant. Skull. Sun. Serpent. If, like The Father insisted, those markings were some sort of code to a treasure map, there had to be a common denominator between them. A key she could use to decipher their meaning.

But what?

Her captors shoved her into the cell. She sank onto the cold concrete and buried her face in her hands.

"He said you would know." The Father's words from their first confrontation slithered through her mind.

He'd been talking about her dad.

Donald Hewitt wasn't the careless type. He would have made sure the code was deliberate and personal— something only those closest to him would know how to interpret. Which meant…

Her head snapped up.

She was the key.

Miss Hewitt was every bit as spiteful as her father.

Jude massaged sanitizer into his dead cheek. Dabbed at it with a tissue. Oh, Donald Hewitt had put on a grand pretense of love and kindness, but beneath the surface he'd been no better than the Reverend. Only Jude's mother had practiced what she preached.

He opened his desk drawer and rooted around until his fingers closed over a smooth, oval-shaped object. The miniature likeness of Angela Larkin never failed to soothe him. He could still remember the way she smelled, a combination of oranges and jasmine that floated around the air as she had spread aloe on his cuts and bruises.

"He loves you, baby," she'd say. "He just doesn't know how to show it. All he wants is for you to be your best."

Then she'd take the next beating for him.

He'd do right by the Reverend for as long as he could, and his mom would smile like Jude had given her the most precious gift, but he never measured up to his dad's standards. Sooner or later, no matter how hard he tried, he crumbled under the weight of his dad's mandates and the vicious cycle started all over again.

His mother never once complained. Never once blamed Jude when her entire back turned black and blue or when her legs hurt too much to walk unassisted to church. No. She thought him perfect. Always. She loved him when his shortcomings made him unlovable.

She'd loved Donald Hewitt with that same selfless love, and he'd taken advantage of it. He'd had to pay for that. Both him and the Reverend.

A knock on the door brought his head up. He swiped a hand over his eyes. "Come in."

Chann entered the room, tugging at his missionary collar. The action never failed to make Jude smile. Chann hated his role in The Trinity, but he was the only one who could pull it off. He had grown up as one of the Khmer. With his short stature, broad face and darker skin he blended in, commandeering their trust with the ease of a pious missionary, then turning on them as fast as a chameleon snake. "Leo tells me you've been looking for me."

Jude shrugged, choosing his words carefully, probing for unspoken truths, shifts in loyalty. "You've been scarce."

"I can't very well do my job if I'm not visible among the villagers." Chann folded his arms across his chest. "They trust me because I commune with them."

"As long as it's your job you're doing."

"What's that supposed to mean?"

"Three new children in the last month, and not one of them worthy." Jude tightened his jaw. "I count on you to bring me the chosen ones, not rejects I have to cast out."

"You work them to an early grave, Jude. No child can withstand—"

"Do you remember my mother?" Jude ran his thumb over his mother's miniature, stroking her long blond hair.

Chann blinked. "Yes. Of course. She taught me how to write my name."

"She was always so nice to everyone." He dropped the picture back into the drawer, sealing it inside. "I don't think I'm like her."

THE WHIMPERS REMINDED Leo of a pack of howling coyotes as he made one more round through the camp. Perspiration clung to him. His skin prickled, not from a chill, but from the high-pitched keening that pierced the night.

Stepping around a jig adjacent to one of the larger mining pits, he approached the low building that housed the children. He undid the latch securing the rough-hewn door and shoved it open. The creak of hinges sliced across the cry, cutting the child off in mid-shriek.

Bless my fucking ears.

Leo fumbled along the wall until his fingers grazed the light switch and flipped it on. Twenty pairs of dark, empty eyes blinked against the sudden brightness. The stench of sickness and unwashed bodies hit him. He drew in a mouthful of clean air and started down the narrow strip of dirt floor separating each side of the room.

For a brief moment the space remained blessedly silent except for the whisper of his own footfalls. Children ranging in age from seven to their late teens huddled together on dingy mats. Filthy rags hung on their lean frames—shirts and pants that had once been clean and stiff. The children's hair was kept shorn close to their head, making it difficult to determine their gender without a closer look.

He narrowed his eyes at them and tried to find some compassion. Annoyance tugged at him instead. While Jude and Chann slept peacefully in their soft beds night after night, his rest was constantly disturbed by this pack of brats. Their hungry moans. Their endless needs. If he got a decent day's work out of them, that would be one thing, but more often than not, they came up empty handed and he was forced to report to Jude that only a handful of zircons had been found.

Served Jude right. He was the one who'd insisted on using children in the first place. Claimed they were his disciples. Leo snorted. As far as he could see, they met the only criteria that mattered—free labor, easy to control and dispensable. Until they'd recently started getting sick, they'd also always been plentiful.

One child reached out and snagged the hem of his pants. He shook her off, but another grabbed for him, and another, each of them wrapping their puny arms around his leg.

"I'm hungry—"

"My throat hurts—"

"I'm hot—"

"I'm cold—"

The complaints escalated until he could no longer distinguish the individual words in the collective hum.

He raised his fists to his ears, glowered, and shook off the children. "Quiet!"

Immediately a hush fell over the room. The children tucked their hands between their knees and shrank back against each other.

Better.

Leo sent them all one more glare to ensure their silence for the rest of the night and spun on his heel. He hadn't taken more than a few steps when a soft voice stopped him cold.

"Samnang is very sick."

He turned to the back of the room. That girl—their newest recruit—stood in the middle of a group of cowering children. Her hair had yet to be cut, and the inky black strands dipped into her brown eyes. She clenched her dirt-streaked hands in front of her chest and raised her chin a notch. An almost imperceptible tremor ran through her.

"Who?" He stalked forward. The sea of children parted.

"S—Samnang." She gestured to a boy at the front of the group.

Leo stopped in front of him and looked down into the boy's hollow gaze. He rocked back and forth as if trying to combat the shivers that wracked his bony body. Clearly the boy was burning up.

Another case of dengue fever. Had to be.

Leo sank onto his haunches and gripped the boy's sallow cheeks. "Open your mouth."

The boy's lips tightened. He shook his head.

Leo squeezed tighter. "Open. Up."

Once more the boy hesitated, but finally he dropped his jaw a fraction.

He yanked the child's head back to catch the light, forcing his mouth open wider. Something shiny winked back at him. "What the fuck?"

Leo pulled the boy's lips away from his teeth. Tucked in the side of his mouth down by the gums was a crude sapphire, the size of a pea.

He yanked it out of the child's mouth. Held it in his face. "What is this? Where did you get this?"

The boy whimpered.

Leo shot to his feet and yanked the boy into his arms. His anger bubbled over, searing his veins. He stalked to the door and swung around to face the children one last time.

"Samnang won't be back."

While the rest of the children buried their faces in their knees, the girl didn't physically react to his guttural hiss. She stared at him with wide, penetrating eyes that dared to curse him to hell.

"If I catch anyone else stealing what's ours…" He drew his finger across his throat, then tightened his hold on Samnang and ducked out the door.

JOCELYN PRESSED HER palm to her throbbing temple. Why couldn't she think? Time wouldn't slow down to give her a chance to make sense of her dad's pictograms. Forty-eight hours wasn't long at all. What would happen if she couldn't give The Father an answer? Could she stall him? Find a way to buy more time?

She'd always believed good triumphed over evil. But in this dark and desolate place, evil ruled. Despair weighed on her. She didn't understand any of this. What kind of sickos kept ancient prison cells in the middle of the jungle? The kind that wouldn't hesitate to kill her even if she gave them what they were after.

She didn't want to die.

Don't think like that. There is good here. You just have to find it.

She swallowed hard, scooted over to the small hole in the wall and leaned her head on the cool metal to bring her mouth near the opening.

"Hey...are...are you still there?" She held her breath and listened to the scrape of movement on the other side.

"Jocelyn?" The man's breath seemed to shudder against the wall. "I thought you were dead."

Dead? She dipped her head and peeked into the hole, hoping to catch a glimpse of the man whose jagged words could have cut the tin separating them. But she could see nothing except the barest hint of shadowy light.

"No. No! Why would you think that?"

"You were gone. They moved you. They never move anyone unless—" he choked off the rest of his statement, but it echoed in the air anyway.

The low rasp of his voice was like a guitar string being plucked after years of disuse. She flattened her palm against the metal, wishing she could find a way to prove to him that she was all right. The wall felt so cold, so impersonal. She needed the warm reality of his touch.

"I'm right here." She slid two fingers through the hole. "See?"

Her fingers started to prickle as she waited for him to reach out, and just when she decided it was a lost cause, his warm, calloused fingertips brushed hers. She closed her eyes, not wanting to relinquish the strength that came from him. If he retreated, she'd go back to that cold, dark place where loneliness had the power to destroy her. She could endure anything—fight any-thing—as long as she didn't have to do it alone.

She swallowed hard. "What's your name?"

He yanked his hand back. "It's better if you don't know."

Frowning, she pulled her own hand from the wall. "How could it be better not to know your name? What am I supposed to call you?"

"Why would you want to call me anything?"

"Because…" Why? It wasn't like they'd met over a drink at some cozy bar. What did it matter who he was? She folded her knees. It didn't. Except, not know-ing somehow dehumanized both her and him. And she couldn't bear to sacrifice any part of who she was to this horrific situation. "Because we're people," she said, trying to put her feelings into words. "Not just face-less captives."

"I haven't been anything other than a faceless cap-tive in a long time."

She laid her cheek on her knee. "How long have you been here?"

"Long enough to know I should've been dead a long time ago."

An ache spread through her. "How long is that?"

"Two years. Maybe a little more. I lost count of the days for a time."

She'd been here less than a week and wanted out. Now. Two years was like an eternity. Did he have fam-ily waiting for him back home? Was anyone still looking for him? She wanted to bombard him with questions, but he wouldn't even tell her his name and she didn't want to risk him shutting her out if she got too personal.

"What do they want from you?" she asked, steering the questions to something he might be willing to answer.

He laughed. Bitter, sharp. "The Trinity? They don't want anything from me. Not anymore. They could come in and kill me at any time and there wouldn't be a damn thing I could do to stop it."

"But they wanted something from you once."

"I wanted something from them too. Their location." She heard the scuff of him moving closer, settling himself against the wall. "I'm—" he hesitated and when he spoke again his voice was just a hint rougher than before, "I *was* an undercover agent with the CIA's Special Activities Division. The Trinity has been on the CIA's radar for years for funneling money to terrorist groups. FARC, Hamas, Hezbollah. It doesn't matter who gets the money, as long as they use it for destruction."

Goose bumps rose on her skin. "Oh, God. That's... crazy."

"Two years ago we'd finally caught a break and traced the source of the money back to a sapphire mine in Cambodia," Oliver continued. "The CIA assembled a small team of agents from around the globe—CIA, MI-6, Mossad—to ferret out their location. Once we found their base, we were to call the coordinates in and leave Spec Ops to take out both the mine and The Trinity. The plan was supposed to be a simple reconnaissance mission."

"But something went wrong." The words rushed out on a single breath she hadn't realized she'd been holding.

"Yes."

His affirmation fell between them with a finality that told her he wouldn't welcome further probing into the details of the failed mission. But she couldn't let it go.

"Didn't you ever think about trying to escape?"

OLIVER INHALED SHARPLY, Jocelyn's question finding its target deep into his heart. When hadn't he thought about escaping? He'd made it his singular purpose from the moment The Trinity had captured him. He'd sacrificed the rest of his team because of his determination to escape.

He still saw his friends' faces in his nightmares. Heard their screams. They shackled him to this cell more effectively than any iron could.

He shoved his hands through his hair and opted to give her a watered-down answer. "I tried several times and failed. It's not worth the risk."

"So…you just stopped trying? I'd think freedom's worth just about any risk."

Censure colored her words. He should stop talking, just move to the other side of the cell and ignore her from this point forward. He didn't owe her any explanations, certainly didn't owe her a peek into his shriveled soul.

"Freedom's just another prison." He hadn't intended to voice his opinion on the matter, but the words resonated within him, drawing a fire in his gut.

"If everyone thought like that, the world would be a sad place."

"Better sad than unrealistic."

His statement was met with silence. From the way it lengthened, he thought he'd succeeded in driving her away.

But then she spoke again, and he had to lean closer to the hole to catch her words. "Maybe you're right."

He clenched his jaw, digging his fingernails into the concrete floor. Damn it, no, he didn't want to be right. He wanted to hear her convince him otherwise in that voice of hers—the one that was so full of goodness he feared he was fast becoming obsessed with hearing her speak.

Just one more word. One more sentence. Enough to sustain him when he plunged back into the darkness.

"You asked what The Trinity wanted with me," he said, desperate to keep her talking for another minute. "What about you?"

"I just want to bring my father home."

"He lives here in Cambodia?"

"No. I'm a forensic anthropologist with the Joint POW-MIA Accounting Command. They sent a team to recover my father's remains and I…"

His heart dropped into his stomach. "You what?"

"Wasn't even supposed to be here." Her voice thickened. "My boss refused to put me on the team because the mission was too personal. But, I—I couldn't let someone else be the one to bring my dad home, you know? It had to be me. I made a promise to my mother before she died, that I would finally get answers to his disappearance. And now the rest of my team is dead and I'm…"

She trailed off, getting very quiet, but he didn't need to see her to feel the tears coursing down her cheeks. They filled the hollow place inside him.

"Someone will come looking for you." The lie rolled off his tongue so smoothly. He should've choked on it, but she didn't need to know the chances of finding her in this hellhole were next to none. Those brought here never left. "They'll discover you're missing and they'll send a team of experts who won't rest until they find you."

She sniffed. "Is the CIA still out looking for you?"

"To look for me, they'd have to acknowledge my

existence. They couldn't jeopardize the entire Special Activities Division for me or any other team member."

"So they just left you here? To die?"

He almost laughed at the outrage that sparked in her voice. She didn't understand that dying was the easy part. It was the living that was a bitch. "If I was any kind of agent, I would've found a way to accommodate them by now."

"But what about your family? Surely they would've insisted the CIA look for you."

"No family." His mom had died when he was eight, and his dad, days after his high school graduation. He'd enlisted right after the funeral, hoping to find his place in the Army, but once a loner, always a loner. "I was prime S.A.D. material and well aware of the risks when I signed on. I've spent years becoming whoever they needed me to be."

"Is that why you won't tell me your name? You don't know which one to give?"

What was in a name? He'd had many identities over the years that felt more real than his own. Maybe he should just give her one of those and be done with it. It would solve so many things…

He closed his eyes, leaned his head against the wall. "It's—Oliver—the name on my birth certificate. Oliver Shaw."

"Oliver." She repeated it again, softer, her voice caressing his name. "Thank you for telling me."

He shrugged. "Yeah, well…"

Why *had* he told her? What happened to keeping it impersonal? To not getting involved? Too late for that. He'd let her get under his skin in the space of a few short minutes and there was no turning back.

He was linked with her. If The Father found out…

Oliver shuddered, drawing the worn fabric of his shirt closer around him. "We shouldn't be talking."

She didn't say anything for a long time and he figured she'd gotten his not-so-subtle hint. He crouched to his feet, flattened his palms on the wall and prepared to move back to the shadowy corner of his cell where he could write in his journal and visit his beachfront home in his head.

"Oliver?"

He leaned his forehead against the pitted metal, drinking in the lovely cadence of her voice. "Yeah?"

"I need you to help me find a way out of here."

HIS FAVORED CHILDREN were stealing from him.

Jude rolled the tiny sapphire Leo had brought him between his fingers. He gripped the gem in his fist and thumped it against his chest. After all he'd done to give those pitiful waifs a future, this is how they repaid his love. With deception and betrayal.

What disappointments. He should cast them all out. Tell Leo to take them into the jungle and get rid of them. Maybe if he started over he'd find children that would finally appreciate him and the lessons he was trying so hard to instill.

No, he didn't have time. If this measly rock was the best the mine was producing, they were in worse trouble than he'd thought.

Once the sapphires were so plentiful it took no effort to pluck them out of the ground and turn them into cash. His money had secured guns, bombs, chemical warfare, new identities—whatever necessary to orchestrate global destruction. He'd bought his status as one of the most powerful lords of chaos, and the depletion of the sapphire mine meant someone else could step in and take his place.

Unless he found Kala's Ashes.

With a wealth of sacred red diamonds at his disposal, no one would dare question his supremacy.

He spread Donald Hewitt's letters out on the table beside the open flight log and carefully scanned the pages. Each pictogram was drawn in its own precise block, eight blocks in all. Four of them had been scattered throughout the logbook, the other four dispersed amongst Hewitt's letters.

The pictogram of a serpent eating its own tail had to refer to Kala. Cambodian folklore depicted the great Kala as a jawless monster commanded by the gods to devour his own body. Why else include such a reference if not to point the way to Kala's shrine?

Yet as he looked at the remaining seven pictograms, ranging from a sun to an elephant to some innocuous-looking squiggles, he couldn't find a common thread to any of them.

No, that wasn't exactly true. There was one common thread, but she wasn't talking.

He slammed the book closed, fluttering the photograph that lay facedown in the desk lamp's halo of light. Jude snagged the picture, warm from the lamp, and held it at eye level. A young Miss Hewitt—no more than seven or eight—smiled back at him from the Polaroid, her brown hair in pigtails, a light dusting of freckles across her nose. So innocent. So happy. Looking into the camera as if she didn't have a clue about the harsh realities of this world. She'd probably never taken a caning for forgetting morning prayers or been forced to skip a meal.

But he had.

He still remembered the sharp sting of a rod across his back, the laceration that had been his breaking point. Everyone had one. The Reverend had taught him that, and it was one lesson he sought to pass onto the children.

He would find Miss Hewitt's, no matter what it took.

Jude sat back in his chair, folding his hands across his chest. "I trust you've taken care of our little problem?"

Chann's mouth curled in distaste. "I've had a talk with the children. Leo did his best to scare some sense into them. As for the boy... Leo made sure he won't be stealing from anyone ever again."

"Excellent." Jude stared hard at Chann's bowed head and the slump of his shoulders. If he didn't know better, he'd worry at the waves of aversion that rippled off his friend's posture. Surely Chann couldn't be having second thoughts? Not when they were so close to the pinnacle of their kingdom. He drummed his fingers on the desk, giving in to the hunch that had started to take root in his gut. "I'm sending a team out scouting. East of Ta Veaeng Lu."

The sun in Donald Hewitt's pictogram had to act like a compass, pointing in a direction—toward the sunrise.

Chann straightened. His thick brows rose. "So, the woman...she's cooperating then?"

Jude scraped his teeth together. "You just let me worry about the woman."

A lesser man would've missed Chann's slight hesitation. Had his friend forgotten whom he was dealing with? Nothing slipped past Jude's notice—least of all a faltering that could jeopardize the very foundation of power he'd spent his life erecting.

The unease passed in a flash, and Chann executed a tight mock bow, his palms pressed together as if in supplication. "As always, Father. But you should know,

I heard voices as I came up the tunnel. Just faint murmurs, but most definitely Shaw and the woman."

"Let them talk." Jude shoved himself out of his chair, ignoring the acid that rolled through his stomach.

He could stand to be patient a little longer. Let them form a bond and grow to care about one another. There was nothing more thrilling than pitting friend against friend and watching as they tore each other apart.

SIX

As soon as Jocelyn had asked Oliver for his help in escaping, he'd stopped talking. More than stopped talking. No movement came from the other side of the wall. No shuffling or cursing. He'd just…withdrawn. It was as if he'd vanished, or maybe even morphed into stone, turning a deaf ear to anything she might've said to persuade him.

Now, hours later, his voice came back, faint but unmistakably infused with conviction. "I can't do it."

She sat up, moved from the scrap of bamboo that served as her bed, and crawled over to the wall. "Why? Don't you want to get out of here?"

"Want?" He snorted softly. "Wanting is destructive. I *can't* want. And neither should you."

She curved her hand against the wall, tightening it into a fist. Being stuck in the same horrific situation didn't give her the right to presume she knew Oliver at all. She didn't know what he looked like or who he'd once been before captivity stripped him, yet she had to believe he hadn't always been this apathetic. If she could get him to look beyond this place, maybe he would remember something worth fighting for.

"Tell me about your life. Before you got captured."

"Why?" Suspicion clouded the question.

"Why not?" She struggled to make her voice casual. "What else do you have to do?"

"There's nothing to tell."

"Nothing? What about where you're from? How you ended up working with the CIA?"

Why was she so compelled to know him when he didn't want her prying into his life? There was something so raw and jagged about him, like he didn't believe in goodness anymore, and it made her heart hurt to think of him lying in a squalid cell, without hope.

He chuckled—a hard, mirthless sound. "You're something else, you know that? My past doesn't matter. There is no past here. There's nothing but a great big void."

She stared hard at the dingy wall directly across from her. "No past, no future, just the here and now. How can you think like that?" A fissure of rust running along the metal caught her attention. If she let this place tear her down, she'd corrode in much the same way. She had to stay positive. "You're alive. The rest of your team wasn't so lucky."

"Lucky." His voice sharpened. "Luck had nothing to do with it. I killed them as sure as if I put a bullet through their heart."

"No." Remorse gripped her stomach and twisted. He was right. She wasn't alive because of luck either. Her friends had paid for her life with their blood.

"You have family waiting back home for you?"

Oliver's question gave the guilt a tighter hold. "My friends were my family. We spent months at a time together in the field, so we learned to take care of each other. Claire could make the most awesome brownies over an open fire—"

"I don't even remember what those taste like."

"You don't? They taste like…" She bit her lip, fighting the urge to cry. "The best day of your life."

"I can't remember that either."

Her nose started to run and she swiped at it with her sleeve. "And Matt, he—he was always playing tricks on us. One time he managed to switch all our things around while we were sleeping. I woke up and thought I was in Jason's tent. And Jason. Oh, God, Jason came out of his tent wearing Claire's shirt. He'd dressed in the dark and thought it was his." She smiled at the memory. "It was hot pink with High Maintenance Diva written on it. I laughed so hard Jason wouldn't speak to me for weeks."

"Matt. Your voice changes when you speak of him." A beat of silence fell between them. "Was he your boyfriend?"

"No. Just my best friend. I loved him, though." She ran her sleeve across her damp eyes. "I loved all of them. My mom passed away earlier this year and my sister… we haven't talked for a long, long time."

She crossed her arms, gripping her shoulders. More connections lost, more pain that set her further adrift. She truly had no one now. "Maybe my sister was right. Maybe I should've stopped searching for answers to our dad's disappearance. Tasha couldn't understand why my mom and I wouldn't let go of his death. She was only three years old when his plane went down and never really had the chance to know him." Jocelyn closed her eyes, digging her fingers into her skin. "Mom and I used to sit for hours poring over dad's letters, looking for clues to his whereabouts, wondering whether he could be alive out there, somewhere. It made Tasha furious. She just wanted us to get on with our lives. But… how can you get on with your life when you're missing a huge chunk of who you are?"

She sighed, dropping her hands and burying them between her knees. "I want that chunk back. I want the truth. Because it sure isn't what I've believed all these

years. Where does my dad fit in with this group—The...
Trinity? Is that what you called them? Why does their
leader have my dad's logbook?"

"Maybe you mistook what you saw. These walls have
a way of making things unclear. It only gets worse as
time goes on and you start to doubt yourself and everything around you."

"No. The book was my dad's. I held it in my hands.
Saw his handwriting. That man, the one they call The
Father, insists my dad was putting together some sort
of coded map before he died. My dad ran supply routes
for the Air Force. What reason could he possibly have
for all this cloak and dagger—?"

"Wait a minute. Did you just say map?" The lash of
Oliver's voice cut through her musings. "Son of a bitch."

"What? What is it?"

"I only know of one map The Father would do anything to find. Kala's Ashes. A mine rumored to hold
the biggest, rarest gems in the world. Cambodian legend has it that when the great Kala died, his fiery ashes
turned into red diamonds and sank into the earth or
some shit like that."

Kala's Ashes. Could her dad have been looking for
the diamonds? She frowned. What for? Donald Hewitt
wasn't a treasure seeker.

But he never could resist a good legend.

Kala's Ashes was just the sort of tale her dad
would've found fascinating. "So...this mine? It's not a
real place, then?"

"Some believe it is. The CIA was operating under the
assumption that it existed. The story goes that one of the
first Khmer tribes took the map and scattered it in eight
directions. They believed if the markers were divided

amongst the elders of the tribes, each one only know-ing their own piece, they could protect Kala's legacy."

Markers. Symbols.

She shook her head. "That couldn't be it, then. These drawings don't even remotely resemble some form of ancient script."

"What do they look like?"

"They're...ordinary." She bit her lip, trying to put the feel of the doodles into words. "Primitive. Almost... childlike. One was an elephant, then there was a sun—I remember seeing a serpent too when I flipped through his logbook."

"Are you sure they weren't some sort of glyphs? The Egyptian alphabet is about as primitive as you can get."

"They don't resemble glyphs at all. They're just... scribbles."

Her cheeks warmed. The idea of those hastily scrawled markings pointing the way to some priceless cache of diamonds sounded even more foolish after voicing it out loud. Oliver must've thought so too, be-cause he fell silent. Why couldn't The Father see the absurdity?

Absurd or not, he demanded an answer. One she still couldn't come up with.

She looked around the cell, and let silence stretch be-tween her and Oliver. The shadows dulled her senses, but the stale smell and damp air put her on edge. They were a reminder that her friends lay in an unmarked grave somewhere while she at least had a semblance of shelter. Even if that shelter suffocated her. A mere five days in this place seemed like an eternity. She couldn't learn to adapt the way Oliver had. Every day she'd think of Claire and Jason and Matt and how she'd failed to

save them. She had to find them and bring them home
to their families.

She straightened, twisting to speak directly into the
hole in the wall. "I have to get out of here. You're the
only one I can trust who knows the layout of this place.
I need your help, Oliver, but if you refuse—I—I'll do it
myself. I won't stay here. I can't."

JOCELYN'S FRANTIC PLEA struck a chord within Oliver.
He'd felt the same way when he'd first been taken cap-
tive. At wit's end. Desperate for a way out. But now...
he couldn't seem to think how anything would be better if he attempted another escape.

If he failed, The Trinity would punish them both.
Swift torture that alternated between the emotional
and the physical, yet never crossed the ultimate line.
The Trinity's power came from harsh punishments that
stopped just short of death. He couldn't go through that
again. Wouldn't put Jocelyn through an even worse hell
for nothing.

But what if he didn't fail? What if this time they succeeded—together?

The thought crashed into him. God, it had been so
long since he'd thought positively about anything. Now
that the idea grabbed onto him, it didn't want to let go.

He wrapped his fingers in his hair and yanked, hoping the discomfort would ground him. Even if they succeeded in getting out, where would they go? They were
hidden in a jungle so thick they'd never know which end
was up. And The Trinity wouldn't just sit back and wave
goodbye. They would sic their mercenaries on them. He
and Josie would die somewhere amongst the trees, their
blood spilling out on the ground.

So what? Was that any worse than what they were

currently enduring? What if they took a chance and it paid off? What if they found their way out of the jungle and were…free?

Free.

He shuddered as the word cut straight through him. Free. Sweat popped out on his brow, and he swiped it away with his palm. His pulse spiked. He had to squeeze his eyes shut and focus on his breathing to rein it back in.

Freedom. The idea sounded so sweet, but it was just another kind of hell. He slouched down, leaning his head against the wall.

"Oliver? Are you okay?"

He stifled the jaded comment that stung his tongue. "Yeah."

"Can you just…think about it?"

No. He couldn't think about getting out of this place. Couldn't wish for it, or plan for it. Hope had crushed him once.

"I won't change my mind," he said after a long minute. "You're better off forgetting the whole thing. Wait it out. Someone will come and find you."

"Really? Is that what you've been telling yourself? It's been two years and no one has come for you."

"It's different."

"How?"

"It just is." He knew he sounded like a two-year-old in the throes of a tantrum, but he had to end the discussion. Immediately.

"I won't wait," she fired right back. "I'll fight my way out of here if I have to. With or without your help."

"Without." The word was a curse, a strangled denial that pushed him to his feet.

If his chest got any tighter, he'd have to fight to draw

breath. The knot in his lungs twisted, urging him to put some distance between him and Jocelyn. He couldn't help her. He should've never spoken.

A key turned in the lock and his door swung open. Petey hovered on the threshold, wary, the familiar chains clutched in his gnarled grip like a weapon. Oliver swallowed thickly. He'd done that to him. Forced a hardened old man to fear him.

What would he do to someone like Jocelyn if he continued to chip away at her vitality?

He grazed his fingers along the wall, the apologetic caress he wished he could give her, then he dropped his hands in front of him in a show of acquiescence.

"You're late today." He met Petey's curious stare for a fraction of a second before bowing his head and holding out his hands.

Petey closed the chains around his wrists. Oliver waited for the oppressive burden of the iron to drag him down. As he passed the threshold, he looked back and wondered, which prison was worse—the physical nine-by-nine or the fear wrapped around his heart.

THE FATHER HAD destroyed Oliver's painting.

The tortured face he'd painted was gone and in its place, waiting for him atop the easel, sat a clean, blank canvas. He moved in front of it and let the smell of pungent oil-based paint once again fill his nostrils. But this time when the fumes went to his head, they didn't calm him.

Thoughts of Jocelyn swirled inside him. He had to find a way to talk her out of escaping. She didn't know what she was getting into, and he couldn't let her find out the way he had. He swallowed the fist of apprehension that lodged in his throat and reached for the brush on the easel's ledge. He paused, his fingers pressing against wood, and stared down at his shackled wrists.

He squeezed the brush between his fingers, shaking off the panic that pelted his chest like gunfire. Damn Jocelyn for making him question himself. For making him wish for the man he used to be. Unscarred, untroubled. Worthy. He wasn't any of those things anymore. What good did it do to pretend he was?

"I'm in the mood for a Cathedral today, but I don't have much time, so start painting." The Father snapped Oliver out of his thoughts.

Oliver dipped his brush in the paint, not in the frame of mind to argue. He fixed his gaze on the canvas and swept a swatch of gray across the surface. The Father would not be deterred from a confrontation. He circled behind the canvas and forced his way into Oliver's line of vision.

"I've heard you and Miss Hewitt have been having a nice chat." He smirked, the damaged side of his face twisting. "It must be nice to have someone to talk to again."

Oliver stiffened his spine, narrowed his eyes on the canvas, and drew his brows tight as he set to adding a bit of brown to the gray.

Ignore him. He's trying to goad you.

"It's just like old times. When you and—what was her name again?—" The Father snapped his fingers, "—ah, yes. Catrina. You two were always whispering back and forth, planning our demise as if you might actually get out of here alive."

Oliver dug his fingers into the wood of the brush until his grip physically hurt. "Don't."

"Yes, don't." The Father shot him with a menacing whisper. "Don't get too attached to Miss Hewitt."

Too late. *He was already in danger of getting far more attached to her than was wise.*

"I don't want to see you suffer." The Father squeezed his shoulder in a gesture normally reserved for friends. Oliver fought the urge to shove him off. "We have such a nice arrangement here—you paint, I keep you alive— I'd hate to have to change all that because of a woman who isn't going to be here long enough to warrant your concern."

"You're letting her go?"

The question rushed out of Oliver's mouth before he could stop it. He was rewarded with a fist to the back of the head. His brush slipped, making a jagged swipe of brown where the Cathedral's spire should've been. He cursed the show of emotion. Welcomed the discomfort that reminded him to keep his thoughts in check.

Of course The Trinity wasn't going to let Jocelyn go.

"Paint." The Father's command chafed in his ears.

He painted until his arm grew heavy, but no matter how much he immersed himself in his art he couldn't escape the dread that collected in his stomach.

The Father had a plan for Jocelyn. And it wasn't good.

Oliver stepped back to survey the finished Cathedral. The spire was slightly crooked from his earlier slip with the brush, but he doubted it would be noticeable to an untrained eye. He wiped his brush off and dipped it into the pot of turpentine.

"Your Cathedral." He flicked his stiff fingers at the painting. "May I go back now?"

The Father stepped alongside him without answering. A reverent hush fell over the room and when Oliver turned for confirmation that The Father was done with him, the man looked lost in memories. His face white and taut, his dark and turbulent eyes fixated on the Cathedral, he reached out a shaky hand to the painting, stopping just short of grazing the wet paint.

He stayed that way, his body suspended in freeze-frame for several long beats. Then he curled his fingers inward, drew back his arm and executed a sharp, deliberate sign of the cross, muttering the rosary prayer.

Oliver's ears hung on one word. Forgive.

The entreaty vibrated through him as he turned and stumbled to the old guard waiting by the door. Had he ever said those words? To Catrina or—or Davis, or Ezra? While their screams echoed through the hall, had he ever begged their forgiveness?

Catrina had deserved the words most of all, but he hadn't been able to say them. And still she'd fought against her death that last day to try and convince him he wasn't to blame. But he was. A hundred years wouldn't have been enough time for her to ever forgive him for the things he'd caused her to endure.

Now he was being forced to relive the same pain all over again.

The Trinity wasn't going to let Jocelyn go. The Father would kill her. Tomorrow, three months from now, a year. Every day she would wake up wondering if today was the day she would die, and every day she'd curse Oliver for refusing to help her escape.

But he still couldn't change his mind.

Without his help she'd surely die.

With it, she'd die slower and much more painfully.

SEVEN

JOCELYN CHIPPED A SMALL chunk from the eroded concrete floor and added it to the eleven other pieces piled in the corner.

Twelve days. Her stomach clenched, a gnawing hunger clawed at her belly. When was the last time she'd eaten? She curled into a ball. The fresh cuts on her back sent fire racing up her spine. The forty-eight-hour ultimatum had come and gone, earning her a beating and a new level of hell. Slow death by starvation.

She'd tried so hard to come up with an answer for The Father, torn apart every memory of her dad, hoping for a clue. How they decorated the makeshift graveyard in the flowerbed every Halloween, the afternoons she'd climbed on his back for elephant rides—elephant instead of piggy because he was such a brawny man. All those nights tucked beneath her fuzzy blanket as he'd read to her from Pippi Longstocking and Robinson Crusoe.

For days, she'd lain awake going over every letter in her mind, but if secret meanings were hidden in his lush descriptions of Cambodia and its people, she couldn't find them. With a groan, she crawled over to the door and pounded at it with a fist.

"Help. Please." She swallowed, her mouth void of saliva, and pressed her face to the cool iron. "Water."

Minutes ticked by in endless silence. No footsteps. No low murmurs. No one was coming to feed her or quench her thirst. Her throat ached. She squeezed her eyes shut and tried to ignore the pain, but the craving got worse, searing its way up her esophagus.

She scooted over to the wall that separated her cell from Oliver's. A faint scratching drifted through the hole in the metal, like pencil on paper.

Scribbling, always scribbling.

"Oliver?" she croaked.

The pencil clattered to the floor. He shuffled into place beside the hole. "Yeah?"

Jocelyn touched the wall with her fingertips. "You have to help me get out of here."

Silence. "No."

His voice had started to lose some of its scratchy rasp, his responses given with less and less hesitation, but in this he was still as gruff and unbending as always.

"I have no food." She flattened her palms against the wall, trying to calm the tremors. "They won't give me water—"

"Here. Put your mouth to the wall. I'll give you some of mine."

She aligned her lips over the jagged crack. A moment later a slow trickle seeped through. The tepid water collected in her mouth. She swallowed, savoring the tang of rust that filled her throat.

She grimaced. "If I had a better imagination, I could almost pretend that was a nice, cold glass of iced tea."

Oliver's cup clattered to the floor on the other side of the wall. "No tea."

"I'm sorry, I—"

"No tea. No crumpets. No books." The metal wall rattled. "No fucking trees. Not now. Not one last time. Never."

Her pulse kicked up a notch. "Oliver, I don't understand—"

"Davis liked tea." Each word scraped against the air.

She inched closer to the wall. This was the first time he'd talked about one of his friends by name. "Who's Davis?"

"Jonathan Davis. MI-6 agent. He contracted pneumonia. He had this amazingly dry, British wit, you know? Even when he was so sick he could barely talk he'd manage to crack these one-liners. We tried to get him to eat, but all he wanted was a spot of tea." A strangled breath cut through the wall. "He said it just like that, too. A spot of tea. As if he was in the finest parlor in England instead of this damp, crumbling hellhole."

"Did he ever get it?"

"I...The Father kept a Camellia sinensi plant on the windowsill in his room. I ripped off the leaves when he wasn't looking and as soon as I got back to our cell, I steeped them in water. It wasn't ideal. I couldn't boil it. I'm sure it tasted like absolute shit, but Davis drank every drop."

Jocelyn hugged her arms. "It wasn't a matter of taste. He appreciated what you'd done for him."

He laughed. Short. Hollow. "Oh, yeah. Until The Father found out. He sent his minions in with buckets of scalding tea and they poured it down Davis's throat until he drowned in the one thing he loved best." His voice hardened. "If I hadn't stolen the tea leaves—"

"No." She wiggled closer, pressed her cheek near the jagged hole. "His death was not your fault."

"He deserved to die with dignity. I robbed him of that."

"I don't see it like that."

"Of course not. You think people are all good and

life is sunshine and rainbows. Truth is, I was selfish. I hated hearing Davis go on and on about his bloody tea. I just wanted to shut him up. How's that for your rose-colored glasses?"

She rested her cheek on her knees, trying to ignore the damage his words had done, but she couldn't. "It tarnishes them. Is that what you want to hear?"

He didn't answer and she was happy to let the subject drop. Was it so wrong that she wanted to believe in him? The light bulb flickered overhead. Shadows lengthened across the floor, tendrils of darkness that threatened to swallow her.

She shuddered. "What…what do you miss the most? You know, on the outside?"

Oliver grunted. "You really want to go there?"

"I have nowhere else to go." Her throat throbbed. "Nothing to do but think. How can you stand it?"

"I don't mind being alone with my thoughts. My memories…they're filed away, waiting for me to take them out and re-examine them. The sand beneath my bare feet, the first time I held a paintbrush, sneaking my dad's Harley out of the garage when I was sixteen. I control them, not the other way around."

"How?"

"Don't let memories crowd you. Pick one."

She closed her eyes, slowly exhaled and focused on calling up one specific happy memory. Before her mom got sick. Before her sister left to join the Peace Corps and all but disappeared from her life.

"We joined a Polynesian dance class once—my mom, sister and I. It was right after we'd moved to Hawaii. We thought it would be fun to learn the hula. It was a disaster. None of us could learn how to roll our hips. Apparently the Hewitts were at the back of the line when

God passed out the graceful gene. My mom—she was actually the best at it, not that that's saying much. Her laughter came back during that class." A smile slipped past her despair. She touched her fingers to her mouth, surprised to feel the slight curve to her lips. "You're right. That did help. Thanks."

Silence floated between them. For once it wasn't the usual void that set her on edge. It was comfortable. Calming.

She still couldn't resist breaking it. "You never did answer my question. About what you missed the most."

Oliver guarded his privacy so carefully. She didn't really expect him to give her a response, so when he went back to his scribbling, she figured that was the end of it. But minutes later, a lumpy pebble sailed through the hole and bounced to the floor.

Her fingers closed over it and met a small scrap of paper wrapped around the stone. She pulled it out and held it up to the meager light. One word was scrawled across it in sharp, decisive handwriting.

She blinked. "Sex?" She dropped the fragment into her lap, curved her hands around her knees. "God, that's such a guy response."

"What, you think I'm talking about getting off? I could take care of that myself without too much trouble. It's…" His voice frayed. "It's the smell of a woman's hair, the feel of her skin beneath my palm, her breath across my cheek. The heat, the closeness—"

"Two people making that special connection for one moment in time," she cut in. "Just the two of them, no walls, no pretense…"

Kind of like right now.

She tangled her fingers in her hair, dragging a strand in front of her nose and inhaling sharply. She grimaced

at the musty smell, shoved the matted hunk back behind her ears.

No. Not like now.

These four rusty walls were her personal hell. Her
heart shouldn't flutter at the husky timbre of Oliver's
voice. She shouldn't be wondering what the warmth of
his body would feel like against hers or how his embrace
would shield her from the loneliness and fear.

She swallowed the lump in her throat and plucked
at the scrap of paper in her lap. Barely visible along the
top edge was a faded typeset title and a page number.
She frowned. "The Count of Monte Cristo?"

OLIVER GRIPPED THE worn book between his hands and
ran his thumb over the shabby cover, imagining what
it would be like if it were Jocelyn's hand instead. He
shouldn't need her like this. Like a soldier hunkered in
a ditch, waiting for fighter jets to streak the dark sky
with their brilliant return fire, he lived for basking in the
light of Jocelyn's voice. Even if she was too damn naïve.

"'There is neither happiness nor misery in the
world,'" he quoted, trying to knock that innocence
down another peg, "'there is only the comparison of
one state with another, nothing more.' Dantes says that.
In the book."

"Do you think it's true?" There was that tone again.
Soft. Reproachful. "That there's no real measure of happiness?"

He shrugged. "One person's happiness is another's
misery. All that separates them is their ability to be
grateful for what they have."

"Are you?"

He hesitated. Part of him wanted to pretend not to
understand what she was asking. Was he grateful for

what he had? The inadequate food, sleeping on the hard ground, a leaky roof over his head. Mental and physical torture.

The horrors he'd seen. Friends he'd failed.

But he was alive. He had the caress of Jocelyn's voice to keep him company amidst the darkness. The illusion that one day they'd be together in a better time and place.

He gripped the book tighter, but couldn't seem to ground his thoughts. "Right now…yeah. Yeah, I think I am."

Silence. A shaky breath. "So am I."

The pebble he'd shot through the hole earlier came bouncing back at him. It hit the cement and rolled next to his bare foot. He picked it up, rolled it between his thumb and forefinger, learning the rock's uneven contours before palming it and fisting his hand against his chest.

OLIVER KNEW THE moment Jocelyn woke to the note wrapped around the pebble. She laughed, a sweet hush of breath that filtered through the wall.

"Good morning to you, too."

"I would've asked if you'd slept well…" he trailed off with a hard swallow.

"I didn't. I kept having nightmares. Of The Father sending someone to kill me."

"Don't talk like that." He didn't like hearing the harsh truth through her lips. It told him this place had started to taint her too, and as much as she needed a strong dose of reality, he didn't want it to poison her.

"I can't give him what he wants. Those symbols in my dad's letters? They mean nothing to me. I wish they

did. I wish I could tell The Father and be done with it."
Her voice cracked. "I don't know what to do."

He had no answer, at least not the one she wanted.

"Help me, Oliver." The tip of her fingers pushed past
the hole in the wall, the pebble balanced atop them.
"C'mon. Let's get out of here and go home."

He clenched his jaw. *Back away, fool.* His heart leapt.
He lunged forward, plucked the stone from her fingers
and crushed it in his palm. The rough edges dug into
his skin, much like her plea. But he remained silent.

"Truth or dare." Jocelyn pulled her hand away. "You
have the pebble, so that means you're up. Which do
you want?"

He rolled the pebble between his palms. "Neither."

"Fine. Then I'll pick." A pause. "Dare. I dare you to
escape with me."

His gaze snagged on the line of rust bisecting the
wall. "I can't."

"Fine. Truth, then."

The brusque refusal should've deterred her, but
of course it didn't. She was like a mosquito, buzzing
around and around, refusing to leave him alone until
he swatted her with cold, hard terror. "What do you
want to know?"

"Why?"

He ran a finger along the pitted stone and tried to
play dumb. "Why, what?"

"I know it's risky," she said, making it clear she
hadn't bought his act. "I know there's a good chance
we won't make it out alive. It's not dying that scares me,
Oliver. It's doing nothing."

"You think I'm scared of dying?" A bitter grunt
pushed up from his chest. "'He who dies, gains. He

who sees others die, loses.' That's another Alexandre Dumas quote, from *The Man in the Iron Mask*."

"What is it with you and Dumas? His words are not gold. Doing nothing doesn't always keep you from pain."

She didn't need to tell him that. "This building housed some kind of library once. There was this guard—he used to go up there to smoke, and one time he took me up to the room before bringing me back to my cell. The place was trashed, but the complete work of Dumas was untouched, all neatly lined up on this crumbling piece of wood." Oliver wrapped a hand around *The Count of Monte Cristo* and tugged it into his lap. The weighty feel, the tattered pages, calmed the violent memories swirling inside of him. But they begged for a voice. "Ezra, he—he loved books, loved nothing better than waxing philosophical with us 'kids.' He was a seasoned Mossad agent, one of their best. Not just because he knew how to do his job. He was a wise old soul. You know the type. Catrina and I nicknamed him 'Dadra' because he took his role as a father figure so seriously."

He waited for Jocelyn to ask about Cat, but instead, she simply said, "He sounds like a great man."

"He was." His voice clotted. "I never should've told him about the books. If it wasn't for me, he wouldn't have sought them out."

"They're just books, Oliver, what could anyone possibly have against him reading them?"

"He snuck out. I still don't know how he did it." Maybe if he'd known, he could have stopped Ezra, before it was too late. "He...he got caught. Up in the library. The Father knew the guard was the only one who went up there, and it didn't take much for the guard to cave and spill that I'd been up there with him too."

"And Ezra?"

"They took him outside and burned him. With the books."

"Oh, my God. Oliver, no!"

"I watched. Chained to a post, unable to do anything else. I—I couldn't look away. Looking away would've meant dismissing him and I—" His voice broke. He gripped the book tighter. "—I couldn't do that to him. After it was over, only one book was left untouched by the fire. I took it. To remember him by."

"*The Count of Monte Cristo.*"

He shrugged off the sympathy in her voice, locked the memories up tight. "The Father will always find a way to use what you love most against you." He pushed the pebble back through the hole, sending it to her cell. "What do you love, Jocelyn?"

JOCELYN SNAGGED THE pebble off the ground and stared at the uneven grooves across its surface. If Oliver had been trying to scare her, he'd succeeded, but not in the way he'd hoped. Hearing about Ezra made her all the more determined to make sure she escaped before she ended up like him.

"What do I love most?" She pressed her lips together. "I don't know."

"Come on, that's a cop-out. And I cry foul." His callous voice scraped across her already tender heart.

"I love many things. My job, my friends, my family. History. I don't really have a—a passion like your friends did, I just like—"

"People." Something vibrated against the wall, like he'd thumped a fist against metal. "Your passion is people."

He made it sound like an accusation.

"Maybe you're right." Her chest tightened, not in annoyance, but in fear. He'd pegged her so easily, without even needing to see her face-to-face. How much easier had it been for The Father to get a read on her? "I'll just have to make sure he can't use that against me."

"He already has. He's put you next to me, made you… care about me. He knows you won't just walk away."

"Who says I care what happens to you?" She jammed the pebble back through the hole, hoping to distract him from calling her on the lie.

"You care." The stone came sailing back to her. "You can't help it. That's just who you are."

Her cheeks flamed. "So what."

"Out there—it's different. It's okay to care. In here— you'd do well to forget about me. Your friends. All of it."

She shot to her feet. "Why don't I just give up, while I'm at it?" She kicked the wall. The vibration sent a spurt of satisfaction through her veins. She kicked the metal again. "Might as well accept my fate, right? I'm never getting out of here, anyhow. I've lost count of the last time I had anything decent to eat. I'm exhausted, and sore, and thirsty, and every time I hear a faint scuffling down the hall, I think it's the last time I'm going to draw breath. So why don't I just man up and wait for them to come and kill me."

"Josie—"

He thought he could pull her nickname on her now? "Tell me you weren't always like this, Oliver. Tell me that somewhere, deep inside of you, there's the man you used to be."

"You don't even know me." His whisper was ragged.

She put her toes to the wall, touched her forehead to the metal, flattening her palms on either side of her head. "I know you loved your friends. I know you'd trade places with them in a heartbeat if it meant they would still be alive. I know you think you don't deserve more than waiting to die in this awful place." She squeezed her eyes shut, listening to the scuffle on the other side of the wall as he moved closer. "I know you're trying to discourage me from escaping because you're afraid for me. That's all I need to know."

"You don't know everything."

"Then tell me," she whispered. "Help me understand why you've given up hope."

The wall shuddered under her palms, and though she had no way of knowing for sure, she imagined his posture matched hers, foreheads touching, hands meeting, as if neither the physical nor emotional wall stood between them.

"Don't ask that of me." The metal muffled his ragged voice. "I'll give you anything else, but that's one memory I can't bear to relive."

EIGHT

"The Father wants to see you."

Jocelyn looked up at Pheakdei. Severe lines were etched beside his tight mouth. Seventeen days had passed since her last interrogation, and something told her this time wouldn't be like the others. The Father wouldn't be sending her back to her cell with only a beating or the threat of starvation. He'd finally lost patience.

She ran her fingers over the pebble one last time. The edges had slowly worn smooth from passing it back and forth with Oliver. What had started out as a way to get him to open up about himself had turned into a ritual to survive each day. He scribbled her notes on scraps of paper, anything from the mundane "how are you?" to the shattering "talk to me." Yet whenever she probed too close to that one remaining memory, he'd clam up and it would take hours to coax him into talking again.

Tomorrow marked her thirtieth day in captivity. Maybe JPAC had sent out a search party by now, but chances of finding her were slim at best. She had to face the truth—Oliver wasn't going to change his mind about helping her escape. She had no choice but to try on her own.

The pebble slipped from her shaking hand and hit the floor with a ping. She stood and nudged the stone with her foot, bringing it in line with the hole in the wall. If Oliver peered into her cell, hopefully he'd see it.

She splayed her hand on the metal. Her muscles quivered, a blatant reminder that she wasn't as strong after almost a month of barely any food and limited exercise. She clenched her fists, feeling adrenaline race through her veins.

Somehow, she'd get out of this place. She'd contact Commander Norris over at JPAC, find her friends, and bring them home to their families for a proper burial.

Only a brutal band of captors and miles of jungle separated her from her goal.

Her heart hammered against her ribs.

Don't think about the odds. Just put one foot in front of the other.

"Come." Pheakdei gestured at her with weathered fingers, his stoop more prominent than usual.

"Goodbye, Oliver." She tapped the wall once, and stepped forward, bowing her head. Avoiding Pheakdei's dark gaze.

If he suspected she planned to make a run for it, he might shackle or blindfold her. So far he'd perceived her as quiet and unthreatening. She had no wish to hurt the elderly guard. He'd been good to her. But she couldn't risk tipping him off.

He led her into the hallway and down the corridor in the direction of the shower. At the doorway, she hesitated, dragging the moist air into her lungs. Pheakdei gave her a gentle prod across the threshold. Her feet met the slick concrete of the shower stall. She blinked the chipped enclosure into focus, her gaze snagging on a bent piece of steel that used to serve as a towel bar. Something stuck out of the jagged end.

A piece of paper?

A rivulet of cold water ran over her toes on its way toward the rusty drain and spurred her forward. She snatched the scrap and started to unroll it. As soon as she spied the beginnings of the typeset *Cristo* her heart leapt.

Oliver. He'd left her a note.

Jocelyn straightened the last edge of the paper and the sight of his firm handwriting made her eyes burn. *One good memory gets you through the day.* When had he scribbled this?

She tipped her head back, squeezed her eyes shut. After nearly thirty days of bonding through nothing more than a cold metal wall, he'd become her whole world. How could she do this without him? How could she just leave him behind when she wanted so much to save him?

He won't try to escape. And you can't stay here.

"Shower." Pheakdei's frantic voice bounced off the walls. "Hurry. We must not keep The Father waiting."

Wrong. She had to keep the sicko waiting. Forever, if possible. She crumpled the note, shoved it back into the towel bar, and turned toward Pheakdei. He hovered in the doorway. His gaze pulled sideways, his hands clenched in front of him as if standing there made him uncomfortable.

So give him a reason to leave.

"Um…could I…" She looked at her toes, curled them into the floor and watched her skin bleach white. "Could I have a bit of privacy? Just to shower?" Keeping her head down, she glanced up at him. Gripped the front of her shirt and raised it a few inches. Just enough to make him more uncomfortable. "A few minutes. Please? I'll be quick."

Pheakdei tensed, shuffled his feet.

She held her breath. *Oh God, don't say no. Please don't say—*

"Fine. Three minutes. That's all I give you." He disappeared around the corner.

She reached over and turned on the water, then sidestepped the spray and pressed her back to the wall. Her lungs constricted, pushing out short, choppy breaths.

Three minutes to save her life.

Would it be enough?

OLIVER PRESSED HIS eye to the rough opening in the wall. A sliver of light gleamed off the discarded pebble lying on Jocelyn's floor.

"Jocelyn?"

He sat back, listened. The finality of her goodbye rang in his ears. They'd developed a system—if one of them was taken from their cell, they sent the pebble over. It was their way of reassuring the other they'd be back. But she'd left the pebble on the floor. What did that mean?

His pulse sped into a frantic rhythm. He pressed the palms of his hands against his eyes.

"Josie." Her nickname—so familiar, so quick to spring on his tongue—scraped past his throat. He jumped to his feet. Pounded on the metal. "Josie!"

She's gone.

The thought punched him in the gut. No, not just gone. She never said goodbye when she knew she'd be back. The pebble always served as their means of communication. And her voice had rung with finality. She was going to escape. He reeled away from the wall, running a hand down his face to wipe away the wash of perspiration across his skin.

No. She wouldn't.

She would. She'd been saying as much for weeks despite his attempts to discourage her.

Discourage her? How? *You're all talk and no action, Shaw.* He may have argued with her and tried to scare her with grisly details of his friends' death, but he sure as shit hadn't done anything. *Yeah? What could I have done? Hell and damnation, stuck in a nine-by-nine, what could I have realistically done?*

Something. He could've done something. He could've done…

This.

He ran to the door and slammed his fists against the iron. "Guards! Open up! Open the damn door!"

With each word, the quaking in his stomach grew. It undulated to his heart, snagged on his breath. After nearly a year of bowed heads and compliance, here he was, baiting the guards again.

He had to. For her.

Fear warred with the fire in his veins. Crazy, irrational, risky. If Jocelyn were out there, somewhere, running for her life, he needed to give her more time. Had to create a diversion. Something to take the heat off her.

Unless he was already too late.

No. He wouldn't accept that.

He rushed back to the corner of his cell and scooped his tin plate off the floor. His breakfast of undercooked rice scattered like snow flurries in his wake as he returned to the door. He banged the plate against the impenetrable barrier. The clash reverberated in his ears.

Clang. Clang. Clang.

"Come on, you bastards!" he roared over the noise. "Come and get me!" He leaned his forehead against the door and closed his eyes, breath ragged. "Please, God. Come and get me."

Footsteps echoed outside. He stepped back, dropped the plate and tensed. The clatter of metal against concrete mingled with the clack of a key sliding into the lock. The slow, deliberate tick of seconds pounded in his head.

Open the door already.

He flexed his fingers, curled them into fists. The iron barrier swung inward. A boot came into view, then the short, wiry body of one of the more hateful guards. Veha possessed a thirst for blood and creativity with torture.

Oliver's hands jerked up to cover his ears, but the phantom screams still rushed his eardrums at the sight of the stocky man. Violent images flashed in front of his eyes. Veha's wicked smile, his taunts, the glint of light off his machete, shackles, blood. So much blood…

"What you want?" At Veha's growled question the memories scattered back to the dark corners of Oliver's mind.

He yanked his hands away from his face, caught Veha's scowl and the flare of his wide nose. Oliver's own fury ruptured. He lunged for Veha and rammed a shoulder into the guard's chest. The short man spun, losing his balance and crashing against the wall. Oliver ran for the door before Veha could recover. Shoving the cumbersome iron aside, he slipped through the opening and careened into the dark hallway.

The corridor stretched before him. He knew the way, had taken the same route countless times in his mind, had even managed to make it to the top floor once for real, but indecision suddenly gripped him.

What the hell was he doing?

He glanced back at his cell. Veha stalked toward him, reaching for the pistol holstered at his side. Oliver clenched his jaw, drawing a stilted breath through his nose.

Do it for Josie.
He ran.

TENDRILS OF STEAM began to billow up from the ground
as hot water met cold, moist concrete. Jocelyn rubbed
her slick palms along the sides of her pants. Precious
seconds ticked by. Pheakdei could return at any moment and announce her time was up. She had to make
her move.

But how? Did she just make a run for it? Catch him
off guard?

She might be able to outrun the older man. Surprise
was on her side. He wouldn't be expecting her to come
barreling out of the shower stall. It wasn't much of a
plan, but it was all she had.

Her gaze settled on the broken towel bar and she
darted over to the wall. Water sprayed her in the face
and she swiped it away with her sleeve. She reached for
the bar. Gave it a tug. The rod wobbled in its mounting
bracket. If she could break it free, she could—

What? Her stomach rolled at the thought of using it
on Pheakdei. She'd never be able to go through with it.
Didn't have time to waste trying to pry it from the wall.

She gave the bar one last forceful, desperate jerk. Her
hands slipped from the wet bar, feet losing traction. She
fell back and collided with an unexpected blockade.

Pheakdei.

The roar of the water had masked his footsteps. The
back of her skull connected with his face. The crunch
of bone and cartilage cracked above the din of the
shower. She scrambled off Pheakdei, and turned. Horror bloomed in her chest. Blood poured from his nose.
He choked and grabbed blindly for his face, his dark
eyes dazed and unfocused.

Jocelyn gasped and reached a shaky hand out to him.
Get out of here, Josie. You're wasting time.

She snatched her hand back. "I'm sorry."

Run.

She vaulted out of the stall, wincing at the force of her feet scraping against the concrete floor, and fled into the hallway. Which way? One hallway looked the same as any other. Was her cell in front of or behind her? God, she was all turned around and she didn't know—

Pick a direction. Go!

She darted left. Her strides ate up the distance between the shower and the unknown. Her stomach cramped. Don't think about what's up there. Just run. She widened her eyes, trying to discern the shape of the shadows up ahead.

Don't blink. Don't miss a thing.

Goose bumps pebbled on her skin. Another hallway came into view. She skidded to a stop. Right or left. Her blood rumbled in her ears. Right or left!

Oh, God, which way should she go?

PHEAKDEI ROLLED OVER. A moan tore from him. Blood poured from his nose and splashed to the floor, mixing with water and swirling toward the drain. He pressed his palm against his nose and tried to crawl to his feet.

He got as far as his knees before nausea and blinding pain hit him and he had to sit back down.

The woman was gone. She'd fled. But he hadn't missed the concern that had crumpled her pale face before she'd turned and made her escape. She hadn't meant to strike him. He could hardly blame her for what she'd done.

Which made what he had to do all the harder.

He blinked away the black, fuzzy spots in his vision and reached for the radio clipped to his belt. His trembling hand hovered over the black casing. What if he didn't sound the alarm? What if he waited to report her escape?

She didn't belong here. He'd heard whispers. The Father was growing weary of her. If she could reach the jungle she could find a way to Siem Reap. Surely The Trinity wouldn't waste time and resources going after one small woman.

Maybe not, but they would find it worthwhile to go after him, and his family, just for the sheer pleasure of punishing him. An act of defiance as big as this would wipe out any goodwill that lingered.

Why had he saved Jude's life that day at the mine? He should've left the bastard to bleed to death when his arm got caught in the jig. But the missionary doctors had inspired respect for the Hippocratic Oath and his conscience hadn't allowed him to do nothing. The act had earned his family's freedom, but not Pheakdei's. His skill had tethered him to The Trinity's very long reach.

Was it worth the lives of his wife and children to go up against The Trinity now?

Yes.

He wanted to say the word. Wanted to fight for something—to stand tall and proud again. But his family...

Pheakdei gripped the radio, squeezing it until his knuckles hurt. His family. He couldn't live with himself if he betrayed them. But could he live with himself if The Trinity caught the woman and slaughtered her?

What would his family say then?

He yanked the radio from his belt. They wouldn't say a thing. They depended on him to keep them safe. And so he would.

Whatever it took.

He pulled in a slow, viscous breath, tasting the tang of his own blood, and depressed the talk button. Lifting the radio to his mouth, he squeezed his eyes shut and choked out the words, "The woman has escaped. She's on the run."

JOCELYN PEERED AROUND the corner. Nothing but gloomy shadows down either side. How long were these stupid hallways anyway? She hung another left, ignoring the burn sizzling in her lungs as she ran.

Footsteps pounded the concrete, heavy and faster than hers. Behind or up ahead? She couldn't tell. A bulb hung from the ceiling illuminating a circle of the hallway in front of her, but beyond the patch of light, darkness engulfed the corridor.

Something shifted out of the shadows. *Someone.* She skidded to a halt, chafing her feet further. A scream ripped from her. Oh, God, they'd caught up with her.

She spun to retreat—

"Josie!"

—And froze.

That husky timbre could only belong to one man.

"Oliver?" she whispered and turned in the direction of his footsteps. Her heart beat a fast cadence against her ribs.

He moved into the halo of light. Tall and lean, his build hinted at the broad stature he must've possessed before his time in captivity. Black hair hung to his shoulders and at least a month's worth of dark scruffy beard covered his sharp jaw. Green eyes, as fathomless as the jungle foliage, bored into hers for a fraction of a second before shouts echoed all around them.

Guards closed in from both sides. Someone grabbed her from behind and yanked her away from Oliver.

She stumbled, her knees collapsing beneath her. Oliver reached out to catch her, but two guards wrestled him to the ground and shackled his hands behind his back. She was pushed to the ground in a similar manner. Her chin scraped the concrete and the sting of the cut fueled her anger. She bucked and kicked out. Her foot connected with one of the guard's thighs.

"Let her up." The scratchy voice came out of the darkness.

Her skin crawled. The Father.

The guard hauled her to her feet, wound an arm around her shoulders and stuck a knife to her throat.

The Father stepped into the light, illuminating his narrowed eyes, his disfigured cheek, and twisted lips. "Going somewhere?"

"I—"

The Father grabbed her by the chin. "No one leaves until I say they leave."

He snapped his fingers and two more guards came forward, dragging Pheakdei between them. Blood flowed over his mouth and down his chin.

She gasped. "Pheakdei."

The Father stared at her. His face hardened. He whirled on Pheakdei and cuffed the old guard across the forehead. Pheakdei stumbled.

The guards tightened their hold on him, forcing him upright. Fresh blood welled on his skin from where The Father's ring had cut into his flesh.

"I do not tolerate incompetence here." The Father's voice vibrated with rage.

The sadistic bastard drew back his hand and struck Pheakdei again. And again.

Oh, God. He was going to kill the guard. And it would be her fault. All her fault. Why didn't she think?

Pheakdei hadn't done anything to hurt her. He'd helped her when she was sick. Brought her food and water. He was the only one who treated her with decency.

What had she done?

"Stop! Don't! Please. It's my fault. I—"

The Father reeled on her. "No. He was supposed to watch you. He failed. And he will be punished." He snapped his fingers and one of the guards produced the length of bamboo. The Father snatched it out of the man's hand and slapped it against his palm. "Petey will reap the consequences. And you will watch."

The blood drained from her face. "No!" She flinched at the slice of bamboo on Pheakdei's flesh. Bile rose in her throat. "Please, no. He did nothing wrong." Her fingers flexed, desperate to cover her ears, but the guard still held her tight. "Stop!" she screamed. "Please stop. I'll do anything—"

The bamboo halted in mid-air. "Anything?"

No. Not anything. Please, God, not—

"Yes." What other answer was there? "Anything."

The Father emitted a low sound. Like a purr. "Even take his punishment?"

Jocelyn squeezed her eyes shut. If she said yes, she'd be the one caned. If she said no, Pheakdei would suffer for her reckless actions. No, not reckless. She was only doing what she had to in order to survive.

She opened her eyes to find Oliver's troubled frown leveled at her. Is this how he felt? Torn between compassion and self-preservation. How could she ever choose between her own suffering and Pheakdei's?

She had no choice.

Oliver's body went rigid. "Josie, no."

She hesitated.

"No?" The Father chuckled. Bamboo whistled through the air, screaming in her ears. "I didn't think so."

"Okay!" Her voice cracked. "Okay. Yes. I'll take his punishment. Please, just…stop."

The Father dropped the bamboo.

From his position on the floor, Pheakdei trembled, reached out a shaky hand and locked his coffee-brown gaze on her. "No…"

The Father smiled, showing off white teeth. He kicked Pheakdei aside. "Bring her."

One of the guards shoved her forward and she fell to her knees. She clenched her hands at her sides. Out of the corner of her eye she saw Oliver shift, agitated and tense. He growled.

Without warning, The Father brought the length of bamboo across her back. Pain split up her spine. She screamed, covered her face with her hands and braced for the next blow.

"Stop!" Oliver's bellow tore through the corridor, leaving aftershocks in its wake. "Don't hurt her. She didn't know. Let me take her place. Beat me instead." His command was no more than a whisper, but it rang with authority.

The Father chuckled. "Oh, this is getting good. How far will you people go to protect one another?" He snapped his fingers. "I'm no longer in the mood to beat you. I've got something much better in mind."

NINE

He should've known better than to open his mouth.

The bastards had taken Jocelyn to a small window-less room and strapped her down on some sort of contraption. It resembled a bench press, with two metal poles running up the sides at the head. A metal bar stretched between the welded cradles at the top of the rods.

Oliver wrenched free of the guards at the doorway and sank to his knees between the poles. Two bright bulbs hung down from the ceiling. He couldn't see Jocelyn's eyes through her squint, but she wasn't hard to read by the taut lines etched around her mouth. Her hands were fisted at her sides, her breath rising and falling rapidly beneath the strips of leather taut against her chest.

Before he could completely register their intent, the guards hauled him back to his feet, thrust his arms upward and dumped the metal bar into his hands. His fingers automatically clenched around the rubber grips, bracing the weight. Iron clamped around his wrists, shackling him to the poles.

He reared back, the cuffs biting into his skin, and snarled at The Father. "Unchain me! I'm done playing your fucking games."

He started to lower the bar. A switch clicked and a low hum reverberated in the air.

"If you let the bar hit the cradle, the lovely Miss Hewitt will get a nice jolt." The puckered skin above

The Father's right eye creased in lieu of a raised brow. "It won't kill her. The voltage is only at fifty percent. For now. But do you really want to cause pain to one more person who was foolish enough to trust you?"

Oliver jammed his arms back above his head, locking his elbows. His heart slipped, the beats racing and tumbling over each other. Sweat beaded on his brow and pooled against his palms. His fingers tightened around the grips. He found the thin black wires entwined around the pole and followed their path to a small black box near The Father's feet.

He clenched his teeth. If he didn't react—didn't feel—The Father couldn't hurt him. But then again, he wasn't the one on the receiving end. The rubber grips would prevent him from feeling the electric shock. Instead, he would be forced to act as the conduit to Jocelyn's suffering.

She'd been trying so hard to convince him redemption wasn't out of reach. He'd almost started to think he could grasp for it, but after The Father was through playing out whatever sick game he'd concocted, she'd never look at him the same way.

If she was still alive.

Don't you dare drop that bar, damn it.

"I've been more than patient—" The Father cut in, "—but I still don't have what I want. I could try to beat the answers out of Miss Hewitt, but I've already done that, and it's starting to get tedious. So, I think I'll just sit back and watch this play out. Get her to decipher her father's code, and I'll turn off the electricity. If she still refuses to cooperate—well, I guess we'll all have to hope your arms hold out, won't we?"

"I could just drop the bar. Refuse to participate." His stomach twisted as he choked out the words.

"But you won't." The Father's lips curled into a smirk. "I know you, Oliver."

"You don't know shit about me," he retorted, but he feared The Father was right.

The Father knew that he'd kept silent when he could've spoken up and prevented his friends' suffering. He knew that he'd learned to watch their torture with a dry eye and an aching heart. And worst of all, he knew that Oliver wasn't strong enough to keep the bar above his head indefinitely.

Jocelyn threw back her head, her attention darting between him and The Father. Oliver stared at the pale column of her neck, watching the tendons tighten beneath her skin, too much of a coward to look her in the eye. She gasped his name. The sound went straight through him.

He found her gaze. Steady, pleading, trusting.

Oliver swallowed the dry lump in his throat, looked away. "Why'd you do it?"

"Do what?" Jocelyn's voice rippled with confusion.

Aware of The Father standing off to the side, listening in on them, Oliver lowered his voice. "Offer to take the old man's punishment. He wouldn't have faulted you for staying silent, you know."

"Could you have?"

He forced himself to keep looking her in the eye when he uttered the truth. "Yeah. In a blink." He'd done it before.

"Liar." She let out a breath on a long, slow exhale. "You stepped in for me."

"The old man can take care of himself."

A drop of sweat trickled over his eyebrow and into his eye. He blinked, the sting giving him an excuse to turn his focus to the wall across from him. If he continued to look at Jocelyn he might fracture. He couldn't risk it.

"His name is Pheakdei," she corrected in a voice suddenly tinged with steel.

"Pheakdei?" He frowned at the dirty chipped plaster. "You sure? I thought I heard him called Petey."

"You mean you never asked his name?"

"I never saw the point."

"Did he ever…hurt you—I mean, he isn't like the others—?"

"The old—" he shook his head, "—Pheakdei's never once harmed me."

"Isn't that reason enough to treat him with respect?"

Her quiet question kicked him in the gut. How had he forgotten something as simple as asking a person's name? He'd done as much to Jocelyn when she'd first been captured. Treated her like her name wasn't important, like *she* wasn't important.

Under the guise of coping, he'd sacrificed the one thing that separated him from the rats that sometimes scurried through the corridors.

"It seems I've forgotten how to act like a human being."

But it was slowly starting to come back. Because of her. Small glimmers of the humanity he'd thought long dead had found their way through the cracks in his soul, and now he was torn between letting them burst inside of him and shoving them all back into the darkest corner of himself.

He tightened his hands around the bar and concentrated on the burn spreading across his shoulders instead of the one filling his heart.

JOCELYN COULDN'T BE sure how long they'd sat there in silence—her strapped to the hard bench, Oliver forced to hold up that wretched bar above her head.

Six hours? Longer? Without windows to gauge the angle of the sun, she could only judge by the comings and goings of the guards that morning had given way to late afternoon.

She closed her eyes, wishing for some sort of reassurance from Oliver. She needed to hear his voice, but he'd retreated into himself to a place she didn't think she could reach with mere words. And with The Father watching them, she couldn't bring herself to speak freely.

The faint smell of cooked meat suddenly drifted around her and she craned her head toward the door to see a boy carry a tray of food into the room. He couldn't have been more than seven or eight. His dark hair was shaved in uneven patches and his dark eyes looked huge in his gaunt face. He wore a faded shirt, tattered at the ends, and a dirt-streaked pair of pants. His feet were bare. A rope was cinched tight around his waist, showing off his scrawny frame.

She tracked him around the room and watched as he handed the tray to The Father. The smug bastard took it without a word and slouched in his chair, shoveling food into his mouth. Her stomach clenched.

He plucked a chicken leg from the tray and bit into it with a twisted smile. "Oh, you're not hungry are you?"

Jocelyn glared back at him. She wouldn't give him the satisfaction of an answer.

He took a few more bites of the chicken before tossing the half finished leg on the floor. The boy let out a moan, his fingers twitching to restrain himself from reaching for the food.

The Father grimaced around a bite of rice. He turned and flung the contents of the tray in the boy's face. "It's cold."

Instead of wiping away the rice and bits of vegetables, the boy carefully scraped them into his hand and shoved the food into his mouth. His belly rumbled. Hers twisted.

"He's hungry!" Tears filled her eyes. She longed to draw the boy into a hug. "Can't you see that?"

The Father grunted, cuffed the boy in the back of the head. "Get out of here."

The boy stumbled, but regained his footing quickly and scrambled out of the room.

She choked on the ball of revulsion. Were there more children like that boy? Ragged, starved, mistreated. Did The Trinity's cruelty extend to preying on the small and defenseless?

"How dare you," she whispered.

The Father leaned over to the black box at his feet and turned up the voltage. "Sixty percent."

Above her, chains began to rattle. She leaned her head back as far as it would go to bring Oliver into her line of vision. His arms quaked, the wiry muscles in his biceps straining with fatigue. A thick blue vein blazed a trail under his skin.

"I'm trying, Josie. God, I'm trying. But I don't know how much longer I can hold on." He spoke through gritted teeth. "End this. Tell The Father what you know."

The raw pain in his voice tied her into knots. "If I knew how to decipher the code, I'd do it in a heartbeat."

"Think."

"I'm trying!"

"Try harder." The entire bench shook from Oliver's tremors. "What could the sun mean? A direction? Think of the compass on a map. Which way would it point? How does the elephant tie in—?"

"I don't—"

The grate of metal on metal shrieked in her ears, breaking into her thoughts. A wallop of electricity slammed into her. Her back arched away from the bench, triggering a painful stutter in her sternum. The jolt triggered vibrations through her entire body. Her eyes stung and her teeth clacked together.

She bit down on her tongue so hard blood filled her mouth.

"Fuck!" Oliver's low, drawn-out roar was punctuated with a jerk. He disengaged the bar from its cradle. The buzz of electrical current immediately stopped.

She gasped for breath. It wouldn't come. Pinpricks tingled across her nerves. She tried to claw at the leather straps, but her limbs were numb. Uncooperative. She went still, panic tumbling through her mind, her muscles like jelly.

Slowly, her heart rate settled back to normal. Her breath started to return. She shifted her gaze to the bar above her head. It wobbled in Oliver's hands.

"I'm sorry. God, Josie, I'm so sorry. I can't—"

The muscles in his neck constricted as he swallowed. With a strength he could've only dredged up from deep within, he clenched the bar in one hand and tore at the cylindrical piece of rubber with the other. He worked the strip down to the end of the bar then yanked it free, tossing it to the floor. Breath choppy, he transferred the bar to the other hand and performed the same task on the matching grip, until it too fluttered to the floor.

He curled his hands around the bare metal. He'd just made sure if the bar slipped again, she wouldn't suffer through the next electric shock alone.

"If you...hurt...I hurt."

A chuckle rumbled from the corner of the room. The Father clapped. "Bravo. Very well done, Shaw. I didn't think you had it in you."

A fresh wash of moisture stung Jocelyn's eyes, leaking out from the corners and raining down her cheeks in hot rivulets. Oliver did have it in him. He wasn't as far gone as he claimed. The darkness hadn't won. And to make sure it wouldn't, she did the only thing she could think of to end both their pain.

She lied.

"Lumphat." The name of the bombed-out village popped into her head and she ran with it. "My dad's markings point the way to the ruins east of the Srepok River. That's all I know."

The Father hit the switch and the grating hum of electricity stopped. He snapped his fingers and the guards came forward to release her and Oliver from the bench. She yelped as one of the guards yanked off her straps and hauled her to her feet. Her legs wobbled out from under her. She would've hit the concrete if the man hadn't wrapped an arm around her middle to keep her upright.

Her breath rattled in her ears. No, not her breath. Chains. More chains. Always chains. She saw them in her nightmares, heard them clanking in her head. She licked her dry lips and tried to swallow past the lump that had wedged in her throat. Her gaze darted to the doorway, anticipating the appearance of a guard, shackles in hand. Oliver shifted into her line of vision. His face was tight, impassive. But his eyes...

Those green eyes darkened like burnt jade. Things were about to get worse, not better.

The guard stepped into the light, shackles dripping

from his grip. Oliver bared his clenched teeth. She shuddered. Her already racing heart ratcheted another notch. She frowned at the chains. Those shackles...something was wrong—different—about them. They were far too big to clamp around either wrists or ankles. But how could that be? It didn't make sense. She blinked, shook her head.

"While we're checking out the information you gave us, we'll keep you close." The Father smiled. "Consider it an insurance policy."

Realization speared through her, crystallizing in her veins.

Oh, God, those weren't cuffs.

They were neck shackles.

OLIVER STARTED TO shake. Fresh sweat broke out on his brow. He knew what was coming. Didn't want any part of it. Hadn't he already hurt Jocelyn enough without her having to suffer the indignity of being chained to him like a dog?

The guard swung the neck shackles in his hand and stepped under the low-watt bulb. Gritty light sifted across the irons. Their clink rattled in his head.

"Oh, God, no." He reared backward, spun, breaking the guards' hold on him. "No fucking way in hell."

His protest wasn't just for Jocelyn's sake. He couldn't endure this torment a second time. The first had nearly killed him. He still fought the nightmares. Still heard echoes of Catrina drawing her last, painful breath.

His stomach heaved, shoving him forward, but before he'd succeeded in taking more than a couple of steps, the guards jumped him. An arm came around his throat, a nightstick cracked across his knees and he staggered. His legs collapsed and he fell to the floor. One of the guards planted a knee in his back, a boot pressed down on his skull, smashing his cheek into the concrete.

Oliver jammed his eyes shut. The move blocked out the light, but not the vivid images that flickered behind his eyelids.

Catrina. Bleeding. Dying. All over again.

But, wait. That face…not Catrina after all. Jocelyn. Bleeding, dying—

"What…is this?" Jocelyn's voice, fractured and trembling.

He jerked his eyes open. His heart thumped hard until his gaze found Jocelyn standing a few feet away. A strand of her chin-length dark brown hair lay against her bruised cheek. Wide hazel eyes darted around the corridor before coming to rest on him.

She looked just as he'd imagined, her pale face full of that fresh girl-next-door innocence, but…God, her tears cut him to the quick. He'd done that to her. He should've been stronger, fought harder.

She yelped as the guard fit the wide chain around her neck and squeezed the latch closed. The sound of her terror poured salt into his open wounds.

The guards yanked him to his feet. Pushed him closer to Jocelyn. Closer to the other end of the chain. He snarled, hyperventilating through clenched teeth.

Stay away from the chain!

He dug his heels into the ground and tried to shake free, but the bastard holding the chain swung the end and caught him in the shoulder. Pain radiated through him. He doubled over. Cold metal pressed against his neck.

He jerked. The latch snicked shut.

"No!" His denial clung to the stale air, echoing in the hall.

Jocelyn's eyes widened further. She sucked in a sharp breath. "O—Oliver?"

Raw fear tightened her face, her eyes darkening. It wasn't just the guards that had her scared. It was—him. His yelling, his agitation. For all his time spent in this hellhole, he hadn't allowed himself to lose his mind. He couldn't start now. He had to hold it together. For Jocelyn. It would be okay. Josie wasn't like Catrina. She wasn't...*dying*.

Oliver forced his heart rate back to normal.

He raised his eyes to meet Jocelyn's, willed his gaze to remain strong and steady. She stared at him like she could see all the way to his charred soul. What she found there was likely to send her even further into a panic.

He tensed. Waited for her to break eye contact.

She didn't.

The bastard guards sniggered and shoved her hard. She stumbled to her knees. The chain between them pulled taut and jerked Oliver off balance. He righted himself and leaned forward to help Jocelyn stand, but the guards hauled her to her feet and dragged them out of the room and down the hall.

He'd taken about a dozen steps before he realized where they were headed. Solitary confinement. A chill swept over him. The cell was down a long dark, narrow corridor, barely wide enough to traverse single file.

One of the guards opened the door. The squeak of hinges chased up Oliver's spine. He stepped into the room. It was half the size of his normal cell. Damp rotting leaves assailed his nostrils. The muted glow from the single hanging light added shadows to the stained concrete walls.

Catrina had died here. And he...

He'd warred with his own survival. Right there, under that same grubby light bulb.

The door slammed shut, sealing him and Jocelyn inside like a coffin. He could feel her confusion and shock through the three feet of chain that separated their neck irons. He refused to look at her. "I warned you. You shouldn't have tried to escape." His stomach knotted. He'd meant to ask her if she was okay, not make her feel worse. But he was so afraid what had just happened in that other room had caused her to lose faith in him. Anger seemed a much more preferable emotion to fear.

"What were you doing in the hall, then?" She hadn't risen to his bait. Instead, her voice was gentle, luring him closer with forgiveness. "If not coming after me."

"Trying to keep you from doing something stupid."

"You can't." Ah, there was a bit of anger. She lifted her chin and shot him a glare that looked watered-down in her too-pale face. "I'm going to keep fighting to get out of here. Even if it kills me. *You* can continue to give up hope, if you like."

She stepped closer and the light spilled over her, highlighting high cheekbones and the stubborn hitch of her mouth. Her chestnut hair was badly in need of a comb, but he could imagine her in a different setting, one where she'd be perfectly put together and knee deep in dirt, sifting through some poor dead guy's remains, trying to save him from the injustice of an unmarked grave.

Oliver cleared his throat and turned a cold shoulder, determined not to give in to her warmth. "Give it another month. Sooner or later you'll find you're more afraid of what's outside these walls. At least in here you know what's expected of you."

"And what's that?"

"Obedience," he said flatly. "Haven't you learned yet? Escaping isn't an option."

His fingers itched for his pencil and he started to pace, desperate for some way to bring order to the chaos swirling inside him. A sharp tug on his neck brought him up short. He glanced at Jocelyn, the chain now taut between them.

Where he went she had to follow.

He swore under his breath. He couldn't do this. Bonding with her when a solid wall stood between them was one thing, sharing the same cell, the same chain, breathing the same damn air—brought him down to a whole different level of slavery. Emotional.

His lungs wrenched tight. He doubled over, the clatter of chains ringing in his ears.

Jocelyn stepped into view and put her shackled hands on his back. "I don't blame you, you know. No one could've held the bar any longer—"

The warmth of her touch scorched through the thin material of his shirt. He flinched, jerking upright and knocking into her. She stumbled, caught herself. He wanted to reach out to steady her but didn't know how.

How long had it been since someone touched him with a soft, comforting hand? Flashes went off in his head, fired along his nerves. He wanted to jump out of his skin to escape before his body had the chance to remember the power of a simple touch and started to crave the connection.

Too late.

"I'm sorry. I—" He curled his fingers inward, dug his nails into his palms and met her gaze only to find her close, much too close, staring back at him, those hazel irises ringed in gray.

Words deserted him. He swallowed. His skin tingled

from her nearness and he knew it wouldn't stop unless he moved far away from her—preferably to another room with a thick wall for a barrier.

But that was no longer possible.

He tried to put some distance between them anyhow. She matched every step he took. No matter how much he wanted to outrun her, a measly three feet would remain the sum total of their separation.

"How long has it been? Since you've…" She fluttered her hands.

"Had contact with someone besides the guards?" He tried to shove the tightness aside with a shrug. "A year and a half. Maybe more."

He wandered over to the back wall, well aware that Jocelyn was stuck following him. The concrete still bore faded remnants of the orange-red sunset he'd painted more than seven months ago. Lack of sunlight had kept it from completely disappearing. He touched one of the wide streaks, closed his eyes and ran his fingertips along the bold stroke. The familiar texture immersed him in the past. Cold seeped into his veins.

"WHAT HAPPENED to you in here?"

The question spilled out of Jocelyn's mouth on a rush of breath. Oliver had gone through something big in this room. Something that put the rigidity in his posture and the fractured rasp back in his voice. This place was at the core of the one memory he'd refused to discuss.

"Nothing."

She caught his brooding stare, and had to swallow the tension that squeezed her throat. "I don't believe you."

Now that she'd had time to study him, she couldn't deny that there was something arresting about him with all that dark hair brushing his shoulders and the beard darkening his jaw. But it was his eyes that drew her in the most. Intense and fathomless green, a lifetime of pain laid bare in their depths.

"Haven't you heard enough? Didn't Davis and Ezra's deaths give you plenty of reasons to stop thinking of making an escape? Do you really need more?" His voice fragmented on the plea. "You haven't learned from my mistakes at all. You just keep pushing and pushing, doing whatever you think is right no matter how it affects others." He ran his shackled hands down his face. "I don't want to remember. It hurts to remember."

"I know." She waited for him to look at her. "When I think of Claire and Jason and—and Matt, I can't even breathe for the pain. But that's not going to change just because I don't talk about them. Remembering them is keeping me alive."

He glanced back at the pale mural on the wall. "I wanted to die." Such a simple statement, but the halting, anguished way in which he said it told its own tangled, complex tale. "But she made sure—" He cut himself off, pressed his trembling lips into a hard, straight line.

"She made sure of what?"

He clenched his jaw, gave one hard shake of his head.

"Who made sure, Oliver?" Not that she needed him to voice the woman's name out loud. He'd only mentioned her once in passing, but it had stuck with Jocelyn.

She closed the distance between them, reached over and sandwiched his hands between hers. Though he still flinched at her touch, he didn't pull away this time. "Talk to me."

He pulled his calloused hands out of her grasp. "Her name was Catrina Nim. She was a fellow CIA operative and a—friend. The CIA needed someone who could blend in here, someone who wouldn't raise any red flags.

When Catrina heard about the mission, she jumped at the chance. She was Cambodian, you see, and, being a woman to boot—she was the perfect cover. We could go in as a couple, her as a woman desperately seeking her roots, me as the boyfriend along for the ride. With Ezra and Davis on our side, the two international agents we'd brought in, the CIA believed we could covertly uncover the location of The Trinity's headquarters."

He paused, lost in his own thoughts for a long beat. "I tried to talk Catrina out of it. I warned her the mission was different than anything we'd tackled before. We expected to spend months in the jungle and our communication would only be spotty at best. But she wanted it so badly. She was…so fired up about doing something good for the country."

Oliver's sharp emphasis on the word "good" squeezed at Jocelyn's heart. No wonder he'd tried to disillusion her. "So you let her come?"

"Yeah. It wasn't my call. I couldn't go above her head without raising a few flags about our…relationship. So I kept my mouth shut. After six months in Cambodia we still had no luck. We'd tramped all over this godforsaken jungle, and I…was tired of coming up empty handed. I thought if I dangled a big enough carrot in front of the Trinity, something I knew they were hot after, I could trap them into giving up their location."

"So you baited them. With Kala's Ashes." Her stomach flip-flopped. Just as she'd done when she'd lied to The Father.

"We'd come into contact with some of their mercenaries—lowlifes that spent their pay on cheap booze and prostitutes. I convinced the team to follow the scum into the bar. Dropped some not-so-subtle hints that I knew the location and would be willing to give it up. For a price." He hunched over as if the burden of his decision dumped a sudden weight on his shoulders. "And that error cost my teammates their freedom. On the way back to our hotel we were ambushed and brought here. After a year of pure hell, Catrina and I were the only ones left. By then, I'd already tried escaping half a dozen times on my own, and each time I failed The Trinity punished me by forcing me to—" his voice started to break, "—to watch as my friends were beaten. Tortured.

"I was done, but Catrina—she wanted to see the trees. Just once more before she died. She couldn't walk anymore, they'd broken both her legs, and she loved the outdoors more than anything. It was her last request." His words started coming faster, rougher. "She begged and I—even if I'd wanted to say no—how could I deny her? It was such a simple desire. The next time the guard came to get me, I took him out and locked him in my cell. I grabbed Catrina from hers and carried her outside." He swallowed. "The door was right there in front of us, less than a yard away. I thought we had it. But another guard came in from the outside and saw us. He took us before The Father. Instead of turning on Catrina as I expected, he started to beat me. I welcomed it, wanted it. Finally, they were going after the one who really deserved it."

"You didn't deserve that," she whispered. "You know that, right?"

Oliver blinked at her, almost as if he'd forgotten she was there. "Cat…she knew she was done and she—damn it, she took my place. I tried to stop them. They ganged up on me and dragged me out of the room. The bastards weren't gentle with her. They left her hanging on by a thread. And then we were chained together by the neck, just like this and thrown here, in this room.

The guards didn't come back. Catrina was in so much pain. I couldn't help her. She just kept telling me that I had to make sure I survived. Three days later, she died in my arms."

He moved over to the wall, braced his palms against the concrete, and laid his forehead against the painted sun. "I broke my promise. I'd survived as long as I could, but I couldn't bear to live any longer. I made sure the fuckers were all too happy to oblige my wishes. They beat me until my body collapsed, but when I came to—" he drew a shuddering breath, stared hard at the mural, "—I was still here."

So much guilt in that simple whisper. Jocelyn closed the small gap between them, surprised to find her limbs still rubbery. Her calves trembled with the residual effects of the electric shock and forced her to slide down into a sitting position, knowing Oliver would have to do the same.

"Your voice changes when you talk about her," she said, echoing his words when he'd first asked her about Matt. "She was your girlfriend, yes?"

"We never acted on it." The chains rattled as he sat down next to her. "No, that's not—once. One night. But the CIA was everything, to both of us. We weren't ready to retire and if they'd known about it, they would've farmed us out in a blink. We thought we had plenty of time. We thought we could wait."

So much regret. "Tell me. What's the one thing you loved best about her?"

"I can't remember." He buried his head in his knees, closing himself off when she would've reached for him.

She chewed on her lip, not knowing what to say. It was probably better that way. He wasn't ready to accept her comfort, and she was too raw to be able to separate her tangled emotions.

Jocelyn twisted her hands in the folds of her shirt and vowed to stay silent, but the quiet caused her mind to race, one question jumping into the forefront and demanding voice. "Have you ever seen children with The Father before, like that boy who brought his food?"

He shook his head. "Catrina did. She tried to tell me but I—I wouldn't listen."

"Why not?"

"I didn't want to hurt them."

She frowned. "How could you have possibly hurt them?"

He lifted his head, pierced her with a gaze that churned with residual sparks from the electrical current that had passed through them. "I hurt you, didn't I?"

TEN

THE BITCH HAD lied to him.

He'd sent a team out to Lumphat to comb every inch of both banks of the river. They'd found no trace of any such ruins.

Jude scratched furiously at the scar tissue on his right hand and paced the length of his room. He could tolerate disobedience, even ignorance, but lying—that was one insult he couldn't overlook.

If he had the time, he'd relish the opportunity to bring her to her knees. But he hadn't expected her to succeed in coaxing both Pheakdei and Shaw into her corner. With that kind of power, she was dangerous. A threat. No telling what Oliver and the old guard would be willing to do on her behalf.

Jocelyn Hewitt had to go.

He would find Kala's Ashes some other way.

He stopped in front of the easel and raised his gaze to Oliver's painting. The Cathedral was a study in control with its sharp edges and angles. Not a line out of place, no uneven splotches of paint marring the surface. Calm poured through his veins. Only the church could hold the anarchy at bay and stop the madness.

Jude reached up to touch the damaged skin on his face, ever grateful for the purification by fire that had showed him the way. His focus strayed to the painted sky and he blinked, noticing the break in the clouds for the first time. A hint of sunshine peeked through the darkness. He gasped. The hint of lemony yellow happiness drove through him like a stake.

Wrong. All wrong.

The clouds had been dark and purple the day he'd torched the primitive mission church and sent both his father and Donald Hewitt straight to hell. He rubbed his cheek. The cleansing had given him a rebirth. A purpose in life. He'd known then, when he'd survived his trial by fire, that raising a temple built on chaos was his destiny.

Bedlam renewed in his gut, boiling over, choking him. He ripped the canvas off the easel and smashed it over his knee. He growled, tossed it aside.

The door opened behind him.

He spun, breathing hard. "What do you want?"

Leo stared at him with flat, translucent eyes. "I want to talk to you about Chann. He's become a liability. His heart's not in this anymore."

He dared question Chann's loyalty? Jude gritted his teeth and took a step toward Leo, cutting his hand through the air. "Chann is the lifeblood of The Trinity. Without him we have no way of infiltrating the villages. Are you vying for his job? Because I assure you, you'd stick out like a vampire in a room full of virgins."

"I don't want Chann's job." A spark of rebellion tightened Leo's face. "Day after day I watch over the brats. I listen to their cries and their endless demands. When they fall out of favor, I'm the one that deals with them." He thumped his chest. "I keep the mine running smoothly. For once, *I* want to be recognized as a valuable member of this team."

"You think I don't value you?" Jude could hardly push the question past his distress. He reached for Leo. "You have no idea what I've done for you. How I've kept you from going astray. We're true brothers, thicker than any blood." He curled his fingers into Leo's shoulder. "I created us. I made us a family."

Leo stiffened. "What do you mean?"

"Oh, come on. You remember how it was. All those lost souls in need of saving, all the people of these backward tribes that desperately needed an education. There wasn't time for our parents to look after us, too."

"My mother wasn't like that. She—"

"Was putting out for the great Reverend Larkin," Jude snapped.

Leo wrenched out of Jude's grip. "That's not true!"

"Why do you think the Reverend spared you?" Had Leo really been completely blind? Why did he have to go and force Jude to shatter his illusions? "Everyone else had to stand still and take their weekly penance, but not you. Sweet, oblivious Leonard always got to run off and go play in the dirt."

Leo's nostrils flared. "You're wrong."

"No. I was right." His hand crept up to caress the twisted flesh at his jaw. "And I was the only one with the balls to do something about it."

LEO SUCKED IN a breath. "The fire."

"Not even twenty-four hours after my father murdered my mother, those pious bastards filed into the church as if nothing happened, lining up to hear a sermon about love and honor. Delivered by the very man who had just stabbed his wife thirty-six times and dumped her body in the jungle." Jude stalked behind his desk, squirted sanitizer into his palm and furiously rubbed it into his skin. "What kind of heavenly kingdom allows such evil hearts past its pearly gates? We were better off without them."

Leo swallowed hard, backed into the wall to keep

from vaulting at Jude. He'd always thought the fire that had robbed him of his mother was an accident. After all, Jude had almost died himself. Now... "All this talk of we, and I don't even know who you are."

"Don't you dare say that." Jude pressed a hand to his heart. "Look at all we've done together. We're The Trinity. Three in one. Forget the heavenly kingdom, we've built a far superior one here on earth. As soon as we find Kala's Ashes—"

Kala's Ashes? Jude didn't love him. He'd never cared about Leo. Everything Jude had done was for his agenda alone. Why hadn't Leo seen he was just another pawn in Jude's machinations?

Leo barked out a laugh. "You'll never get your hands on Kala's Ashes."

Jude's head snapped back. "It's the woman isn't it? She's gotten to you too. We have to get rid of her." He pointed a shaking finger. "Just like that shameful harlot, Ruth. She—she tried to lead you astray as well and I—I almost lost you."

"What about Ruth?" Pain spread across Leo's chest.

"She was going to take you away. Ruin everything we'd been working for."

No. Not Ruth. Jude wouldn't have—

"What are you saying?"

"I had to, Leo." Jude held out his hands. "The Trinity can't exist without you."

There it was. The validation Leo had wanted. Proof that he was more than The Ghost, more than the grunt who shadowed the important players. The acknowledgment should've filled him with purpose.

Ruth hadn't left him. Jude took her away. "How?"

"What?" Jude's gaze darted around the room. He shook his head, turning to his desk. "I'm busy, Leo—"

"How?" He gritted his teeth. Jude couldn't pretend to misunderstand this time.

Jude froze.

Leo stared at his back and waited.

He inched around, hands thrown wide. "I strangled her in her sleep," he whispered, raising his eyes.

Rage roared through Leo, heating his blood, pulling his hands into fists. Jude had taken everything from him. His mother, Ruthie, every ounce of his energy and blind obedience. His knife tingled against his hip. He could slit Jude's throat, plunge the blade into his heart. Make the bastard drown in his own blood.

But, no.

Jude had taken something precious from him.

Leo would exact something equally precious in return.

Kala's Ashes.

He gulped air into his lungs and straightened. His hands stung from being clenched so tight. He willed his fingers to unfurl and pressed his palms against his pants. If he'd learned anything from Jude over the years, it was to filter his anger. Wait for the perfect moment to unleash it.

"You're right, Jude. She wasn't worth losing everything we've worked so hard for. The Trinity comes first. Isn't that what we always vowed?"

Jude nodded, his lips curling into a smile. The fucker. "Yes, yes. I knew you'd understand. You know I love you, right?"

"Of course. Just as I love you, my brother." Leo pushed away from the wall, spun on his heel and left the room.

KILL HER. They were going to kill the woman.

Pheakdei waited until Leo and Jude left the room before sliding out of the darkness behind the hidden door. He'd heard enough.

A numb cold settled into his creaky bones as he shuffled down the hall. The woman was the first person to treat him like something other than scum, the first to ask his name and give him back his dignity.

His feet slapped against the concrete on the way to the iron stairs that descended into the bowels of the prison, but he hesitated on the second step.

What you think you're doing? Keep your head down. You're no cowboy. You can't save the day.

Pheakdei backed up. No, he wasn't a cowboy. He wasn't anything but a gutless wonder, as John Wayne in the movie *Chisum* would say.

Do something.

But what could he do?

"OLIVER?"

Necessity prompted Jocelyn to call out his name in the silence. She'd tried to convince him that what happened in The Father's room hadn't been his fault. If the electricity hadn't succeeded, The Father would have found some other way to hurt her. But Oliver couldn't get past the fact that his hands had inflicted the pain.

He sat with his back against the wall, as far from her as the chain would allow. "Yeah?" He looked up, regret muddying his gaze.

Her cheeks burned. Maybe she didn't have to tell him. She crossed her legs, clenched her muscles tight. If she could just wait it out, until one of the guards came for her…who knew how long that would be? She shifted against the hard concrete. Nope. She couldn't wait that long.

"I…" She bit her lip and turned away from Oliver's hard stare. Her cheeks flamed hotter. "I have to…I need…" *Just get it out already. It's nothing he hasn't heard before.* "I have to pee."

The admission crackled between them. Humiliation crawled up her throat, but she forced herself to meet the intense jade of his eyes. They softened, and with a nod he climbed to his feet, in sync with her. She shuffled to the back corner, aware of him echoing her, to where a dented bucket waited.

Though the shackles on her wrists made the movement awkward, she quickly skimmed her fingers to the elastic waistband of her pants. She hesitated. How could she be expected to just drop her pants with Oliver three feet away, his gaze boring into her?

"Can you…turn around?" She flicked a glance at him.

His solemn face pulled tighter. "I can't." The position of the shackles didn't allow for him to fully turn his back on her.

Her trembling fingers dug tighter into her waistband. She couldn't let this get to her. It was nothing, just a normal bodily function. Her modesty had no place here.

Oliver closed his eyes, squeezing them so tight she could see the creases across his eyelids, as if he wanted to make sure she knew he was giving her as much privacy as he possibly could. She yanked down her pants and straddled the bucket. Fixing her gaze on the painted wall next to her, she took care of business as quick as possible, trying not to think about the noise.

Her cheeks flared again. She tugged up her pants, moved away from the bucket. "Um…okay."

Oliver's eyes opened slowly, his dark irises centered on her. "I'm sorry."

She exhaled a shaky breath and turned her attention to the mural. Turbulent gray-blue waves crashed against the sand, an orange sunset hovered above the water. She touched the bird that soared neared the sun. "Such beauty in such a miserable place."

"It's home."

Oliver's simple, knowing words slammed into her. She whipped her head around.

"You painted this?" Another beat hit her—the paintings in The Father's room. "The churches…did you paint those too?"

"Yeah." His jaw clenched. "I wish you hadn't seen those."

"But why? They're wonderful. Evocative."

"It means you've been in The Father's room. Nobody should have to go in there." A muscle twitched in his cheek. "All my friends, they died for what they couldn't live without. But for me…what I couldn't live without is what keeps me alive."

"Your painting?"

Oliver nodded sharply. "I should've died the first time I stole a pencil and piece of paper, but when The Father learned I could I paint, he spared me. Every day he summons me to paint, and every day, my hatred of taking brush to canvas grows."

Jocelyn stared at the scene in front of her, almost tasting the salt air and feeling the caress of the ocean breeze. "Maybe you need to remember why you loved it in the first place." She tilted her head to the mural. "Where is home?"

"Monterey Bay. A big, empty house of steel and glass right on the beach." His voice gentled as he became lost in another time and place. "When I was a kid I used to sit on a stool and watch as my father turned a blank page into another world. I experienced my first crush the day he brought Peg Digby's face to life on paper. I was ten at the time. It took me years to understand she wasn't a real person."

Her jaw dropped. "Your father was Charles Shaw? *The Perilous Journey* was my favorite book as a child. I still have a tattered copy of it at home somewhere. It's the reason I became an anthropologist."

She'd loved the adventurous, gutsy spirit of Peg Digby, the way the girl went around helping others and making the world a better place.

"Yeah, well, she's the reason my dad often forgot I was around. He chose the imaginary world over reality more often than not. His studio was a lonely place, even with him in it. But there was nowhere else I wanted to be. He died just after I turned eighteen. Car accident."

"I'm sure he loved you very much."

A strangled chuckle leaked out of him. "You are so— good. Do you ever once stop looking on the bright side?"

"Why should I? What purpose does negativity serve?"

"Negativity?" His mouth curled into a scowl. "Call it reality."

"Life is what you make it." She reached for him even though his words scored into her optimism, but the iron clamped around her wrists wouldn't allow for the embrace.

"Yeah?" He pulled back, arched a brow. "How's that working out for you?"

She flinched. "Not so good."

"I didn't think so."

"Doesn't mean we should stop trying to make it better."

She glanced up at him, and he must've read the intent in her gaze. His eyes darkened with something raw and primal, something that urged her to back off even as he strained toward her.

OLIVER'S SKIN PRICKLED under Jocelyn's stare. How could he stay unmoved under that kind of passion? The way her voice blanketed him, her guileless face and big hazel eyes…she was so—clean. And he didn't mean her appearance. It was her heart, her squeaky clean soul. She had the power to wash his dirt away.

Her unwillingness to see the darker realities of life had put them both in jeopardy. The grounded part of him knew that. But the other part—the part that was winning—wanted him to hop right out of his skin and become someone different. Someone better.

"I used to believe that way."

She bit her lip. "I lied, you know. About my dad's map. I don't have a clue where Kala's Ashes is."

He'd suspected. "Maybe you just don't remember. Your dad wouldn't have gone through the trouble of scattering symbols through his letters if he didn't believe you or your mother would be able to decipher them."

"My mother's dead." Fresh grief creased her face.

"I know."

"And when The Father realizes I've lied…"

He'd kill her.

Oliver didn't know who moved first. He suspected it was he, and should've been shocked at how natural the movement felt. His heart hammered. They were standing toe-to-toe, fingers entwined, her soft palms meeting his calloused ones.

"I won't let that happen."

His fierce declaration was swallowed by the scrape of a key in the lock. The door creaked on its hinges and swung open. The albino stood in the doorway. Piercing translucent eyes raked over them, his pale lips parted in a snarl, his chest heaving.

A trench knife gleamed in his hands.

ELEVEN

THE PALE MAN stalked toward Jocelyn, his hungry gaze roving over her body.

She took a step back at the same time Oliver inched forward, trying to shield her from view. The man moved so swift and smooth. Before she had time to react further, his pasty fingers closed over her arm and wrenched her forward.

The chain between her and Oliver rattled, telling her the move had jerked him off balance as well. She cried out and stumbled into the man's broad chest. He wrapped his arms around her and drew her flush against his body. She squirmed against the hardness she found there, her stomach lurching violently.

"Let her go." Oliver advanced, his hands clenched in the air, despite the wrist shackles.

The Ghost dug his fingers into her shoulder. "Stay back." He pressed the point of the knife to her throat, forcing Oliver to retreat. "She's coming with me."

She winced and froze. "I'm not going anywhere with you."

He gripped Jocelyn's chin and tilted her face. His thumb scraped over her mouth. "Oh, yes you are. We're going to take a little road trip to Kala's Ashes."

"You're crazy." She wheezed out the words. "I don't know where that stupid mine is, and even if I did—"

He lowered his head to nip at her lips. "Shush. Together, we'll work Kala's Ashes and make sure Jude never gets his hands on one red sliver. Maybe we'll even start a family. I'll finally have what Jude robbed from me and Ruthie—"

Bile rose in her throat. She shoved at him. "Stay away from me!"

Oliver lunged, but the creep sidestepped, taking her with him. The movement dragged Oliver forward. His knees struck the floor near her feet. Pain etched on his face. She leaned forward, intent on giving him a hand up, but the tip of the knife pricked against her skin. A bead of warmth trickled down her throat.

Blood.

The albino's eyes went cold and glassy. He turned on Oliver. "Look what you made me do!" Jamming the knife into the sheath at his waist, he bent and licked away the blood.

She shuddered, the heat leeching from her face. "Please. Leave me alone."

He lifted his head, ignoring her plea. A crazed, ravenous light flared in his eyes. His fingers tangled in the front of her shirt. "She's the one I want." His whisper chilled her to the bone. He turned to Oliver. "Just her. You can earn your freedom, right here, right now. Keep quiet. Agree to leave her with me. I'll undo your chains and let you go."

Oliver climbed to his feet. "Just like that?"

"Yes."

A hush fell over the room. She swallowed and forced herself to look at Oliver. Would he take the deal? She wouldn't blame him if he did. He'd endured more than two hellish years in this place. He'd paid his dues. Earned his freedom. But, God, she didn't want him to leave her.

His gaze turned the green of his eyes the color of wet moss. "No."

The word held a tormented promise—she would never be alone. She closed her eyes, selfish relief filling her.

"So be it." The man shoved at Oliver with a growl, flashing a silver key between his fingers.

"No, wait." The plea was out of her mouth before she realized her intent.

How could she deny Oliver the chance to go free? He knew these jungles. By his own admission he'd spent six months backpacking through Cambodia. How long would it take him to reach a village and call in help? A few days? Maybe a week at most. Could she endure—?

She had to. Whatever this man had in store for her, whatever The Father would throw at her, her will to survive was far stronger. If she could buy some time, just enough for Oliver to call in reinforcements, she could save them both.

"I—" she swallowed, trying to calm her stomach, and met the albino's narrowed eyes. "I'll stay. I want you to let him go."

"No!"

"You should go," she said, raising her gaze to Oliver's. "This is your chance."

"I CAN'T." Tremors rippled through Oliver's hands.

Jocelyn was putting far too much faith in him. Freedom loomed so close. All he had to do was take it.

"Don't pin your hopes on me, Josie. I am not the man you think I am." He had no intention of letting her continue to hold him in such high regard. "If I get out of this hellhole, I may not have the courage to come back."

To his surprise she didn't even flinch.

"Bullshit." Her whispered curse made him rear back. "If you don't go, neither one of us will make it out of the jungle alive. You have to do this."

Didn't she understand that he'd been here before? Once he'd been cocky and self-assured, so certain he could save everyone. He'd thought himself invincible. But now he knew better.

If he left without her, she'd die. Somewhere along the way he'd crumble and fail her. And that was a risk he wasn't willing to take.

"Not without you. Either we both go or—"

"Oliver, no, you have to—"

The albino's low, keening wail cut off Jocelyn's plea. "So that's how it is? You want this bastard instead of me? I'll show you. I'm every bit as good as him."

He threw Oliver back, pinning him against the wall. Jocelyn stumbled and bounced next to him. Her head smacked the wall and she gasped.

Oliver felt the jam of the key in one of his shackles. The iron popped free. He swung his fist, hoping to catch the asshole in the jaw, but the man blocked the blow and twisted, snapping the loose shackle around a rusty ring that protruded from the cement block.

He curled his colorless lips. "Watch and learn."

Oliver looked down. The bastard had chained him to the wall.

He jiggled the chain and tried to lash out. With less than six inches of slack, he had nowhere to go. His teammates flashed before his eyes in a jumble of faces— Davis, Ezra, Catrina. Screams of terror, rivers of blood. He wanted to close his eyes, squeeze them tight until every image had been obliterated, but Jocelyn yelped beside him and he couldn't bring himself to shut her out.

The albino crushed her against the wall, smashing his

mouth on hers. He fisted his hand in her shirt and ripped the thin linen down her body. She kicked out, but he caught her leg, twisted it, and forced her to the ground.

Oliver swallowed his heart, which had taken root in his throat. The shackle around his neck jerked and tugged, rubbing against his skin with each of Jocelyn's struggles. The bastard was going to rape her. Right in front of Oliver. While he was tethered to her, helpless to fight for her, forced to feel her panic through the vibrations in the chain.

Not this time.

His stomach kicked up a cloud of emotion. Fear. Anger. But mostly fear. He'd let it rule his actions for so long—afraid to die, afraid to live—hell, after all the botched escape attempts, the beatings, the mental and physical torture, he'd just been afraid. Period.

Little by little he'd lost himself. He'd allowed himself to forget what it was like to fight for something, to put someone else's life ahead of his own. But Jocelyn hadn't forgotten. She could still escape unscathed.

Yanking at his chains, he began wiggling the rusty ring back and forth, slowly at first then with increased speed. Sweat broke out on his forehead and dripped into his eyes. No telling how long the iron loop had been anchored to the concrete block.

But he would break it free.

JOCELYN HUNCHED HER shoulders in an attempt to hide her exposed breasts. The man climbed on top of her, pinning her to the floor. She shoved at his chest. No use. She couldn't budge him. Not with her hands chained in front of her and the weight of his body pressing her palms into her stomach.

He raked a clammy hand over her breast.

She recoiled. "Get off me!"

His breath hit her full in the face. "Don't you think you should call me Leo? I want to hear you say it." He scraped a finger down her cheek. "You'll see. We belong together. Just wait. It'll be good between us."

"No."

She turned her head, but he angled it back with brute force then bent to nip hard at her lips. The tang of blood filled her mouth. She fought the compulsion to squeeze her eyes shut. She had to keep her wits about her, look for an opening.

The creak and rattle of chains drew her attention. Out of the corner of her eye she saw Oliver working to free himself from the wall. As if he felt the weight of her gaze on him, he stilled, his eyes settled on her and darkened.

"Hang on," he mouthed.

"Hurry." She bit her lip. She hadn't meant to say the plea out loud.

The scum on top of her took the appeal as an invitation and grabbed her breast again, this time giving her nipple a bruising pinch before sliding his hand between the waistband of her pants.

She bucked, squeezed her thighs tight. "Don't touch me!"

Hot tears boiled over onto her cheeks. *Please, God, no.*

The bastard yanked her pants down, exposing her fully not only for his own benefit but for Oliver's as well. Her cheeks burned. The guards had taken her undergarments the first day she'd arrived. She turned her head, not wanting to see Oliver's reaction to her complete humiliation.

Leo jammed his hand past her tight legs. Panic exploded in her chest. She clawed at his arm. Raked her fingernails down his skin. He didn't so much as flinch. Who the hell was this man? She curled her hands together into one fist and hammered at his shoulder. The loop of chain bumped awkwardly between them then bounced back to strike her in the face. Spots danced in front of her eyes.

Hands came around her and clenched at her windpipe. "Go ahead and fight. I'll take it rough."

She gasped for breath. Her vision clouded. She could feel his hard length pressed against her thigh. She tried to strike out at him. Her limbs wouldn't cooperate. Dizzy nausea swamped her. A strange ping rang in her ears. The iron around her neck vibrated sharply.

She blinked hard, hoping to clear the fuzziness from her head. A figure wavered into view over Leo's shoulder. *Oliver.* He lunged, knocking Leo off her. She hauled up her pants as best as she could despite her bound hands.

Run. Run for the door.

Jocelyn tried to inch backward on her butt away from the scuffle, but the chain connecting her and Oliver pulled taut, drawing her up sharp. The albino planted his fist in Oliver's face. The cuff around her neck scraped at her skin as he fell to the concrete, Leo rolling atop him.

Oliver curled his free hands around the length of chain dangling from his shackled wrist and wrapped the links tight around Leo's throat. The man's eyes bulged, the slightest bit of color flushing his translucent cheeks. He grabbed for the chain, but his broad fingers couldn't slip beneath the iron. His hands jerked and went to his waist, fumbling for the leather sheath attached to his belt.

The knife.

She opened her mouth to scream a warning, but no sound came out. Leo swung the blade. The dingy light managed to catch the sharp metal and give itself away with a glint. Oliver's head snapped back, he dropped the chain and rolled, trying to throw Leo off him.

Too late.

The blade sliced across Oliver's upper arm. He grunted. Clamped a hand over the cut. Leo raised the knife for another attempt. She crawled forward and barreled into Leo. Surprise was on her side. The direct hit had no impact on his bulk, but the knife flew out of his hand and clattered to the ground. He swung and backhanded her across the face. She fell to the floor next to Oliver. Her head bounced against the concrete. She blinked away the lightning pain across the back of her skull, trying to catch her breath. A hand clamped around her arm.

"No!" She dug her nails into the pitted cement.

Leo shifted off Oliver and climbed on top of her instead, swiping a hand across his mouth. "I'm sorry." He touched her throbbing cheek, sending a chill down her spine. "I didn't want to hurt you. Once I get you all to myself, I promise to make it up to you."

"Get…your hands…off her."

Oliver's steely voice registered a second before she saw him roll. He raised his arm, the knife clutched in his fist, and plunged the blade into Leo's back. The man's eyes popped wide, his mouth falling slack. He strangled on his saliva, blood bubbled up on his lips. His body went rigid and he collapsed, sprawling on top of her.

"Oh, my God." She pushed at his weight. Her useless, bound hands wouldn't cooperate. "Oh, God, oh, God. Get him off of me."

Oliver knelt by her side and heaved the dead man off her, but she couldn't stop trembling.

"Get him off of me. Please get him off. Get him off."

"Jocelyn." Oliver touched her shoulder.

She yelped.

"Josie. Stop."

The way he barked her name brought her to her senses. It was over. She clenched her hands to her chest and rolled onto her side, away from him, curling into a ball.

"Josie." He touched her hair, so light and so brief, she wasn't sure if she imagined it. "We have to get out of here. Now."

He was right. They had no way of knowing if anyone heard the commotion. Their window of escape was small. It might be their only chance. She tried to stand, but her quivering legs wouldn't cooperate.

Oliver tugged on her hands and helped her to her feet.

Once she gained her balance, the nausea and jumbled thoughts receded. Her gaze strayed to the sleeve of his shirt. A trail of blood soaked the linen from bicep to wrist.

She swallowed hard. "Your arm."

He barely spared it a glance. "It's fine." He turned, bent over Leo and snapped the key ring off his belt. "Come here. Hurry."

She shuffled closer, and he gripped her wrists steady, slipping the key into the lock. The shackles sprang open and fell to the ground. He popped his own cuff off. Before she could revel in the freedom of movement, he leaned in, nudged her chin and hunched down to work on the iron band around her neck. She held her breath, clutching her torn shirt closed, as he tried one key, then another, and finally the third without success.

"Shit!" He threw the key ring to the floor, raked his hands through his hair. "The key's not here."

"What? No. It has to be." She made a move to retrieve the set of keys, but he stopped her with a hand on her arm.

"It's not here."

His gentle voice undid her. To come so far…

She looked up at him. "What are we going to do?"

His face tightened, his lips turning down into a grim slash. "We have no other choice. We're running in chains."

TWELVE

"How ARE WE going to escape—like this?" Jocelyn gestured to her shackled neck. The torn fabric of her shirt fell away from her breasts, exposing them.

Oliver's gaze slid over her. Her cheeks flushed. She bowed her head and yanked the ragged shirt closed.

"Here." She looked up at the sound of his strained voice and met his eyes, dark with compassion. "Take mine."

He hastily undid the buttons, slid it off and held it out to her.

"Thank you." She snatched it out of his hand and made fast work of shedding the ruined shirt.

The fabric still held the warmth from his body and when she slipped it on, the shirt hung on her much smaller frame. The left sleeve, wet from his blood, clung to her arm. She swallowed, trying hard to ignore the sharp metallic scent, and glanced up at him. Blood still dripped from the gash in his bicep. A wide path of crimson streaked the length of his arm.

"We have to do something about that arm." She wasn't a trained medic by any stretch, but she knew basic emergency first aid. It would have to do.

Retrieving her ruined shirt, she tore a strip from the hem and wrapped the fabric tight around his arm in a makeshift tourniquet. Oliver stayed silent the entire time, the only sound in the cell his harsh breathing. "Let's go." The command rumbled up from his chest.

"Keep your hands on the chain. We've got to muffle the sound as best we can."

She wrapped her hands around the iron, and shadowed him to the door. He pulled it open with a creak that scuttled along her spine. What if the guards were out there? Waiting for them?

Oliver dragged her into the dark corridor. Empty. For now. Getting out of the cell was the easy part. Thousands of steps still lay between them and freedom. More shadowy hallways where guards might lurk. The first stirrings of doubt swam through her. She struggled to push them aside. She had to stay alert. Be prepared for anything.

They neared the end of the hall. Right or left? Which way? Her sense of direction was all turned around. They needed to retrace their steps, find their cells, and continue on to the stairwell that led to the ground level. But every corridor looked the same.

Muffled footsteps echoed against concrete, growing louder. Oliver shoved her back into the shadows with a whispered curse and set her against the wall. His body pressed flush to hers, and she realized he was trembling every bit as badly as she. Jocelyn held her breath and hung on, her face against his chest. The pounding of his heart drummed in her ear, the warmth of his bare skin clung to her cheek.

Footsteps slowed and a guard came into view in the adjacent hall. The slice of weak light cut across his face long enough for her to determine he was one of the more ruthless of the mercenaries, the one who had delighted in scrubbing her down that first day with deliberate force. Something clattered against the floor and he stopped, just feet from their hiding spot.

She bit her lip to keep from crying out. *Oh, God,*

please don't let him see us. Her hands started to shake. She curled them tighter around the chain to stop the tremors from clanking the links together. Oliver herded her into the wall, trapping her hands between their bodies.

The guard bent and retrieved the dropped object. He straightened. A small flame snicked to life in his hands. A lighter. He jammed a cigarette between his lips and lit it. After taking a few drags, he moved down the hall. His footsteps faded, the echo dissipating into silence once again. Still, Jocelyn couldn't bring herself to release her pent-up breath.

Oliver finally broke the hush with his own ragged breath. "Time to make a run for it."

Her heart skipped a beat. "What if we run into the guard?"

"Opposite direction. Hopefully he's well out of earshot."

And if he wasn't?

"Stick close." He pulled her away from the wall and darted into the corridor.

Her legs had no choice but to work hard to keep up with his longer strides. He slowed to match her steps, but finding a rhythm while chained at the neck proved much more difficult than she'd thought. The chain bounced between them. Even with both their hands gripping the length, the iron still clanked.

In minutes they came to another hallway. She recognized the series of pipes that ran up the wall. Ahead she could make out the shadowed doorways of their cells. Oliver slowed when he came to his. He looked inside, his eyes roving over the interior, his face etched with hollow regret.

Leaving their cells behind, they followed another serpentine hallway until it ended in a narrow stairway, the steps obscured by the gloom. Oliver shot up the stairs, his long strides eating them up two at a time. She tried to match him, and miscalculated. Her foot slipped on the edge of the slick metal. She went down. Her fingers tangled in the chain, her chin struck the step. Pain exploded in her jaw. She gritted her teeth to keep from making a sound. Bit down on her tongue.

"Damn it." Oliver knelt beside her, his whisper near her ear. "You okay?"

She nodded, not trusting herself to speak. He grabbed her arm, helped her to her feet and together they mounted the remaining stairs. She paused at the top, letting the tension in her chest ease just a fraction.

Out of the bowels of hell. One level closer to freedom.

She looked at Oliver to see his reaction to leaving two years of his life behind, but the darkness gave nothing away, least of all his state of mind. He continued down the hall without so much as a backward glance. And stopped before a slightly ajar door. A faded wash of light leaked out around it. "Keys," he huffed. "We can't keep on running like this."

She agreed, but the thought of finding someone on the other side of the door made her skin crawl. He pushed at the door with his fingertips, sending a squeak into the silence. The light from the single desk lamp speared into her eyes. She blinked away the spots, the impression of a man hunched over the desk. Her pulse sped, perspiration dampening her palms. She felt Oliver tugging her forward.

She groped for his arm. "No, wait—"

Empty. The room was empty.

The space snapped into clearer focus. The Father. His room—his evil—stamped on every inch of his domain.

"What are we doing in here?" Her voice cracked. She wanted nothing more than to bolt, even as she was drawn inside, forced to keep pace with Oliver.

"He has to have the keys. Look around. Quickly."

She headed for the desk. He had the same idea. The surface was littered with papers. She immediately recognized her dad's letters, his leather-bound logbook next to a thick manila file folder. She snatched the bundle up, feeling the paper's familiar worn texture against her fingertips.

"You can't take those."

"I'm not leaving them behind. They're all I have left of my dad."

"Your dad's dead." He grabbed her shoulders and shook her. "You will be too if you take what belongs to The Father."

She jerked her head back, feeling as if he'd just slapped her. Her hip bumped into the desk and sent the file folder careening off the desk. "They belong to me. Not The Father. And he has all the information he needs. They're useless to him—" Her gaze snagged on the contents of the folder splayed out on the tile floor.

Jocelyn knelt for a closer look, tugging Oliver down beside her. Photos. She plucked several from the floor. A young Khmer girl smiled up at the camera as she washed clothes in a stream, another photo showed a boy climbing a tree, and a third depicted a father pushing his son in a wooden cart—a boy that looked remarkably like the undernourished child that had brought The Father a tray of food. She couldn't be sure, but the shape of those eyes—

"Don't touch those. Grab your dad's things, let's find the damn key and get out of here."

She scooped the documents into the folder and settled

it back onto the desk, but she couldn't let go of the photos. These children were somebody's daughters. Their sons. Had The Trinity taken kids from their parents and forced them to live under The Father's tyranny?

Oliver reached for the drawers and yanked two open at a time. He rifled through the contents, tossed her a worn messenger bag that had been tucked at the bottom. She grabbed the sack, dumped everything she had in her hands inside, and slung the bag over her shoulder.

One shallow drawer sat anchored in the middle of the desk. She jerked it open. A small oval object lay in the otherwise empty drawer. She scooped the piece of wood into her hand and turned it over. A woman's face stared up at her from the miniature portrait.

Oliver finished his search. "Nothing." He hopped to his feet and motioned to the blank wall. "In there."

She frowned, slapped the miniature on the desk and slammed the drawer shut. In where? There wasn't anything over...

Wait a minute—the secret door. The first time she'd been brought before The Father he'd come through a door hidden in that wall. What better place to hide the keys? She joined Oliver at the wall and helped him tug at the nearly invisible seams until the door popped free with a click.

He pushed it open to reveal a walk-in closet, empty, except for the three-foot-wide metal safe that sat in the middle. A keypad was mounted next to it on the wall. The green light on the control panel suddenly went red and started blinking, slowly at first then growing increasingly rapid as if waiting for input. Or signaling a countdown.

Oliver hissed out a breath. "Oh, shit."

Her pulse kicked into high gear. She backed out of

the closet as fast as her feet would carry her, but by the time they both turned around and headed for the door it was too late.

An insistent shrieking split the air, wailing its steady stream of rage.

They had tripped an alarm.

OLIVER GRABBED JOCELYN'S hand and tore off down the hallway. Their only hope now was speed. The faster they got the hell out of here, the better.

He glanced over to gauge how she was faring, and was struck by the hard set of her jaw. The screaming siren pounded in his head and unraveled his nerves. It had to be doing the same to her, but the concentration etched across her profile hid everything except her determination to succeed. She would fight until the end, no matter the outcome. He could not let her down.

The hallway suddenly ended in a large open room. Dim lights rested in wall sconces, bathing the high, cracked ceiling in an eerie glow. The green paint crumbled on the eroded cement floor. Two corridors broke off from the corners. He chose one and started down the dark path.

Several steps in, he froze. Unease gripped his spine and crackled the hair at the back of his neck.

Jocelyn sidled closer, her arm pressing into his. "What is it?"

He matched her hushed tone. "Do you hear it too?"

Footsteps. Faint, nearly drowned out by the shrill alarm, but echoing in his head just the same.

She stiffened. "Someone's coming."

He clamped an arm around her waist and reeled, retracing their steps to the room. They darted for the hall at the other corner. Shouts arose from down the long passage. More footsteps.

"Go." He backed out of the corridor, Jocelyn in tow.

The walls of the room started to close in on him. He spun, bringing her with him. The action brought a rush of blood to his head. He blinked away the dizziness, clenched his teeth against the sudden throb of his arm.

Where could they go? Where could they hide?

Both passages were blocked. The third led them back to where they'd come. The corridor was probably crawling with guards by now. They couldn't stay here. The empty room provided zero coverage.

Precious seconds ticked down. Jocelyn's hand found his and squeezed tight. To come so far, only to fail her…

No. He wouldn't accept that.

He pulled her over to the wall and sank into a crouch. The alarm suddenly cut short on a wail. Footsteps thundered closer.

"They're coming and there's nowhere to go." She curled into him. The pressure of her cheek against his bare arm made his throat tighten.

"So we rush 'em and hope for the best."

He felt her nod against his shoulder. There it was again, that undeserved trust, as if he knew what the hell he was doing and would somehow get them out of this alive. Her breath blew across his skin in warm, shallow bursts, and he knew—he would protect her until his last gasp left his body. If he could do nothing else, he would make sure she didn't go through this alone.

A low creak whined off to his right. He flinched and whipped his head in the direction of the sound. He squinted into the shadows. A panel had slid back from the wall revealing the dark shape of a man. His hunched shoulders gave him away before he even spoke.

Pheakdei.

"Come. Quickly." The man's whisper fired in their direction.

Oliver hesitated. Could they trust the old man? He'd never gone against The Trinity before, why do so now? What if it was just a trap?

"I help you. I know a way out. Come." His voice rang with sincerity, but Oliver had been fooled before. He couldn't risk Jocelyn's fate on mere words, and yet, he'd rather take his chances with the old man over any of The Trinity's other goons.

"We're out of options." Jocelyn spoke in his ear. "We have to trust him."

He nodded and they darted into the passageway. Pheakdei closed the panel, sealing them in the pitch-black tunnel. He flicked on a flashlight and the beam danced around the small space until he pointed it toward the ground.

"This way. Hurry."

Oliver dogged his heels, as close as he could get without tripping the old man.

"What is this place?" Jocelyn's hushed voice still managed to resonate in the narrow corridor.

"Emergency escape. Many here in building, if you know where to look."

Oliver wrapped his fingers around the chain that dangled from his neck, his muscles tensing. "Who else knows about them?"

Pheakdei threw a glance over his shoulder. "Hard to say. Old building. Abandoned long time before The Trinity take over. I spend much hours here. Find many things, but tell no one. Maybe others do the same."

Not exactly the reassurance he'd hoped for, but he appreciated the man's honesty. He urged Pheakdei to increase his pace, listening hard for the sound of guards crashing through the wall. The tunnel shrunk, the air turned humid. He found it difficult to draw breath. And then he saw it, in the beam of Pheakdei's flashlight. The metal rungs of a ladder.

Pheakdei stopped, turned to them, fumbling for his belt. "Go." He yanked the ring of keys off and pressed them into Oliver's hand.

The key ring burned in his palm. The weight of freedom came with heavy responsibility. He knew exactly what Pheakdei was risking by helping them, and yet he'd have to turn his back on the old man and leave him to accept The Trinity's ruthless consequences.

Jocelyn, on the other hand, reached for the old man's hands and pressed them between hers. "Come with us."

In the soft glow of the flashlight, Pheakdei's eyes shone. He shook his head.

"But they'll kill you! You can't stay here—"

He pulled his hands free. "My family would not be proud of what I become. It's time to start doing what is right."

"We can't just leave you here." She stared at Oliver like she wanted him to agree.

He looked away. The old man would slow them down. He'd vowed to get her out of here alive. The odds were stacked against them already. He couldn't tip them in The Trinity's favor. But maybe there was something he could do to help Pheakdei.

"Give me your nightstick."

Pheakdei pulled it from his belt and passed it to Oliver.

He grimaced. "This is going to hurt."

"What—?"

He drew back the nightstick and swung it across Pheakdei's head.

The man crumpled to the ground, the flashlight dropped out of his hand and rolled across the floor.

"What did you do that for?" Jocelyn bent to help Pheakdei, but Oliver gripped her arm and pulled her to her feet.

"Leave him." He tipped her chin to reach the lock on her shackles. "He'll wake up with a killer headache. But if The Trinity thinks he tried to stop us and we overpowered him, maybe they'll let him live."

He went through the keys until he came to the one that easily slid into the lock. The iron unlatched and he pulled the collar from Jocelyn's neck.

"Here. Do mine." He passed her the key and bent his knees so she could reach the lock.

Her cold hands pressed against his neck as she slipped the key into the lock and turned it. She tugged the cuff free and the shackles fell away. He wanted to revel in that first step to freedom, but adrenaline pumped through his veins, reminding him they were far from home free.

Jocelyn darted over to the ladder and began her ascent. He gripped the rungs, waited to give her a few seconds' lead, then followed.

"The hatch—I can't—it won't budge."

He climbed the remaining rungs. "Hang on."

One step below her, he wrapped his arm around her waist to steady himself and reached to pop the hinge. It gave with a groan. A warm breeze blew across his skin.

"I smell rain." The longing in Jocelyn's voice washed over him.

Rain. How long had it been since he'd felt fat, stormy drops pelt his skin?

"Wait. Let me check it out first."

She scooted to the side to allow him to pass. He scaled the last few rungs and poked his head out from the hatch. They were about a hundred yards from The Trinity's compound. Moonlight bathed the grassy area in a silvery light. Beyond the valley lay the jungle. All things he'd never thought to see again.

"All clear." It was difficult to push out the okay.

He levered himself out of the hatch. Jocelyn was beside him before he had the chance to lend her a hand. He stood to get his bearings and made a break for the narrow road that cut through the patches of grass.

His feet sunk into the moist dirt. "This way. Come on."

An open-air Land Rover was parked near the side of the building. He fell into a crouch and gestured for Jocelyn to do the same. If he could get to the truck he could hotwire the starter. The plan was worth a shot. They'd be much harder to catch if they weren't on foot.

Bright lights suddenly struck him full in the face. He blinked away the spots clouding his vision. Searchlights. The guards were coming for them. They were out of time.

Grabbing Jocelyn's hand, he changed directions, heading for the cover of the jungle. "Keep running. Don't slow down."

Not for the pebbles under their feet, or the pointed branches whipping past their faces.

Not to catch a breath, or relieve the burning in their legs.

Gunfire erupted, rippling the air around them.

They dove beyond the halo of searchlights.

THIRTEEN

THE SHRILL RINGING awakened Jude from a lush dream. He'd been standing in Kala's belly. Red diamonds glittered like coals all around him. His face still tingled with their fire, their power hummed in his veins. He snatched the phone from the nightstand and flipped it open.

"This had better be good."

"It's—the prisoners. They've escaped."

Jude vaulted out of bed. "What? When?"

"Minutes ago. They tripped the alarm, from inside your office, or we might never have known. Thom and Veha have gathered up the men. They're out after them now."

His office? What were Shaw and Hewitt doing in his office? "Why wasn't anyone watching their cell?"

"They shouldn't have been able to get out of there. The place was secure. Sealed up tight."

He flipped on a light switch, grabbed a pair of trousers hanging on the back of a chair. "I'm on my way."

He'd ordered his quarters built close to The Trinity's compound for just this reason. In the event of an emergency he wanted to ensure he was always kept in the loop.

"Sir…" The man hesitated. "There's more."

More? What could be worse?

He rubbed his brow. "What is it?"

"Leo's dead. We found him in the cell. Stabbed in the back. That's…uh…how the prisoners escaped."

Jude reeled so sharply, he had to sit down on the edge of the bed and catch his breath.

Leo. Dead.

All that talk of love? Of understanding? And then he'd gone behind Jude's back and went after the woman. What had he thought to accomplish?

Had he just wanted a piece of ass?

Or had he thought to punish Jude for murdering Ruth?

The little shit.

Jude's eyes stung. "Fifteen minutes," he croaked. "Tell the others to wait for me."

THE TATTOO OF the AK-47 echoed across the silent night.

Oliver flung out an arm, snagging the back of Jocelyn's shirt. He pulled her to the ground and covered her body with his. Wet leaves and mud clung to his clammy skin. His arm throbbed, his head ached, blood roared in his ears.

Don't think it. This isn't like last time. You have to keep going.

He pressed his cheek against Jocelyn's to calm the racing in his heart. Her rapid breaths puffed from her nose, her back rising and falling beneath him in choppy bursts. He strained to hear the dull shush of boots across wet grass.

If he reached out, his fingertips could almost brush the wide leaves of the jungle plants. So close. The tall trees stretched into the inky sky, cocooning all the night creatures from the harsh glare of the moon. Why couldn't the dense foliage hide them as well?

He pressed his lips against Jocelyn's ear. "Stay low.

Run for the trees. On the count of three." He rolled off her and into a crouch. "One." She scrambled onto her hands and knees. "Two. Three."

He waited for her to get a head start and tore after her. Bullets strafed from somewhere off to his left. He urged his burning legs faster. Just a few more seconds. That's all the time he needed for the tangle of trees to swallow him. He burst through the barrier. Noise assaulted his ears—a million tiny chirps, squeaks and flutters—blending together in an undulating cacophony. He could barely see his hand in front of his face, but he felt Jocelyn alongside him, the heat of her, the whisper of her breath. He found her hand and guided her into the dark rainforest.

She hesitated. "Where are we going?"

"Further into the jungle. They'll expect us to run for civilization and will post mercenaries along the road. We stand the best chance if we stick to dense, sparsely populated areas."

He urged her into a trot. When she slipped on a patch of leaves, he slung his arm around her waist and hauled her up. Fire seared across his knife wound. He sucked in a harsh breath and gritted his teeth, waiting until he was sure she'd regained her footing before letting go. Several times they had to slow down, retrace their steps and find an alternate route through an impenetrable section of undergrowth.

Every once in a while he'd catch a glimpse of the moon, but it always seemed stuck in the same position, high in the sky, peering down at them. He had no way to gauge how long they'd been running—thirty minutes or a couple of hours—or if they were wandering in circles rather than putting distance between them and The Trinity's stronghold.

He pulled Jocelyn to a stop and listened. Crickets twittered and a bird warbled in the distance.

No voices, no footsteps. "Hear anything?"

"No. Nothing." Weariness mingled with the hope in her voice, clouding it with a bittersweet thickness.

Even the harsh darkness and eerie jungle couldn't dampen that damn sunny optimism of hers. He started walking again, determined to keep the truth from her. They were far from out of danger. If The Trinity didn't catch up with them, jungle predators might, and though he'd take them over the mercenaries any day, there were an endless number of ways he could still fail to get her out of this alive.

They came to the base of a small rocky creek. By the time they found a place to cross and managed to set foot on the other side, he was feeling lightheaded. He collapsed on the ground, his hands fisting into the massive roots of a large tree. A trail of moonlight filtered through a break in the leaves.

He lifted his head. The tree continued its upward stretch in a tangle of bark and stone. He blinked. Stone? His vision cleared and a small crumbling structure took shape amidst the branches.

"Look." He pointed a shaky hand.

Jocelyn climbed to her feet and he willed his body to do the same. As they drew closer he could see a face emerge out of the eroding rock—a forgotten ruin, abandoned by time and the ancestors of those who had constructed it.

Stepping over roots and broken stone, he found a small opening in the ruin and ducked inside. Moonlight penetrated past the opening. The smell of earth and moss filled his nostrils.

Jocelyn slipped in beside him. "I can't help but think

of all the creepy crawlies that are scurrying around in here."

"Better them than what's crawling around out there. We can rest here. For a bit."

He planted himself near the entrance and slumped to the ground. Now that terror wasn't fueling his body's flight response, he could feel the slow trickle of blood down his arm and the perspiration coating his skin.

Jocelyn pulled the leather bag from her shoulder, dropped it on the ground and squatted. "You're bleeding again, aren't you?"

"That's the least of my concerns."

"Not for me." She leaned forward. "If you pass out, I'll be stuck here all alone. I don't like being alone."

He braced himself for her touch, and when her fingers met his skin he clenched his eyes shut. He couldn't get used to it. Didn't remember what to do. Would he eventually remember how to react, or was he forever doomed to straddle the line between pleasure and agony? Bracing himself against each caress of kindness, wanting, yet undeserving. Fearing the consequences.

"Why don't you like being alone?" he asked, hoping to steer his focus from Jocelyn's soft hands unwinding the crude tourniquet from his arm.

"I don't know." She bent her head to tear off another strip from the hem of her shirt. "I think too much. And sometimes…I don't like my thoughts."

She looked up at him and her dirt splattered, haunted face caught a sliver of moonlight. Her eyes were wet, her mouth trembling. He'd found a chink in her optimism. A place where shadows lurked. He should've found that comforting; she was human after all, not the flawless woman he'd thought her to be. But somehow it made his heart hurt for her. If it weren't for her, he'd still be locked in a dirty cell, content with scribbling his thoughts in a tattered book.

His fingers itched for a chunk of charcoal and a piece of paper with which to capture this moment. "Self-reflection isn't all bad, you know. I've had years to perfect it."

Her eyes widened. "I'm sorry." She smoothed out the strip of cloth and began rewrapping his arm. "I didn't think—I'm not always so insensitive—"

"You weren't." If he could've remembered how to smile, he would've conjured one up. Instead, he leaned his head back against stone. His eyelids drooped, weighted down with grit. He forced them open and watched her caress the flap of the messenger bag. "Why are they so important to you? Your dad's letters?"

She blew out a breath. "They…make me whole. Don't you have anything like that? Something so precious you can't be you without it?"

"No." He couldn't remember a time in all his thirty-six years when he'd ever felt truly whole, and because the very thought made him uncomfortable, he resorted to pointing out the obvious. "They're just things."

"Not to me. These letters are all I've had of my dad since I was eight."

"I don't think he expected you to shackle yourself to them."

Silence stretched between them, broken only by the buzz of insects. He'd stepped over the line. Who was he to talk to her of chains when he still felt bound to the cell he'd left behind? He opened his mouth to apologize, but she shivered, wrapping her arms around her middle.

"Are you…cold?"

"Yeah. A little."

He rubbed his palms against his pants and braced his legs apart. "Come here."

He didn't let himself think about what he was doing until she had scooted into his arms and he'd wrapped them around her. She fit. Far too nicely, and he couldn't help but realize that the coarse comfort of his embrace invited an unwise familiarity between them.

The urge to push her away filled him.

He tightened his arms. "Better?"

"Not yet."

She leaned her head against his chest. He marveled at the way she settled into him as if she knew he'd take care of her.

What was someone like her doing putting her trust in someone like him?

JUDE CLOSED LEO'S sightless eyes, swallowing around a painful lump.

It was real. Leo was dead.

He ran a hand down Leo's cheek. His final act may have been a betrayal, but Jude had loved him. Grief crashed through him. "Rest in peace, my brother."

Chaotic emotions burst in his chest, propelling him to his feet, pushing him out of the chilly, damp cell and fueling his dash up to his office.

"Bitch." He clenched his teeth until his jaw locked.

She'd enticed Leo to stray. Whether Miss Hewitt wielded the knife or not, she was responsible for his death. She had created the rift between him and Jude.

A new fire raged in Jude's veins, one that even Shaw's paintings couldn't quench. No, the only way to quench this inferno was to kill Jocelyn Hewitt. Slowly. Painfully. He would watch the blood seep out of her. It alone could wash away the vengeance that itched inside him.

He flipped on the light and stalked over to his desk. Donald Hewitt's logbook was gone. His letters too. Heat boiled in his cheeks. He slammed his fist atop the metal.

Not only had she taken Leo from him, she'd stolen what was his.

Yes, his.

Takers, keepers, losers, weepers.

He threw back his head and growled. His phone pealed. He snatched it from his pocket, flipped it open.

"Tell me you've found them."

"Not yet."

He gulped in several even breaths, trying to keep from having a stroke. "What are you going to do about it?"

"We're posting mercenaries on every road leading to town. The most skilled trackers are combing the jungle. We'll find them. They can't hide for long."

Jude strode back over to the desk, stroked his hand over the file folder. "I'm not a patient man. Remember that."

He slammed the phone shut and tossed it onto the desk. Opening the folder, he leaned forward and began thumbing through the series of photos taken by Chann. Jude's portfolio. All of these children had claimed their place in The Trinity's mine at one point or another over the years. He liked looking back through them. Each smiling face reminded him of how many he'd nurtured over the years.

A crease scored into his forehead as he counted the stack. Some of the photos were missing. Impossible. He flipped through them again. Had he miscounted?

No, he was right. At least two pictures were missing from the stack.

His eye started to twitch. He reached up to scratch the scar tissue beneath the eye—his hands shaking and perspiring. No, she couldn't have—but what other explanation was there? He slapped the file folder shut, clenching his teeth against the urge to throw it across the room.

She'd stolen some of his photos.

The miniature of his mother lying facedown on his desk caught his eye. He reached over and snatched it up, running a hand over her face. His thumb snagged on her cheek.

What the hell?

He brought the picture to his face and squinted at it.

There. Right next to her nose.

The bitch had chipped the only thing he had left of his mother.

JOCELYN LEANED INTO Oliver's warmth and the adrenaline coursing through her body slowly began to dissipate. She tried to close her eyes, but all she saw was the albino—bared teeth, his hands on her body. The way his eyes had bulged and blood foamed from his mouth when Oliver had stabbed him. She was firmly entrenched in the ugly side of the world now, and it scared her to think she might never get out. That she could die out here and her bones would never be found—two generations of Hewitts lost to Cambodian soil.

She curled her hands around Oliver's forearms, trying to take strength from his warmth. Though he held her tightly, he kept his upper body rigid. Detached. Her eyes burned. He wasn't comfortable holding her, and yet he was doing it. Because it was what she needed.

"Do you think they're close?" Part of her didn't want

to know. She could just stay in Oliver's embrace and pretend that when the sun shone through the ruin opening, life would be back to normal.

But nothing would ever be the same again.

"Yeah, they're close." The surety of his gruff words skittered down her spine.

"We should keep moving." She tried to push off the floor. Her legs shot pain up her calves.

He shifted his hold, surprising her when he rested his chin on the top of her head. "No. Rest. For a couple of hours. We leave again at first light."

She didn't think she'd be able to sleep, but the steady rhythm of Oliver's heartbeat must've lured her eyes closed. When she startled awake sometime later, she found only cool stone at her back and the faint stirrings of daylight creeping into the ruin.

Jocelyn bolted upright. Her fingers sifted into the dirt floor, her gaze catching on a pile of undisturbed rubble at one end of the structure where the wall had caved in years ago.

No Oliver.

Panic jolted through her. "Oliver?"

She crawled outside. The sun was just starting to peek over the horizon, its reddish-orange glow streaking across the silvery sky. Where was he? Why hadn't he woken her?

Last night the temple had been nothing more than shelter, but this morning she could make out the intricate carvings sprinkled with moss and eroded from time. She ran her hand along the scaly texture of one of the stone creatures, its body like a fish with eagle talons and a face like an elephant. Tree trunks wound around the ruin like tentacles.

The surrounding jungle beyond the clearing still

looked dark and foreboding despite the increasing day-light. Were The Trinity's men lurking just beyond the trees? Were they even now getting in position to gun them down?

A gentle breeze disturbed the leaves.

Her skin prickled. She had to find Oliver. Now.

She spun, scanning the landscape, and a dark figure on top of the ruin caught her eye, tearing a gasp from her throat. Her heart slammed against her ribs and her toes curled into the earth, ready to make a run for it. And then he came into focus.

Oliver, sitting on the section of dilapidated stones, legs spread wide. His head was angled back to catch the warm rays of the encroaching sun. So silent and unmov-ing he could've been part of the temple—just another statute chiseled out of the stone.

She hurried up the side of the temple, sharp edges and rough bark poking her feet as she picked her way over stone and tree roots. The perch provided a better view of the treetops, stretching for miles like a lush green car-pet. She squatted beside him and waited. His gaze was fixed on the rising sun, and beneath his scruffy beard his lean, chiseled jaw was tight.

She slipped her hand onto his shoulder. "Oliver?"

"This is the first sunrise I've seen in two years." His voice broke, and he still wouldn't look at her. The sheen in his eyes made hers sting.

"It's gorgeous." Her throat tightened. For all the hor-rors she had witnessed during her time in Cambodia, the land still held a wild, untamed beauty.

"No two sunrises are ever the same. And I've missed close to seven hundred." He finally turned his head and looked at her. "But the worst part is, I no longer see the beauty in them." He swept his hand out. "In any of this."

"What do you see?"

"Bars." He stood. "All I see are bars."

FOURTEEN

"Let's get the hell out of here."

Oliver barked the order and stepped down from the ruins, not waiting for Jocelyn to respond. It was a cowardly thing to do, but he couldn't bear to see disapproval in her eyes. She saw the world as hopeful and beautiful. All he saw were bleak prison bars. He couldn't appreciate the view anymore.

When he looked at the landscape he saw the things he'd done to stay alive these last two years. The times he kept silent when he should've spoken up, the times he'd chosen himself over others. He no longer knew how to react to wide-open spaces. With The Trinity's mercenaries still out there, the vast jungle presented nothing more than a cruel illusion of freedom. One that could shatter as easily as spun glass.

He glanced over his shoulder. Why wasn't Jocelyn following him? She stood, frozen, at the base of the temple, her gaze fixed on the ground. He started to retrace his steps but the sight of a neon green snake slithering near her feet stopped him cold. The deceptively small Hanuman was no more than a foot long, but one bite could kill a man. If it lashed out at Jocelyn, she didn't stand a chance.

He inched forward. "Don't move."

She nodded, her eyes wide and bright with fear.

He crept up on the reptile. The snake's beady eyes

stared in his direction. Its forked tongue lashed out to taste his scent on the air.

That's right. I'm over here. Come and get me.

The snake didn't move. It continued to sit there, watching.

Better him than Jocelyn.

He chanced a glance at her. Still terrified. And though he no longer remembered how to crack a joke, he tried one, for her sake. "I've heard snakes are more afraid of us then we are of them. Sounds like a load of bullshit if you ask me."

No response.

A few more steps and he'd be within striking range. He covered the distance as swiftly as he dared. His fingers twitched. He flexed them and eased into a crouch, and lashed out before he had the chance to fully absorb his intent. Snatching the snake by the tail, he flung it away from Jocelyn as hard and fast as he could. The reptile hit dirt and disappeared into the trees.

He straightened, shaking off the suffocating weight. Jocelyn stumbled into his arms. Her body went limp.

He touched his cheek to the top of her head. "It's gone. You're okay."

She shivered. "I heard this hissing noise and I—I thought I didn't stand a chance." She clutched him tighter, gulped in a breath and looked up at him. "My whole life flashed before my eyes, and all I could think was that I couldn't die when I still had so much more I needed to do."

Oliver stared at her, trying to will his heart rate back to normal, but it wouldn't slow, not with her pressed against him, her words dredging up emotion he thought long dead and buried. Once upon a time he'd dreamed of a life full of accomplishments and good deeds. Had he ever sounded as refreshingly naïve as her?

He swallowed the memories and set her away from him, letting his hands linger at her waist for longer than necessary before breaking contact and tipping his head back to judge the angle of the sun. Their best chance of finding a good-sized village was to head west. He struck off in that direction.

His stomach rumbled. The early morning humidity clung to his skin. He ducked into the jungle shade, pausing to wait for Jocelyn, and began the slow trek west.

"Keep your eyes open for anything we can eat. Wild fruit, plants, even a frog or two."

She had to be hungry too, but she didn't respond. Her melancholy made him oddly uncomfortable. He didn't like thinking that even she could be brought low by this fierce place.

After a time, the trees gave way to a thicket of thorny creeper plants. He looked for a way around them, but they stretched too far in both directions.

They had no choice but to go through them.

He eyed her bare feet. "Here." He gestured to his back. "Hop on."

Her brow wrinkled. "What?"

He bent into a crouch, urging her with a wave. "I won't have you getting thorns in your feet."

The golden flecks in her eyes softened, getting lost in the more prominent gray-brown of her hazel irises. "What about you?"

"Don't worry about me."

He didn't like her looking at him with her heart in her eyes. She was building him up in her mind again, wanting to believe he had her best interests in mind, when all he really wanted was to get the hell out of the jungle. The fastest way possible. He could barrel through the thorns a lot quicker with her on his back than she could on her own.

When she still hesitated, he bumped into her and all but yanked her onto his back. He moved quickly through the thorns, ignoring their stinging bites poking into his feet. Once on smooth earth, she jumped off his back and he collapsed into the dirt.

"Hell." He ground his teeth together, clasped one foot and started to yank the slivers from his skin one by one. Droplets of blood welled in the cuts.

"Don't do that again." Jocelyn dropped next to him and took his foot in her hands. "You made it worse by adding my weight. Next time, just let me get the stupid thorns too."

"No." The shock of her touch made it impossible for him to string together more words than that.

She glared at him, then bent her head to pluck the rest of the thorns from his foot. By the time she succeeded in removing all the thorns, his feet were crisscrossed with streaks of blood.

She looked up, tears swimming in her eyes. "Thanks."

He'd endured far worse than a few scrapes and cuts. She didn't need to cry for him.

His throat squeezed tight. "You'd do the same for me."

"No, I wouldn't." Her mouth trembled into a shaky smile. "You weigh too much."

He shook his head, wanting to laugh. The urge caught him off guard, pulling his mouth into a frown.

He pushed to his feet. "Ready?"

She nodded and they continued walking in silence. As the sun rose higher in the sky, the jungle became a giant steam bath. Sweat poured down his face. The terrain grew steeper. He felt lightheaded from lack of food. The humid breeze irritated his hot skin, the pebbled earth prodded his sore feet. Birds squawked. Somewhere off in the distance, a monkey screeched. All of it put him on sensory overload.

Jocelyn put a hand on his arm. "Do you hear that?"

He stopped, strained to hear beneath the buzz in his ears. "Water?"

Her sweat-streaked face broke into a smile. She hurried in the direction of the sound.

"Thank God." She fell to her knees at the base of a small, bubbling creek. Cupping her hands, she dunked them into the water. Gulped at the clear liquid. "It's warm, but so good."

The excitement in her voice lured him down beside her. He scooped water into his hand, drinking his fill. Splashed some on his face, his hair. He wiped the moisture out of his eyes. Jocelyn was already on her feet, heading for a cactus-like tree near the creek. Stiff jagged leaves sprouted from the top of the barrel and hung down, offering its pink, spiky fruit.

She plucked one off the tree, held it to her nose for a moment before offering it to him.

He joined her. "Dragonfruit." He snagged it from her hands, tore into it with his fingernails, breaking the small fruit in half to reveal the white pulp flecked with black seeds. "It's...kind of a cross between a kiwi and pear, but blander."

"Bland never looked so good." She took the piece he presented and scraped out the pulp with her fingers.

He watched as she brought it to her mouth, licked it from her fingers. She closed her eyes and tipped her head skyward. One would've thought he'd handed her a piece of Godiva instead of a watery, weak-tasting fruit riddled with crunchy seeds. A smile crossed her lips, the curve of her mouth managing to be both shy and bold at the same time. She opened her eyes, and he could see the zest flood back into them. It hit him square in his stone-cold soul, stabbing at embers he'd snuffed out a long time ago.

"We need to keep moving." He handed her the other piece of fruit, plucking off enough extras to fill their bag.

If she wondered at his constant change of moods, she didn't ask. How could he tell her what he was feeling when he didn't even understand it himself? One minute he felt claustrophobic, the next, as if he could soar. He wanted to run. He wanted to shut himself back inside the cell that had been his home for so long. Sometimes, he wanted to do nothing at all, but look at Jocelyn and try to memorize the tilt of her lips and the nuances of color in her lively eyes.

Once again, he yearned for a piece of paper. Maybe he should've found a way to take his battered copy of *The Count of Monte Cristo* and his nub of a pencil with him, yet it had seemed fitting to leave them behind. A part of himself that would always reside in that musty, godforsaken place.

He ducked under a leafy branch, held it aside for Jocelyn. She stepped through the trees and he turned to continue, drawing up short when his feet touched a narrow, dirt path caked with motorbike tracks. His pulse jumped and he scanned the road.

There. Up ahead. A mud-encrusted motorbike was blocking the road. A man with an M16 gripped in his hands leaned against the bike, his gaze fixed on the opposite direction. Jocelyn gasped and the sound exploded like a gunshot in the silence. The man spun, tensing when he saw them.

Oliver pushed her back into the trees and she fled the way they had come. He dogged her heels. Bullets tore up the plants where they had been standing mere seconds ago. Tugging her into a copse of bushes, he pressed her to the ground and pulled fistfuls of leaves over them. Jocelyn buried her face into his neck, her warm, irregular breaths fanning across his skin.

Footsteps thundered into the jungle. The mercenary was making no attempt at stealth. He ran by in a flash of black and tan, barking into his radio as he passed in front of their hiding place—so close Oliver could've reached out and touched the man. Jocelyn's heart raced beneath Oliver's sweaty palm, her breath no longer pelted him. She was holding it in. He clenched his teeth. Waited.

A new sound assaulted his ears—the familiar thump-thump-thump of a helicopter's rotary blades. He sat up, listening to the purr of the chopper grow closer. If The Trinity was stepping up their search with air surveillance, he and Jocelyn didn't stand a chance.

"A helicopter," she whispered, sitting up beside him and clutching at his arm. "Do you think—could that be one of ours? JPAC should've sent up a search party by now—"

"No." He squashed the false hope that buoyed him. If they took a chance on the helicopter, they'd be left completely defenseless. He raised his gaze to the canopy of trees overhead. "The Trinity's started their aerial surveillance. That's all it is."

He tried to keep his voice calm, casual. *That's all it is.* As if the big metal bird wasn't in the sky waiting to take them out. Footsteps crashed through the jungle floor. Oliver pulled Jocelyn down once more, giving her a gentle squeeze to remain silent.

After a tense, suspended moment, the mercenary darted past again and disappeared through a section of trees. Out of their line of sight. The zip of a motorbike engine broke through the noise of the retreating chopper, and Oliver listened to the mercenary rev off down the road.

When the jungle returned to its familiar buzzing and chirping, Oliver jumped up, pulling Jocelyn to her feet. He motioned in the direction they needed to move and caught the widening of her eyes.

"We need to keep ourselves buried in the jungle for now. Away from the eyes of the helicopter."

She opened her mouth as if to protest, but he turned and started walking with her in tow before the exhaustion and terror etched on her face made him reconsider. Not that they had any other option. The roads weren't safe, the larger villages that sported electricity and phones were most likely being watched. Their only chance was to stick to the more primitive sections of jungle and hope to stay hidden.

But for how long?

KEEP MOVING.

The mantra kept spinning through Oliver's head, but he couldn't seem to put one foot in front of the other. His legs burned, he tried to blink the dust from his eyes and almost missed seeing the gnarled root jutting from the ground in front of him. He stepped over it, swinging out an arm to help Jocelyn. She gripped his fingers to climb over the obstacle and stumbled into him.

He slipped an arm around her and stared at her face, but couldn't make out her features. "You okay?"

She pulled away and kept walking. His gut twisted. She wasn't okay. She'd been walking and running all day without complaint. They'd had little to eat, and even less rest, and neither of them were in top physical form to keep depriving their body's needs.

"Jocelyn, wait—" He pulled up short alongside her. Lantern light flickered through the trees. A village. "Hill people," he murmured.

Tension pulled at him. They should keep going. The less people they encountered the better.

Jocelyn strained toward the light, inching forward until only a few wispy branches separated her and the huts. A sliver of the oil lamp's glow flickered across her pale face, highlighting the depth of her fatigue.

If they kept going now, would they be able to run when it really mattered?

"I know we shouldn't stop," Jocelyn whispered as if reading his thoughts, "but I don't think I can go any further. Not tonight."

"The less we tell them, the better." He took her hand, the simple connection calming him. "We're lost, okay? Separated from our group."

"That shouldn't be too hard." A tremor fluttered through her voice. "We are lost."

They ducked out of the trees and rounded the first hut. It sat on stilts, the walls and roof made out of worn bamboo, the windows and doors uneven and covered by nothing more than burlap. The other two dwellings were in much the same shape. A fire burned and crackled in a ground pit at the center of the community.

"Hello?" He issued the greeting in his best formal Khmer that he'd spent months cramming for before he'd ever first set foot on Cambodian soil. Hopefully whatever dialect these people spoke would be similar enough to make himself understood.

An old woman appeared in the doorway of one of the huts, fear and suspicion wrinkling her brow. Short and barefoot, she wore a plain tunic-like shirt, and a dark, flowing skirt. Her gray hair was scraped away from her face in a loose bun. She made no move to meet them. He didn't blame her. How often did strangers appear in their corner of the jungle?

"We're Americans. Lost." He let go of Jocelyn's hand long enough to make a gesture, both hands clasped then yanked apart. "Separated from our group. We could use something to eat. If you could spare it. I—we don't have any money."

She stared at them with narrowed eyes and he did his best not to reveal the desperation of their circumstances. A frisson of guilt tore into his gut. He was putting these people at risk, just by stopping here, but if he and Jocelyn didn't get some better fuel into them soon, they'd both collapse.

He bowed his head. "Please. We won't trouble you for more than that." They'd eat quickly and get on their way, far from any other people who might get caught in The Trinity's crossfire.

A few seconds of hesitation, then she spun and disappeared back inside the hut.

He blew out a breath. "Looks like we'll have to keep moving, then."

"What did you say to her?"

"I just asked for something to eat."

The woman reappeared, steaming bowls of food in each hand. As she came down the stairs, a man emerged from the hut bearing cups.

"Come." The woman gestured to the fire with her full hands. "Sit. Eat."

The sharp scent of ginger teased Oliver's nostrils. He took a seat near the fire and his stomach immediately started rumbling and wouldn't quit. Relief tipped up the corners of Jocelyn's mouth. She circled the fire and sat in the dirt, removing the bag from her shoulder and placing it on the ground, against her leg.

He took the warm clay bowl from the woman's outstretched hands and murmured his thanks. After serving Jocelyn, she retreated, leaving them with the acrid wood smoke, the warmth of the flames, and a heavy silence that nagged at him.

Steam hit him full in the face when he bent over the bowl. He closed his eyes, reveling in the moist warmth that clung to his skin.

"This is my first hot meal in…" Emotion rolled over him. He dug into the rice and spicy eggplant, letting the flavor seep onto his tongue before swallowing. When he came up for air, he found Jocelyn watching him.

The glow of the fire played across her dirt-streaked face and weary eyes. "Thank you for everything you've—"

"Don't thank me." The rebuke came out sharper than he'd intended, but he didn't want her thanks. Every move he'd made so far was about saving his own hide every bit as much as hers. "I haven't done a damned thing for you."

She flinched. Her hurt slapped across him like the taut end of a whip. She bent her head, shifted the bowl in her hands. "Saving me from the snake, carrying me over the thorns, getting me out of that horrifying prison in the first place…sooner or later you have to take credit for doing a good deed."

He clenched his jaw. "Then save it for when we're back in the United States."

She froze, a handful of food halfway to her lips. "What if we don't make it back?"

His own mouthful of food stuck in his throat. "If we don't make it back, then I really won't deserve your thanks."

She picked at a bite of food and brought it to her mouth, stamping her disagreement into the air without uttering a word.

His gaze strayed to her full lips, and his skin erupted with thousands of prickly sensations. He curled his hands into his bowl, recognizing the phantom stirring that hadn't washed over him in a very long time. Desire. He closed his eyes, pressed the bowl so tightly he thought he might shatter the pottery.

Inappropriate time. Inappropriate feelings. Not even one full day out of captivity and his animalistic instincts were already taking over. He trapped in a breath, but the heat in his veins wouldn't go away.

Just eat your damn food, Shaw.

He opened his eyes, couldn't keep them from glancing over at Jocelyn. She was staring at him as if she felt the same magnetic pull.

I might still get you killed. Don't you dare look at me like that.

He wanted to shout at her. To make her understand that no matter how good his intentions were he had a way of fucking up everything he touched. Jocelyn would not become one more casualty of his own making.

Instead of saying any of that, he concentrated on his food. He didn't want to disillusion her. The selfish part of him liked that she believed he was a better man, and when she looked at him, her eyes shining, she made him want to believe, too.

He downed the contents of his cup in one gulp—some sort of watered-down rice wine that tasted dry and slightly bitter—and frowned into his now empty bowl. He'd hoped filling his belly with food would erase the gnawing hunger of a different kind, but although his stomach was content, the rest of him…wasn't.

The Khmer couple still hovered by their hut. He pushed to his feet and took them the bowls. The woman's arms were laden with a bundle of fabric, so he handed the empty dishes to the man at her side.

"Thank you, Sir. We appreciate your kindness."

The man stared back at him, wary, but the woman beamed, showing him a gap toothed smile. "You stay tonight."

"No, we couldn't. You've already been so kind—"

"Stay."

He shot a glance at Jocelyn.

She climbed to her feet. "What is she saying?"

"She's letting us know it's okay to stay for the night, but…"

Relief mellowed her stance. Unease tightened his shoulders, but how could he deny Jocelyn the chance to get some rest?

As long as they left before the first streaks of dawn.

He would not put these kind people in any more danger.

He turned back to the Khmer woman. "Thank you for the generous offer. We will stay."

Another one of those broad smiles lit her face. She shuffled over to Jocelyn and despite the burden in her arms, managed to tug the empty crockery from Jocelyn and set it on the ground. "Come."

A beat of alarm flickered in Jocelyn's eyes, but she allowed the woman to take her hand and lead her around the outside of the hut. Oliver followed, unwilling to let her out of his sight. Just beyond the huts a dark pond nestled between the trees. Moonlight reflected off its glassy surface. Lotus leaves floated near the bank, and at the far end, branches dipped into the water.

The woman set her bundle on a rickety wooden platform, gestured to the pond and left them alone.

Jocelyn blinked. "What just happened?"

He reached out to touch the coarse array of fabrics, swiped a finger over a chunk of some kind of soap. "I believe she was letting you know you could wash up here. If you wanted."

She sighed, pulling his soiled shirt away from her body. "That sounds wonderful."

Oliver swallowed. "You go ahead. I'll be right around the corner if you need me."

He started to leave, but her voice drew him to a stop.

"Would you…mind sticking close? As beautiful as this place is and as much as I want to bathe…I don't want to be out here alone."

A warm breeze blew across his skin like a caress. *Her caress.*

"Yeah, sure." He squashed the urge to reach for her and tucked his hands behind his back. "I'll stay."

THE HUSKY TIMBRE of Oliver's voice set Jocelyn's heart fluttering.

She fought to hold her ground when she wanted to flee from the way he made her feel. The drumming of her pulse, the heat swirling inside her—their bond was nothing more than a product of shared circumstance. The constant danger, the very real threat of death. It was them against the world, and only natural for her to want him.

He was all she had.

She glanced at him. The planes of his face were shadowed in moonlight, but the white glow reflected in his intense gaze. He stood, stiff and aloof, as if he alone shouldered the burden of their survival. Only his eyes revealed his hunger to connect with her.

She took a step toward him, unsure what she would do once she drew near.

He swung around, presenting her with his back. "I'll be right here if you need me."

How could he talk about losing all of his humanity then go and offer her his back to preserve her modesty? All day he'd alternated between unselfish gentleness and sharp brooding, like he didn't quite know which emotion to feel. She'd concentrate on navigating the terrain and suddenly she'd look up and catch him staring at the sky, or the spindly veins on a leaf. He was caught between the cell and the jungle, struggling to understand where he fit in life. She wanted to help him figure it out.

She turned away and stripped. A murky pond had never looked so inviting, but running over rocks and sharp twigs without shoes had sliced up her skin, and the moisture stung like fire. She forced herself to submerge her feet, stifling a whimper in favor of a hiss.

Biting down on her lip, she eased herself fully into the cool water and waded in up to her waist. The burn of her cuts started to dissipate as her body acclimated and the tension eased. She splashed water on her face and turned, training her gaze on Oliver's back. What was he thinking while he stood there in the grass?

She dunked her hair, washing away the grime of sweat and mud. When she lifted her head, he was still standing in the same place. She squeezed the excess moisture from her hair, hurried to finish the rest of her bathing, and made her way to the bank. The woman had left pieces of cloth to use as towels along with some well-worn, handmade clothes for them on the platform. She rubbed herself dry, donned the clothes and stepped up behind Oliver.

"You can turn around now."

He swiveled slowly, as if still concerned for her modesty. Her heart warmed and she sent him a small smile that faded when the moonlight caught the longing in his gaze. The heat spiraled lower, prodding a shaky breath from her.

"It's all yours."

His brows drew into a frown.

She pressed her lips together. "The pond. You can…"

"Oh. Right."

"Right." She started to move past him, but he caught her arm.

His fingers branded her skin. "Stay?"

"Are you sure?"

His throat worked in a swallow. "Yeah."

"Okay." She tipped her head, wishing she could decipher his thoughts. "I promise to turn my back too."

He slid his hand down her arm and squeezed her wrist briefly before letting go and striding to the pond. Jocelyn watched him walk backward until it became clear he was waiting for her to turn around. She twisted, but her heart thrummed in her ears, and she couldn't resist glancing back. He slipped his thumbs into the waistband of his pants and shoved them to the ground.

She spun, shame heating her cheeks for her blatant spying, but not before she'd caught a long look at his tall—far too lean—frame, and the hint of smooth muscles in his back beneath a crisscross of scars. She blinked up at the stars, smashing her lips together to keep herself from crying out. Oh, God, the things he'd survived. He wouldn't welcome her sympathy. But if she'd needed further motivation to make sure they got out of here alive, she'd just found it.

She listened to the water splash as Oliver washed, and kept her attention focused squarely on the huts in front of her. The rough-hewn stilts kept the structure off the ground. The walls leaned slightly to one side, and the glow of a lantern seeped through tiny cracks in the wood, making the hut both raw and beautiful at the same time.

Kind of like Oliver.

He cleared his throat near her left ear. She whirled. Why hadn't she heard his approach? He stood less than a foot away from her. His long black hair dripped onto the faded shirt he'd been given. The light caught a trail of water sliding down his cheek. He stared at her, not bothering to swipe the moisture away. It disappeared into the shadow of his beard.

"You have a…" he stepped closer, reached out to brush at her jaw, "…leaf."

He held the small, green blade up for her inspection then let it flutter to the ground. His warm breath caressed her face, and she knew she should tuck tail and run before she did something she'd regret.

Her feet refused to move. She leaned toward him and caught the crisp, mossy scent of the pond on his skin. She smoothed a finger over the water droplets clinging to his cheek and felt him tremble. His eyes narrowed. He grasped her shoulders as if to push her away. His fingers tightened. He tugged her into him instead, dipped his head.

His mouth collided with hers.

She rocked up on the balls of her feet, cementing the contact. His lips were cool and rugged until they gentled over hers with a desperate friction that warmed both their mouths. She twined her fingers into his hair and angled her head back, giving fuller access to her mouth. His tongue speared out to lick at the seam of her lips and when she gasped, he thrust his way inside. Fireworks burst to life on her tongue, sending shockwaves rippling through her body.

His hands fisted in her shirt. He nudged her closer and devoured her mouth. She slid her palms over his chest, feeling the rapid thrum of his heartbeat. He stiffened. Cursed into her mouth.

And broke off all contact.

"Josie, I—" He dragged his hands through his hair. "I'm sorry. I shouldn't have—" He broke off with a shake of his head and pushed past her.

She touched her swollen, well-kissed lips and watched him leave. Had she moved first or had he? Now that her head was starting to clear she couldn't be sure who had kissed whom. If it was her...God, what must he think?

Heat burned in her cheeks. She followed the path to the front of the hut. Oliver was unrolling a bamboo pallet near the fire. The flames threw shadows across his sharp face. She snagged the other pallet from the ground, trying to ignore the pang in her heart when he wouldn't look at her.

She smoothed the pallet on the ground, glancing at him from the corner of her eye. He stretched out on his own bedding and turned his back to her. No, she wasn't going to let him ignore what just happened.

"Look." She wrapped her arms around her middle.

"We're both exhausted and running out of adrenaline. It's only natural that after all we've been through—it didn't mean anything. I know that. I certainly don't have any expectations—"

"Jocelyn." He rolled over and pinned her with a hard stare.

Back off. She got that. But, oh, how she hated to be back to Jocelyn after the way Josie had rolled so sweetly off his tongue.

"Good night, then." She lay down and buried her face in her arms, hoping to bury her shame and hurt too.

His footsteps padded over the dirt. He knelt down, his knee brushing her thigh, and let out a sigh that melted some of her hurt.

"I'm not—I haven't…" He grunted. "I can't trust myself right now. There are thoughts running through my head that—urges I haven't felt in years are coursing through my body and I—shit." He stroked her hair in a fleeting touch as if he regretted even that small bit of contact. "Do you understand what I'm trying to say?"

She turned over. He was so close. She wanted to reach out to him, but thought better of it when she met his gaze. Confusion and desire. Not a good combination. Not out here when they both needed each other so desperately. She had to get them back on common ground. Fast. Even if he did just essentially tell her that kissing her was nothing more than his body's response to being denied for so long—as if any woman would've done just as nicely. And maybe they would have.

"I get it." She closed her eyes, but the firelight flickering in front of her eyelids set the memory of their kiss dancing in her mind, so she forced them back open. "It was a mistake. We both know that. Let's just get some sleep."

He shook his head. "You go ahead. I'm going to keep watch." He started to get up.

She grabbed for his hand, unwilling to let him close himself off completely. "Can you keep watch from right here?"

"Yeah, I can do that." He threaded his fingers in hers, tightened his already grim mouth. "Get some sleep. We've got to run again at first light."

She nodded, tucking their entwined hands near her body and closing her eyes, but her heart sliced open at his words. Run again at first light. What she wouldn't give to stay right here, safe in this moment, where only she and Oliver seemed to exist.

FIFTEEN

HE BLAMED IT all on those eyes.

Chann hadn't been able to stop thinking about the girl since he'd helped Leo abduct her. Her eyes haunted his nightmares and stalked him during the day. With Leo dead, the task of monitoring the children had fallen to him. As he made his rounds he'd somehow always circle back to her.

She'd stop whatever she was doing to stare at him with those big, dark-coffee eyes, silently pleading to save her like he hadn't saved his sister. The girl's battered body twisted his insides into knots. He couldn't sleep. Couldn't eat. Not while she was suffering.

He'd done the only thing he could think of to get her out of his sight—freed her. But he had to tell Jude. The Father saw through the most impenetrable lies. Chann needed to make sure he didn't see through this one.

He found Jude standing in the empty cell where Leo was slain, staring at the faded ocean mural on the wall. A dark stain still marred the floor. Leo's blood. Grief welled in Chann's throat, cutting off his ability to speak.

Leo deserved to die. They all did. Redemption would not come for any of them. A special spot in hell awaited their souls. But Chann grieved for the man Leo could have been, before they'd started on this quest for money and power.

Jude turned from the wall, narrowed his eyes at Chann. "What is it?"

He hesitated. "We lost one."

One of Jude's dark brows shot toward his hairline. "What did we lose?"

"One of the children." Chann's stomach curdled. He fought to remain expressionless. "She escaped."

A muscle twitched in Jude's jaw. He reached up to massage his scarred cheek in a gesture that never failed to make Chann's palms grow clammy.

"Why weren't you watching her?"

"That wasn't what I signed up for." Perspiration beaded along his lip. He licked it away, hoping Jude missed the tell. He stiffened his spine, willed a steely ruthlessness into his voice. "I point the way to the brats. I'm not supposed to watch them as well."

"Well, Leo can't very well do it, can he?" Jude choked out the question. To Chann's surprise, a sheen of moisture washed into Jude's eyes. "Can he?"

"I loved him too you know." It was the wrong thing to say. Chann recognized the error as soon as the words left his mouth.

Show no remorse. No softness.

Jude cocked his head. The glint in his eyes no longer revealed a hint of sorrow. He stepped closer. Cool assessment blasted Chann.

"You said the girl escaped?"

Chann forced himself to meet Jude's stare. "Yes. Leo had done a number on her. She was sick. Dying. Trust me, she won't last long out there."

"Trust you?" Jude circled him. His finger was back to rubbing at his scars. "I always thought I could. Now I'm not so sure."

"When have I ever let you down, Jude?" He swallowed.

Jude pulled a butterfly knife from his pocket and casually flipped it open. He ran his thumb along the blade.

Chann backed up a step, his spine scraping the wall. He lifted his hands. "Jude—"

"Tell me something, Chann." He twirled the knife in his fingers. "If the girl was so sick—so close to death as you proclaim—how the hell did she manage to escape?"

He threw the blade.

The sharp steel pierced Chann's wrist. He yanked the knife out, dropped it to the floor. Blood spurted from the wound. His hand shook as he wrapped it around the gushing cut.

"I swear to you, Jude, I don't know." He clenched his teeth, hoping his tongue would not betray him the way it had when he'd blurted the girl's true condition. "Since Leo's death—"

Jude cracked him across the face. Pain shot along his jaw, clouding his vision. He blinked away the spots.

"Please." He gripped his slippery hands together in a plea. The sight of his bloody palms made him light-headed.

Jude swiped the knife off the floor.

Nausea gripped Chann's stomach. His legs collapsed out from under him. The glint of the blade flashed across his eyes.

"No. Jude. Please. I didn't—just listen—you're overwrought. I'll find the girl. I swear to you. I'll find— No!"

The knife sliced into his shoulder, knocking him onto his back. Jude loomed over him, his twisted face flushed, but the heat didn't extend to his eyes which gleamed amidst all that bright red skin. He stabbed downward. Chann tried to roll aside but the blade plunged into his stomach. Jude ripped it free.

Pain spilled into Chann's gut. He couldn't catch his

breath. Didn't have the strength to lift his arms to ward off further attacks.

"You've betrayed me." Jude held the bloody knife aloft in his shaking fist. Tears bloomed in his eyes, spilled down his ravaged cheeks. "You've all betrayed me. The Ghost is dead and The Son...The Son," he choked out, "deserves nothing less than death for what he's done." He raised the knife higher, aiming directly at Chann's heart.

Chann braced himself. Fear strangled his airway, but he refused to close his eyes. The fires of hell licked at his wounds with a barbed tongue. No, he wouldn't look away. He wanted to meet Lucifer with eyes wide open.

"Go ahead, Jude," he rasped. "Finish it."

Jude flinched. He stared down at Chann. His mouth contorted. Short, choppy breaths leaked past his lips. "I—" His grip on the knife wobbled. He tightened his fist, but his hand shook harder. He threw the knife across the room. Stumbled away from Chann. "Go. Get out of my sight."

Chann scrambled to his feet. *Run. Before he changes his mind.* His head spun. He gripped the doorframe for support and looked back at Jude. He was kneeling in the middle of the cell, his hands over his face, rocking back and forth.

The shrill peal of a cell phone broke the tension. Jude snatched it from his pocket. "What?" His thick voice sounded foreign. "Good. Bring them to me. I don't care how you rough up Shaw, but I want the woman un- harmed. Understood?"

They'd found the prisoners. Chann reeled from the room. He looked down at the blood soaking through his shirt. His body shivered hot and cold. He fell to his knees and retched on the concrete.

Face it, you're as good as dead.

Medical help was hours away. A girl with his sister's eyes waited for him just minutes outside of the compound. He'd promised her a rescue. He would make sure she got one.

Jude let out an anguished roar that rippled through Chann's ravaged body. He crawled to his feet and stumbled down the hallway.

The Trinity was no more.

OLIVER WAITED UNTIL Jocelyn's steady breaths indicated she'd fallen asleep, then he lightly tugged his hand from hers. His palm tingled from the heat of her skin, and though he wanted to forget all about the moment at the pond, her rice-wine-flavored kiss still lingered on his tongue.

Her other arm lay tangled around the bag, as if to remind herself, even in dreams, to keep her dad close. Oliver stared into the dying fire, trying not to think about how, if circumstances were different, her hands might be entwined around him.

He had to distance himself. Find a way to convince himself his attraction was only a result of the adrenaline and their close proximity. It was natural that his body would start coming back to life, but he ruled his urges, not the other way around. He needed to channel them into something more productive. Like finding a way to get them home.

His traitorous eyes strayed to her face. He hadn't imagined when he'd first heard her voice on the other side of his wall that she would be beautiful—in every way. He reached over and brushed her cheek. Just the simple touch put him off balance, and pulled him in all different directions. What would happen if he kissed her again?

Nothing. He wouldn't let himself go there.

He turned away, scanning the trees, the huts, trying to focus on anything except Jocelyn, but his senses still reeled with the memory of her in his arms, her soft skin and even softer lips. He could no longer trust himself without four walls to confine him. He rubbed at his burning eyes with the heels of his hands. Exhaustion hung on his shoulders.

Don't close your eyes.

There would be plenty of time for rest later. He had to keep watch. Make sure they were ready to move out in a few hours.

His eyelids grew heavy.

Stay awake. Alert…

Stark visions flashed across his mind of mercenaries armed with guns and machetes slithering through the jungle. Parting the leaves, taking aim at—

Oliver jerked upright.

The fire had gone out, only a faint line of smoke curled into the air. The first tendrils of dawn were beginning to streak across the sky. Shit. He'd fallen asleep. They should've left the village by now.

He hustled to his feet. A prickling sensation danced up his spine, paralyzing him. What had woken him? Surely more than the nightmares. He'd grown accustomed to forcing those aside.

No, it had been a noise. He cocked his head. Like… the rustling of leaves.

Where had it come from? He strained to listen and after a few seconds he heard it again. Off to his left. His heart jumped, but he remained rooted, giving his ears a chance to adjust to the sound.

It could be nothing more than the innocuous breeze disturbing the bushes, or something as jolting as a hungry tiger padding through the undergrowth. Or, so help him God, it could be a predator of a different kind. He didn't plan to stick around to find out.

He leaned over Jocelyn, pressed his palm lightly to her mouth, and spoke into her ear. "Wake up."

She startled. Her eyes flew open and her lips parted beneath his hand, snapping closed when he shook his head.

He helped her to her feet and together they darted toward the cover of the huts, ducking into the shadows beneath the stilted house. Not good enough. They couldn't stay, hoping whatever it was would pass over their hiding spot. The Trinity's trackers were too good for that. He pressed Jocelyn against one of the stilts, hoping to conceal her while he scanned the landscape.

The thwack-thwack of leaves grew louder. The passing seconds thundered in his ears. He flicked his gaze over the pond and spotted the tangle of branches that lay on the far side. It would have to do. He grabbed Jocelyn's hand and ran, keeping as low to the ground as possible.

He pushed her into the small pocket beneath the undergrowth. "Stay here until I come back for you."

She gasped. "Oliver, no—"

He leapt away from the brushwood. His foot slipped on the rocks edging the pond. He caught himself and flattened his body to the ground. The Trinity's men emerged from the forest. They broke apart, one squatting down beside the fire pit to touch the ash, the other sweeping the area with his machine gun gripped in his hands.

Oliver watched the old woman from last night emerge from her hut. She said something that he couldn't make out from his position. Her words became moot in the sharp retort of the mercenary's gun.

Flashes burst from the muzzle and sliced through the woman. Her body dropped like a stone, tumbling down the crooked wooden stairs. She hit the ground and didn't move.

Both mercenaries began peppering the remaining huts with gunfire, sweeping their guns from side to side, the cacophony of bullets riding over the breeze, bamboo walls splintering. They stopped...and silence shrouded the village.

If he'd only refused the woman's offer he could've kept the villagers safe. He clenched his jaw and fought not to react to the anger and regret boiling in his veins. Emotions wouldn't serve him now. He had to keep a lid on them. Sweat pooled in his armpits and along his spine. His fingers dug into the slick rock. He swiped at his brow, watching as the mercs split up and disappeared into different huts, probably hoping to find his and Jocelyn's bullet-riddled bodies.

Sorry to disappoint.

He glanced back to where Jocelyn was hidden from view. *Stay.* The command zinged through him and he willed her to hear the plea. He had one chance to get the jump on these bastards and he couldn't do it if he had to worry about her.

As he slipped out from behind the boulder the sky opened up. Rain sluiced down from the heavens in fat, unforgiving droplets. The drenched fabric of his shirt plastered against him, his hair dripped into his eyes. He blinked the water away and crept around to the front of the hut, the dull roar of the monsoon masking his footsteps.

Years of dormant training kicked in. It surprised him

how easily he slipped back into his old role. His pulse slowed. He ducked under the hut and flattened his back against one of the wooden stilts. The bark pricked his back, tension scratched at his throat. He couldn't look away from the old woman's hand stretching across the ground just beyond the steps.

A mercenary clomped down the stairs, carelessly stepping over the dead woman as if she were nothing more than a nuisance. He paused, back to Oliver, to wipe the rain out of his face. Rage propelled him away from the wooden pillar. He darted under the floor and lunged, wrapping one arm around the man's throat, the other over his mouth, squeezing the air from the bastard's trachea.

Oliver's arms trembled with the effort to hold on to his strength. His palm slipped from the man's mouth for a fraction of a second before he managed to right his position. The man clawed at the headlock, his body arching as he struggled to draw breath. His hands jerked downward to fumble for the AK-47 strapped over his shoulder.

Oliver ground his teeth together and forced the mercenary's body forward, snapping his neck to the side. He heard the sickening crunch of sinew and bone as cartilage and spine severed. The man's knees slumped out from under him. Oliver caught the machine gun and stripped it off the merc as he collapsed to the ground.

He stepped back. Shuddered. From above the steady beat of rain came the squeak of wood, then the thump of boots on the stairs. He spun. The deluge of water had turned the dirt to wet concrete consistency, throwing him off balance. The second mercenary jerked his gun up in surprise. Fired. Oliver stumbled, bringing his own gun into position. His finger found the trigger and he depressed it, holding it down against the recoil vibrating up his arm as he fell onto his back.

The impact knocked the breath from him. The gun bounced out of his hand. He wheezed, rolled onto his feet and prepared to lunge for the gun a second time.

The mercenary lay facedown. Oliver slowly bent to retrieve the AK-47, keeping his gaze trained on the man. His fingers grazed the ridged magazine and he nudged the gun closer. He scooped the weapon into his hand and straightened. The man still hadn't moved. A trail of blood seeped out from under him and ran into a depression in the mud.

Oliver backed up a few paces and turned to find the old woman's body closer than he'd realized. Her dark, sightless eyes stared heavenward. He knelt beside her and arranged her hands across her heart. This woman had been a wife, a daughter, possibly a mother. Hers was a life cruelly cut short, and her death would ripple throughout the Cambodian hills, affecting all who loved her. Jocelyn always spoke to him of connections, but before now he hadn't understood why it mattered so much.

The woman deserved better than being left for predators, but he couldn't stop to give her a proper burial. A prayer rose on his lips, yet when he opened his mouth to voice the benediction, the words hovered just out of reach.

Shaken that he couldn't even give her that much, he stood and climbed the steps to her hut. Her husband lay dead on the floor. Oliver cursed and left the small house, checking the others for survivors. By the time he reached the third hut, a hard stone had settled in the pit of his stomach.

A man and woman—the youngest of the village— were slumped over the crude table at the corner of the hut. Slain while they were eating a simple breakfast of rice porridge. His throat burned. He turned away, squeezing his eyes shut and gripping his head in his hands.

Dead. Every last one of them.

THE ECHO OF gunfire lingered in Jocelyn's ears. She couldn't get it out of her head, even with the steady thrum of rain pelting the foliage. The Trinity had found them and Oliver was out there, defenseless. Alone. Hurt. Maybe even dead. She gripped the slick mossy bark of a tree and lifted her head to peer above the branches.

Where was he? If she could just catch a glimpse of him, she'd know he was okay. But so many shots had been fired. How could he have escaped unscathed?

"Oliver." His name tugged its way past her lips.

She scanned the pond, the trees, the back of the huts. *Come on, Oliver. Where are you?*

He couldn't leave her alone. She needed him.

Water cascaded over her head and seeped into her clothes. Her muscles were numb from holding her crouch for so long. He'd told her to stay put. All their effort to escape couldn't end in vain. She should do as he asked.

No. She wouldn't leave him at The Trinity's mercy. Her friends had already suffered that fate, and she couldn't bear the thought of Oliver becoming another casualty. Because of her. She was the one The Father believed he needed. She'd thought only of herself and her desire to change things and now Oliver might have paid the price.

She straightened and pushed through the shelter of branches. A surge of water pelted her face. Droplets caught her eyelashes, blurring her view of the landscape.

She swiped at her face. Not a flicker of movement disturbed the village.

Show yourself. Let me know you're okay.

Her toe caught on a rock sticking up out of the ground, ripping the tender flesh open. She yelped and fell to her knees. When she lifted her head again, her gaze snagged on a dark form that lay sprawled near the huts in the distance.

It's not Oliver. It can't be him.

She regained her feet and sprinted, slip-sliding in the grass, toward the body. The face came into focus as she drew near. Broad nose, high forehead, sightless black eyes. She stopped short, her arms pinwheeling to hold on to her balance. Her knees quivered, legs buckled, forcing her to sit down in the mud.

Not him. See? He's okay. You just have to find him.

She pushed her head between her knees and tried to suck in gulps of air, but a dark form caught her eye, stealing her focus. On the ground. Off to the right.

Oliver?

No. Female. Elderly.

She crawled over to the woman, and almost vomited at the sight of her ravaged body.

"Oh, God. No." Blood and rain mixed together, churning the rainwater a murky pink as it ran into the ground. This woman had extended them a kindness. And been rewarded with a horrible, senseless death. "I'm sorry. So sorry."

Jocelyn's throat spasmed as she reeled from the woman and continued her search for Oliver. Another body caught her attention near the second hut, robbing her of her breath once more.

Not Oliver. Thank God. Another mercenary from the look of him. Had Oliver killed him?

She whirled in a circle, taking in the splintered huts, the trees dripping with water, the stillness of the jungle surrounding her.

Questions pressed in on her, fear pounded against her temple and shook a scream from her. "Oliver!"

She opened her mouth to scream again, but a raw ache cut into her throat. Before she could assuage it and try again, movement from the doorway of the farthest hut caught her eye. She dug her toes into the mud and prepared to bolt—

"You were supposed to stay hidden." The taut, familiar rumble brought a cry of relief from her lips.

She bounded up the steps and threw herself into Oliver's arms. He stiffened beneath her for a second, then his embrace surrounded her, squeezing her close. She pressed her cheek against his wet shirt and inhaled the clean, earthy scent of the rain on him.

"I told you to wait for me," he murmured into her hair. "I was coming back to get you. After I was finished here."

He set her away, spun on his heel and returned inside the hut. A silent command to stay put. She followed him anyway. The grisly sight that greeted her made her regret the decision. Only stubbornness gave her the willpower to stay. Her gaze swung over the young dead couple at the table. The heat leeched from her cheeks.

She hadn't seen nor spoken to the couple last night, but because she and Oliver had taken advantage of another's generosity, these people would never see another sunrise. She bit back a wave of emotion and moved to the corner of the hut where Oliver sat. He unfolded a faded piece of parchment and spread it across his knees. Spidery brown ink marked off rivers, boundaries, and small footpaths.

Oliver touched their current location on the hand-drawn map, and trailed his finger along the line that led to a crudely sketched symbol of a waterfall. He tapped the location. "See how this waterfall looks like it spills into the nearby river? Most of the rivers in this region will eventually flow into the Mekong. By continuing to avoid the roads and traveling downriver, we'll connect with one of the larger towns, like Stung Treng."

"And bypass any more encounters with The Trinity."

"That's the plan." He refolded the map and stood.

The plan. Those simple words had never sounded so sweet.

They had a shot of getting out of here alive. No more circling the jungle just to stay one step ahead of The Trinity. She took a relieved breath. The metallic stench of spilled blood filled her nostrils.

It wasn't over yet.

Jocelyn gagged and reeled for the door, but her foot slipped on something small and hard. She cried out and looked down. A toy—the crude airplane had been whittled from wood. She reached down and plucked it off the floor, the smell all but forgotten in the face of new questions. New worries. The toy's long-chord wing and single vertical stabilizer looked so much like the Bronco her dad had flown for the Air Force.

She rubbed her thumb over the worn wood, erasing thoughts that threatened to link her dad to this remote village. "Where's the child?"

Oliver frowned. "The what?"

"The child. There's no child." She held up the airplane and strode across the small hut, keeping her eyes averted from the dead. She searched the pallet on the floor. "Do you remember seeing a child last night? Or one leaving the hut this morning? Could they have wandered off somewhere?"

Visions of a lost boy or girl crying in the jungle flashed in her mind. She darted for the door. "If they're out there—we can't leave until we find them."

"There are only two bowls." Oliver's statement hit her like a brick wall.

"What?" she choked out, her gaze skipping over the slain couple at the table and registering the upended pottery on the table.

Two. Just as Oliver had said.

"Two bowls." He repeated. "One pallet. If there was a child here, he or she was gone long before this."

He was right. The lone toy was the only sign that a child had ever resided in the hut. She clutched the airplane tighter, unable to let go. Something had happened here. Long before The Trinity's mercenaries had gunned down these innocent villagers. A pall hung over the hut. Whispers of raw grief were ingrained in the walls. Only time could've put that measure of sadness here.

"Do you think they lost their son?" Her gut told her it had to have been a boy. The way the underside was worn down, as if he'd dragged the plane over the ground hundreds—thousands—of times. She ran her finger over the wings one last time and set it in a place of honor on the shelf near the pallet.

She straightened to find Oliver watching her, his face set into a mask. "It's time to go."

Strapping the machine gun to his shoulder, he walked out of the door, leaving her to follow him underneath the hut where large wooden food storage bins sat sheltered from the rain.

"What are you doing?"

He dumped a handful of potatoes into the sack then

reached across her to open the next container, peering at the medicinal herbs neatly stacked inside. "Supplies."

"You're…taking their things?" After what these people already suffered, Oliver's actions seemed a further indignity. Taking food and herbs to survive wasn't the same as robbing them of precious possessions, but she'd made preserving the legacy of the dead her life's work. She bristled. "Where's your respect?"

"They're dead," he said, not pausing in the act of grabbing a head of cabbage. "We're not."

"They're dead because of us." More deaths added to the guilt that already crushed her heart. If she hadn't been so tired, if they'd just moved on instead of stopping for the night…

If only, if only, if only.

She pressed a hand to her chest. "I refuse to benefit from this atrocity."

Oliver stood, slinging the sack over his shoulder. "Then don't eat."

The sharpness in his voice snapped her head up. If she hadn't been the recipient of his gruff ministrations—and the tender kiss she'd been trying so hard to forget—his attitude would've sent her running. But she stood her ground and looked closer. To the grief etched around his mouth, the rigid muscles in his neck and the white knuckles of the hand clutching the sack.

His struggle to maintain indifference was killing him.

She reached out and put a hand on his arm, stopping him from reaching for the dark brown herb. "Why do you always act like you don't care about people?"

He jerked out of her reach. "I care for my empty belly and my own skin. That's the way it's been for years."

"Out of necessity." She wanted to shake him. "You're more than you think you are."

He slammed the bins shut with a bang. "I've killed bad people and I've let good people die. Sometimes the world really is black and white, and sometimes people deserve their place in hell."

She met his hard gaze without flinching. "I agree. But you're not one of them."

His jaw tightened, and when he continued his voice was rough with anger and pain. "I've just watched more innocent people die, had the taste of their blood fill my mouth. The scent of death and gunpowder clings to my nose. And then I look at you—" He closed his eyes, his throat working in a taut swallow. When he looked at her again, his stare hid nothing. Not the despair, nor the self-loathing, nor the desire that swirled in the shadows of his green eyes. He leaned his forehead against hers, sifted his fingers through her hair. "I look at you, your heart in your sad hazel eyes and your goodness shining in your face—even the rain can't dampen it—and all I want to do is be more like you. To let myself feel something other than this cold, hard lump in my stomach. I want to let myself drown inside of you until I'm washed clean. But I can't."

His lips came within a hairbreadth of hers. He let out a groan and wrenched away from her. Her heart battered against her ribs, his words rooting her to the spot.

Oliver stalked over to the mercenary's body and knelt down to work on the laces of the dead man's boots. He yanked them off and tossed them in her direction.

"Put those on."

She wanted to call him back and finish what he'd started. Did he honestly believe the knowledge that his desire wasn't just some random physical urge would scare her away? He wanted her.

Her.

She made him feel, and she suspected he'd long ago shut himself off from anything that had that kind of power. But he couldn't stay away from her. Not entirely.

She swallowed the ball of emotion and stepped from the shelter of the hut. The rain had tapered off to a drizzle. She shivered inside her soaked clothes and bent to retrieve the boots. The leather was cumbersome, but she managed to work the tongue and laces out of the way to make room for her foot. She slipped her toes inside and pushed down.

Her skin chafed against the boot, knocking a moan from her. She sat and dragged her foot back out, biting the inside of her cheek and cringing at the pain. Raw, pink flesh was visible through the dirt on the soles of her feet. The cuts oozed. Blisters spread across her toes.

Jocelyn looked at Oliver. He was hacking at the tip of the other set of boots with a machete. The muscles in his jaw were bunched beneath his beard and his brows were drawn into a tight frown. He'd thrown up barriers. Ones that didn't invite further conversation beyond their immediate physical needs.

The fact that her feet hurt too much to put on the dead man's shoes qualified as something Oliver would want to know. But she couldn't make herself say a word.

He wasn't the only one afraid of the pull between them.

She forced her feet into the boots, hoping the thin lining would cushion the pain long enough to get to Stung Treng.

SIXTEEN

THE MAN-MADE trail through the twisting trees grew rocky and steep as they'd traveled into the Cambodian hills. It took every ounce of Oliver's concentration to keep his footing sure. He'd had to cut the tips off the boots he'd taken from the mercenary in order to make them fit his feet. His toes hung over the edge, brushing the ground and upsetting his balance with every step.

But only a small part of his off-equilibrium could be blamed on his lack of proper footwear. The other, larger part came from the woman walking behind him. She stripped him raw. When he was with her he lost control—of his emotions, his desires. She made him want more out of life when he'd always been content with less.

He'd lived his life as a minimalist, forming basic relationships when necessary, but always holding himself apart. In the Army he'd worked hard to ensure he had everyone else's back, and yet he'd never felt entirely comfortable when someone tried to return the favor. He'd transitioned to the CIA's Special Activities Division where the job was better suited to a loner. His stay in The Trinity's Heartbreak Hotel had reinforced his belief that detachment was the key ingredient of survival.

Survival.

Jocelyn made him question the very definition of the word.

He stepped up to the crest of the hill and stared out at the panoramic view splayed in front of him. Off to his right, mist rose from the frothy top of a waterfall, the droplets catching the sunlight like a prism. Waves of water rolled and cascaded down dark, mossy rocks, tumbling into a shimmering pool before disappearing over the side of a craggy cliff. To the left, in a wild field of green, sat the village. Huts dotted the landscape, their thatched roofs rippling slightly in the breeze. Clusters of people wearing wide straw hats worked in the large, muddy rice field. Others went about their tasks in front of the huts.

Jocelyn clambered behind him and he turned.

"We made it," she whispered. She gave him a tremulous smile that lit up her eyes. Then her face went pale and her lashes fluttered. Her knees buckled.

"Josie?" He reached for her and guided her to the ground where he pulled her onto his lap and slid his hand against her forehead. Her skin burned beneath his palm. He brushed his fingers across her hot cheek. "Josie. Talk to me. What's wrong?"

Her eyes opened a crack. "M—my feet…"

Cradling her in one arm, he untied her bootlaces as gently as possible and slid the clunky boot off one of her feet. He took one look at her red skin and the oozing cuts and swore. "Why didn't you tell me your feet were this bad?"

"Didn't…want to…slow us down."

He slung the sack off his shoulder and pulled out the flask of watered-down wine he'd taken from the last village. He plucked the stopper off with his teeth, lifted her head. "Here. Drink."

She parted her dry lips and allowed him to pour liquid down her throat. Some of the wine dribbled down her chin and he swiped it aside with his thumb. He replaced the stopper and shoved the flask back into the bag. When she attempted to stand, he tightened his hold and got to his feet, cradling her in his arms.

"Let's get you to the village."

"No!" She stiffened in his arms. "Please, not the village. Can't we just keep going?"

"You're in no shape—"

"Let me be the judge of that."

He gritted his teeth against the weak plea in her voice. "You can't even stand on your own feet."

"If you put me down, I will."

Yeah, and she'd kill herself trying to prove it. "No."

She turned her face up, confronting him with dirt-streaked cheeks and haunted eyes. "I can't watch more innocent people die. Please."

Her words struck his heart. He'd wanted to shelter her from the kind of pain and guilt that tormented him. *You failed, Shaw.*

But he could still keep her from following him further into the dark pit. "We'll just stop there for a few minutes. Let you catch your breath."

He tried to modulate his voice, to keep it from cracking. He had no intention of letting her continue on in her current state. She was burning up and he suspected the cuts on her feet were infected. She needed rest and medical attention before it was too late.

She laid her head on his shoulder and didn't call him on the lie, so maybe he'd managed to sound convincing after all. Either that or she was too sick to protest further. Worry slithered through him, increasing, as she remained silent with every step closer to the village.

The cluster of huts came into clearer view. There were about a dozen of them, telling him this was a bigger tribe than the last one they'd encountered. Chickens pecked the ground, a woman stood near one hut, beating the dust from a colorful braided rug. A tall man embroiled in conversation looked up, then suddenly broke away from the group and strode forward. With his sandy brown hair, fair complexion and his clear Western state of dress he stood out from the Cambodians. Oliver put him somewhere in his fifties.

"Hello." His startled eyes looked Oliver up and down, snagging on the AK-47 slung over his shoulder before moving on to Jocelyn. He studied their shabby appearance in silence. His brows drew into a frown. "You two are a bit far from civilization."

Oliver tightened his hold on Jocelyn. "We got separated from our backpacking group. We've been hiking for days. You wouldn't happen to have a radio in the village?"

"Sorry." The man's gaze drifted back to the AK-47. "You're too far north for radio communications. The Tom Puon guard their culture and traditions well."

"I suspected as much." But, hell, he'd hoped for a break. "Could we trouble you for some food and a place to rest?"

"I may be just a missionary, but this place is home. The safety of the Tom Puon is of utmost importance to me. If you're here for malicious intent, you're not welcome."

"Understood. The gun is just for protection. I would never turn it on you or these kind people. We lost all our belongings and—" he nodded at Jocelyn, "—she could sure use some medical attention. We'll move on as soon as she's able."

Oliver met the man's assessing stare. His cool blue eyes warmed, he inclined his head. "Pastor Joshua Barnes."

"The name's Oliver, Sir."

"Well, then, Oliver, right this way."

Barnes led them into the village and over to one of the huts that leaned precariously to the right. The thatched roof drooped down to shade the slits cut into the wood as windows and the open doorway.

A short woman with honey-colored hair pulled back into a thick braid came outside and descended the ladder steps. Her brown eyes sparkled in her open face. Barnes leaned down and spoke in low tones to her. She nodded and he turned to Oliver.

"This is my wife, Mary. She'll see to your friend."

"Thank you, Sir. Ma'am." The words felt foreign on Oliver's tongue. He dredged up his manners from some long forgotten place. "I...appreciate your assistance."

Mary gestured them inside with a flutter of her hands. Oliver carried Jocelyn up the steps to a wide straw mattress.

"Go ahead and lay her down." Mary prodded him, but his arms disobeyed, tightening around Jocelyn. Mary smiled, dimples denting her round cheeks. "I'll take good care of her."

He swallowed, and lowered Jocelyn to the mattress. Her eyes fluttered open. "What—?"

He slid his arms from beneath her and reached up to smooth the worry line between her brows. "Mary's just going to see to your feet. That's all." There'd be time enough for the truth later.

"Okay." Her pitiful attempt at a smile tore him up.

His chest squeezed. "I'll just be right outside."

He fled, needing to put some distance between himself and Jocelyn. She was too trusting, too strong and beautiful—too everything. He rounded the hut and walked a few feet into the trees, near enough that he could still hear her if she called for him, far enough away that he could block out the effect she had on him.

WHEN HE RETURNED, the sun was beginning its dip below the horizon. Oliver climbed the steps to the hut, the weight of what he was about to do making his legs feel as if they were encased in cement.

Barnes was waiting for him on the porch. "Something tells me there's more to your story," he said quietly.

Oliver stiffened. "There is. But I can't tell you. The less you know the better. I won't risk putting your village in danger."

"You know…" Barnes chewed on the inside of his cheek for a moment as if weighing his words. "The people here believe in listening to the whispers of the jungle. Some claim it tells of a darkness—of a Western evil that makes even the strongest of men scream like women. Think the Tom Puon are just a superstitious bunch?"

"No."

"I didn't think so either. If there's anything I can do—"

"You can keep her safe." He tilted his head toward the hut. "And if I don't make it back, see to it that she gets home, somehow."

He knew that Barnes wanted more, but the need to see Jocelyn took over, and he turned his back on the pastor, stepping into the hut. She was sitting up on the mattress, head leaning against the wall, eyes closed. She'd tucked her dark brown hair behind her ears. The fading sunlight played across her face. Some of her color had returned, but she still looked much too pale and fragile to suit him.

He hadn't meant to make a sound, but he exhaled on

a noisy, ragged breath and Jocelyn's eyes opened. She stared at him.

"How are you feeling?" he asked, tucking his hands behind his back to keep from reaching for her.

She shrugged. "Tired. Sore. But in less pain than I was a few hours ago. I don't want to stay here too long, but I don't think I can handle moving on just yet." Her mouth trembled. "What if The Trinity catches up to us again?"

"They won't."

"How do you know?"

He knelt down in front of her, forcing himself to look her in the eye. "Because I'm going to lead them away from here with a trail they can't possibly miss."

"What are you saying?"

"I think you should stay here." He took one of her bandaged feet in his hands and propped it on his knees, massaging the stiff muscles in her calf. "Rest. Heal. It's at least a three days' walk to a big enough town where they're sure to have a radio or phone. I'll lead The Trinity in the opposite direction and then double back."

"You're…going to leave me here?" Betrayal flashed in her eyes.

He looked away. "Like you said, your feet are hardly up to another dash through the jungle."

"No, but neither are yours. I don't hear you complaining." She shot him a glare that made her chin jut further out.

"You're hurt. I won't risk—"

"It's not your choice to make." She yanked her foot out of his grasp and pushed him back a step. "What if they find you?"

He gripped her chin, swiping his thumbs across her

cheekbones. "Then I'll convince them you died. Barnes will make sure you get home."

"What if they capture you again?"

He flinched. His throat closed, but he managed to push a rasped vow past his lips. "I won't let them take me alive."

Her small fist hit him in the shoulder, once, twice, turning him inside out. "Don't do this. Don't leave me alone here."

"You won't be alone. You have Barnes and a village full of people who will—"

"No." Her palms slid down his arms. She grasped his hands in hers. "I want to stick together."

"And then what? You collapse? Your feet become more infected and raw and soon you can't take another step? I can't let that happen to you. I need to get you out of here."

It was his shot at doing something good for a change. Something worthy. Something that might redeem one small part of himself, even if just in his own eyes. He wanted to do this for himself every bit as much as he needed to do it for her. And if he couldn't bear the thought of failing—of losing her—

He shut down his thoughts. No sense in going there. It would just make this goodbye harder. He drew in a breath and met her gaze. He loved the way her hazel eyes grew brighter when she was pressing her point.

She leaned into him. "We should stay together."

"I'm going." Despite how persuasive she was when her body brushed against his. "And I will not allow you to go with me."

She opened her mouth to argue further but he pressed her to the wall and covered her lips with his. He'd sworn he wasn't going to kiss her again. But what if this was his last chance? He couldn't leave without one more taste of her on his tongue.

His body leapt to life. The blood rushed through his veins and into his groin, setting a fire that he now knew only she could quench. He'd never felt this pure, white-hot longing to be consumed by another before.

Her lips yielded. She gasped against his lips and he couldn't resist sweeping his tongue inside her wet mouth. He stroked his tongue against hers. The kiss reached into him and spread its warmth. He couldn't get enough.

He ran his hands up her arms, reveling in the feel of her silky skin against his calloused palms. She broke away and tipped her head back. He pressed his mouth over the pulse beating at the base of her neck. Opened his mouth to nip at the spot.

"Oliver…" She tangled her hands into his hair and ran her fingers through the strands over and over.

The sensation had him nearly jumping out of his skin. He skimmed his fingers beneath her shirt, lightly grazing her ribcage, before sliding his hands to her back and running his palms up her spine.

She groaned. "Let me come with you."

Her words doused his ardor faster than the sharp sting of a whip. "No."

He untangled himself and immediately missed her warmth.

She settled her cloudy gaze on him. "I'm scared, Oliver."

She scooted over, being careful to avoid putting pressure on her feet. The move reinforced his resolve to allow her the time to heal. He didn't think he could handle her gentle touch so soon after that kiss, but he didn't have the willpower to move away when she reached up and cupped his jaw.

"I'm afraid for you," she said. "I...I don't think I could bear to lose you."

His heart beat wildly against his ribs for an unguarded moment. A band clamped around him, squeezing him, constricting his lungs and his throat. Invisible walls closed in on him like impenetrable prison bars.

Jocelyn stared at him, waiting for a response. He wanted to give her one—the right one—but he couldn't find the words.

She dropped her hands and straightened. "It's not a crime to care about someone, you know."

Her whisper was full of pain, one he couldn't ease. To do so would admit he cared. Confessing something so raw and real would lock him in a place with far greater potential to hurt him. More than every beating and every punishment he'd endured over the last two years.

He swallowed every desire, every craving for her that didn't want to be denied, and found his voice. "Not a crime. Just another form of prison."

Her eyes widened. "You don't believe that."

He wished he didn't. If he stayed with her long enough would she have the power to change his mind? Afraid that she would, he turned to leave. Before he'd taken more than a few steps, Jocelyn's voice halted him.

"It's a lonely world out there. Haven't you ever wanted to share it with someone?"

More than his next breath. But wanting and deserving were two very different things.

"What I want," he said, turning to catch her bleak stare and her slightly downturned mouth, "is for you to stay here while I go for a radio."

"Why?" She crossed her arms in front of her. "Why does it matter so much?"

"It just does." He wouldn't examine the urgency any further than that.

He should've ended it right there, but he couldn't seem to walk away from her even when he wanted to. In fact, his feet moved closer of their own accord. He fingered a lock of her brown hair, pushing it behind her ear, then took a moment to memorize the way her eyes darkened as she looked up at him. He lightly touched a knuckle to the elegant curve of her jaw, moving up to sweep a thumb across her cheekbone so he wouldn't forget the way her skin felt.

He nudged her chin up and took her lips in another kiss, losing his breath and somehow finding his hope.

"I'll be back as soon as I can." His voice shook, unsettling him. "Please, stay here."

He spun on his heel and left the hut.

JOCELYN PRESSED HER back against the wall and squeezed her eyes shut so she wouldn't be able to watch Oliver leave. Rejection stung, and she let it, hoping to burn some sense into her.

Oliver was right. She wasn't fit to travel. Her feet were starting to throb again and chills coursed through her body. She would slow him down, possibly endanger his life, yet even knowing all that, she still wanted to fling herself after him and insist he not leave her behind.

What if he didn't make it back?

She had never expected to find someone like him on the other side of a cell, someone so broken and scarred he shouldn't have an ounce of gentleness left in him. But it was there, buried beneath the cracked surface. He was a man with goodness and strength, a man who had forgotten how to believe in himself. And she was so afraid he'd rather get captured or killed than take a chance with her because he didn't believe he deserved more.

Desperate to do something to keep her mind off her fear for Oliver, she grabbed her bag from the floor and pulled out her dad's letters and the logbook she'd taken from The Father. Setting the letters aside, she took up the book, rubbing her thumbs across the leather cover, swiping over the gold initials engraved at the bottom. She imagined her dad doing the same countless times and felt closer to him.

Instead of the certainty she used to feel over his death, she now wondered why, if he'd survived the plane crash, he hadn't found his way home. She'd always assumed the letters were written before his plane fell out of the sky. But the spark in The Father's eyes whenever he'd mentioned Donald Hewitt spoke of familiar knowledge, not only of the contents of the logbook, but of the man himself.

The answers lay in the cryptic block symbols her dad had scattered throughout the pages. She pulled her knees up and rested the book in her lap, half afraid to know, and yet yearning for the truth.

Dates and coordinates scattered the paper. Lists of cargo. The same set of four symbols. Not one of those things teased her memory or hinted at a connection with *her*. She went back to the beginning and flipped through the book again.

Oliver had suggested the pictograms were glyphs. Okay. Fine. But how would she make an alphabet with the eight symbols divided between the flight log and the letters? And even if she could translate them, there was no way to make a series of words out of what she had here.

Forget the alphabet. Think personal.

Jocelyn scrunched her face up, squeezing her eyes shut. What did she have of her dad's that was hers and hers alone? Not Tasha's or her mother's, but solely hers. She blew out a breath, rubbed at her forehead. And came up empty handed.

She flung the book. It hit the wall with a loud crack and slid to the floor in a warped heap.

Her hand flew to her mouth. What had she done? Why had she been so careless? She'd thrown the book like a piece of trash. If it was permanently damaged, she'd never forgive herself.

She scrambled to her feet and raced after the journal. It lay open to the middle, a jagged fissure running the length of the binding. Remorse twisted her heart. Why hadn't she thought before she acted? Kneeling, she lifted the book off the floor, careful to keep the two halves from ripping further. Maybe she could sew it back together. Have it repaired when she returned home. *If* she returned home.

One small triangle of white stuck out from the cracked spine, turning her attention from the urge to cry. She teased the corner with a finger, realizing it wasn't just a torn scrap from a page. A full piece of paper had been sealed inside the binding, and now that she looked at the book more closely, she could see where the spine had once been glued together.

She unfolded the page. A gasp fell from her lips and her eyes widened at the sight of her dad's handwriting. He'd written another letter, one he'd elected to hide rather than send. Her hands shook as she smoothed away the creases in the paper and began to read.

I hope my previous letters have reached you. I have no way of knowing if they've even been sent, as I entrusted a local villager with their care. Out here in the jungle, mail service is spotty at best.

This will be my last letter from Cambodia. I am leaving tonight. Something is brewing here. An undercurrent of evil I've ignored until it was too late. By now the Air Force has come to your door and told you that I am MIA. I am sorry, my dearest Marianne, for the pain the news has caused.

The plane crash shattered my left leg. I managed to pull myself from the wreckage and remained conscious long enough to realize that I had unearthed something valuable and sacred. After two days of crawling my way through the jungle, I was rescued by the Kavet tribe and brought to their small village, where a group of missionaries welcomed me into their huts and nursed me back to health. I have stayed with them hoping to repay their kindness by helping them build the village's first church.

But the Reverend is like a chameleon, with his ever-changing moods and suspicions. After a time, it became clear he believed I was having an affair with his wife. It's not true, Mari, I swear, but no amount of denial swayed the man.

Baby, he killed her. He killed that poor innocent woman in cold blood.

And the son—I fear the Reverend abuses the boy. I've tried to step in, to show Jude gentleness and affection, but it's too late. There is a darkness inside him...an obsession with fire...a thirst for power. He watches me with hatred in his eyes.

It is time to go.

If I don't make it back, this letter is bound to hurt you, leaving more questions than answers. I am sending you my logbook. It, along with the markings in my other letters, will one day lead you to an ancient legacy of Cambodia that I tried hard to protect. Show the symbols to Josie—my clever girl will know what they mean. I know my disappearance must have hit her hard. Let her know this map is for her. Someday, she'll understand.

I regret that Tasha may never know me the way you and Josie do. Hold tight to her. She will need you. I love you all. The words look inadequate, but their truth is the one constant that has kept me going.

All my devotion,
Donald

Jocelyn traced her dad's signature, lump in her throat. He'd made the map for her. So she'd one day have the answers he knew she'd desperately need. Her memories shifted, like puzzle pieces coming together and finally making her whole. Here, at last, was the connection she'd desperately sought, the answers to the man who'd been everything to her, larger than life, bigger than love…and then gone.

But if the symbols were coded so she'd understand— why couldn't she figure out how to decipher them?

She set the letter aside and picked up the logbook, flipping through the pages until she came to the first pictogram block.

A sun. Oliver had suggested it meant a direction… but something about that didn't feel right. The way the sun was drawn seemed familiar.

She closed her eyes, a memory streaking across her

mind. Her dad's nickname was Sonny. Some of the men in his squadron had given it to him because he'd been the youngest—a fresh, baby-faced recruit. When he'd taken command of his plane, he'd painted a big yellow sun on the tail fin. She'd seen pictures of him standing beside it, wearing his trademark cocky grin. The sun looked exactly like the one he'd drawn here.

Continuing to flip through the logbook, she found three more "blocks". One with a crudely drawn horse, another with two wavy horizontal lines, that could possibly point to a river, and the third with a vertical squiggle that tugged at some long forgotten teaching in her childhood.

But why were all the symbols in blocks? Wouldn't it have been easier for her dad to just scribble them in the margins, instead of going through the trouble of creating precise, almost three-dimensional looking squares for each one?

She rubbed at her eyes. Blocks. Why would her dad…?

Blocks.

Donald Hewitt used to spend hours whittling. He'd carved a set of blocks for her as a child, representing the places and cultures he'd seen. When he'd been home they'd played with them. A treasure hunting game. Using the blocks with numerals on them for direction. The squiggle was the Hindu numeral for one, from the time he'd visited India on leave. And the wavy lines… they weren't for a river at all, but the Chinese numeral for two. One. Two. North. East. Northeast.

She flipped back and forth between the sun and the horse. Not just any horse. A bucking bronc. Her dad had flown an OV-10 Bronco.

Oh, Dad. You're guiding me to your plane, aren't you?

But what did that have to do with Kala's Ashes? Unless…had he crashed near the mine? Had he found it?

She dropped the logbook on the floor, then spread the letters out all around it. Then she set to work deciphering the rest of the symbols.

OLIVER'S BOOT SLIPPED in a muddy dip and his ankle twisted. He caught his fall, his fingers plowing into wet, sticky leaves. Somewhere overhead a monkey let out a piercing screech that rattled his spine. He looked up, but the towering trees hid the moon, keeping everything under the canopy in darkness.

He tromped on through the foliage as best as he could without light, frowning in concentration until pain cut across his forehead. He let out a labored breath as he descended into a valley. His legs screamed for rest, but he ignored them. He'd lain awake in his cell too many nights to count, wishing he could push his body into exhaustion just like this. Now was not the time to complain, nor slow down.

The sooner he reached a town the sooner he could radio for help and return to Jocelyn with military transport. After a month in captivity, her superiors at JPAC had to be actively searching for her. Dropping her name to the right people should bring them running with all sorts of resources at their disposal.

She'd be safe. She could go home.

He leaned against the trunk of a spiny tree and closed his eyes, sucking in even breaths to calm the nausea that suddenly fisted his gut. If he hadn't completely lost all sense of direction, the river should lay directly ahead. He just had to keep putting one foot in front of the other and follow the water.

He swallowed and continued walking. The burble of

water rippled above the chirp of bugs. The trees parted and dabbles of moonlight glistened on the peaks of the river. He knelt at the bank for a drink. It tasted of dirt, but at least it was wet.

He bent for another drink. Halfway there his skin prickled with awareness. He straightened, bringing the gun around from his shoulders and into his hands. He flicked off the safety and tightened his grip, slowly climbing to his feet.

He peered off into the trees and listened. He'd heard something. The snapping of a twig? Footsteps? Where had the noise come from? Following the line of the water, he walked further down the bank where the branches of *Mreah Prew Phnom* trees dipped down, their teardrop-shaped leaves trailing in the water.

A faint moan reached his ears. At first he thought it was just the breeze, but then he heard it again. No, not the wind.

Human. Definitely female.

Young female.

He shifted into a crouch and crept into the shadow of the trees. "Hello? Who's there?"

A sharp intake of breath—then nothing.

He swore. He'd voiced the question in English. He tried again in Khmer. This time, he was rewarded with a muffled sob.

He crawled forward. The cries grew louder the closer he got to the trunk of the largest tree. He reached out and his hand connected with a small, bare foot. The owner screamed and jerked her leg away.

"Shh—" he dropped his gun and held up his hands, hoping she could see the non-threatening gesture in the darkness, "—it's okay. I'm not going to hurt you."

The light breeze ruffled the branch, parting the

leaves enough to send a blessed shaft of moonlight into the shadows. A girl huddled against the trunk of the tree. Her long black hair was tangled and spilling in unruly knots around her shoulders. Even from the scant glow he could see her face was a mixture of yellow and purple bruises. Her feverish eyes darted around and slick perspiration coated her face.

Oliver's stomach churned. He fell back on his heels then realized she was not alone. He fumbled for the gun, but the man next to her was much too still to be any kind of threat. He was also dressed in a priest's garb, the white collar glinting in the moonlight. Reaching over the girl, he pressed his fingers to the man's neck. No pulse. From the temperature of his body, he'd been dead for some time.

He looked at the man's shadowed face, a memory tickling the back of his neck. Where had he seen him before? In the halls of The Trinity's compound. Just once or twice. In passing. But he never forgot a face.

The girl continued to stare at Oliver like she was bracing herself for him to perform unspeakable acts of evil on her. His gut clenched anew. He made a big show of pushing his gun out of reach and clasping his hands in front of him. His gesture had no effect.

She whimpered. Her body trembled from head to toe.

He blew out a breath. What the hell was he supposed to do with her? If Jocelyn were here she'd know exactly how to handle the girl. She'd take her under her wing and have her at ease within minutes.

He cleared his throat. "What's your name?" he asked, speaking slowly in Khmer.

"Maelea." Her voice was barely louder than the wind.

"Maelea?" He repeated her name again, finally managing to coax a faint nod from her. "How old are you, Maelea?"

She sniffled. "Eleven."

Sweet Christ. "How did you get here? Who did this to you?" He pointed to the dead man next to her, but she buried her face in her dirty hands and shook her head. "Who?" he demanded.

But he knew. Deep down, he knew exactly who was responsible. The only question was why.

He reached for her, but she shrank back against the tree and let out a shriek. "Don't take me back to mine. Please. Not there. They'll kill me. They'll kill me dead. Like they did to Samnang."

"I won't take you back there. I just want to help you." He frowned. What mine? And… "Who's…Samnang?"

"A—a boy. He got sick. Ghost come in the night and take him away. He take him away and Samnang no come back. Ghost laugh and say he kill him." She tried to stand, but her legs collapsed out from under her. "I get sick. I think Ghost come kill me too, but Brother Chann—he take me away. Somewhere safe, he say."

"A ghost? What kind of ghost?"

She brought a finger to her lips and started to chew at a ragged nail. He'd get no answers from her about the elusive ghost. Not now.

Instead, he slid a glance at the dead man. "He helped you escape?"

She nodded. "He hid me. But when he come back for me, he badly hurt. We ran and ran and then he couldn't run anymore and I…wait…" She pressed her face into her tattered shirt, choking and hiccupping.

God, the courage that must have taken for an eleven-year-old girl to flee when the odds were so stacked against her. Hearing her story made his gut burn. He was more a coward than even he'd first feared. He'd let The Trinity beat him down, when an eleven-year-old girl still stood tall.

He inched closer, careful to keep his voice low and gentle. "Don't worry. I won't hurt you. And I won't take you back to the mine."

She nodded and slumped against the tree, her eyes fluttering. He smoothed her hair. Touched her forehead. An inferno licked against his hand. He moved his fingers to her neck. Her glands were swollen like golf balls.

He had at least another two days' walk before he reached a town big enough to have some sort of medical clinic. She needed food and water, neither of which he had in great supply in his pack, and medicine, of which he had none. She was in no shape to walk, either, and while he'd carry her the whole way if he had to, the smartest thing to do would be to take her back to the village. Barnes's wife was a nurse. She could help the girl.

But taking her back meant putting Jocelyn in danger. The Trinity's men could be closing in on him as he sat deliberating. They could easily follow him back to the village.

If he forged on to town, the girl would die before they ever reached their destination.

If he went back to the village, he would seal Josie's fate and that of dozens of people.

"Damn it!" He didn't realize he'd shouted out loud until he saw the girl flinch and shrink against the bark of the tree.

He looked into her tear-stained, bruised face, and knew he had to do whatever he could to save her.

He ran his palms down his face and turned to speaking soft Khmer once again. "You're not going back to the mine, do you hear me? You're coming with me. Somewhere safe."

She blinked at him, curling tighter into the tree as if afraid to believe him. He met her wary gaze, holding nothing back, baring his soul to an eleven-year-old in a way he'd never done with anyone else. He didn't know what he'd do if she found him lacking. He couldn't force her to trust him. Wouldn't blame her if she'd rather take her chances on her own.

Her hand slipped inside his. Small and ice cold, despite the fever that was burning her up. He enfolded her in his arms. Something hard burst into a million pieces in his chest.

She collapsed against him, her body wracked with shivers that wouldn't quit no matter how hard he tried to tighten his hold.

"It's going to be okay," he whispered roughly. "You're going to be all right."

SEVENTEEN

JOCELYN STEPPED OUT of the hut, the late morning sunshine shimmering the humid air. She descended the steps, ignoring the twinge in her bandaged feet. At least they were much better than yesterday. The chills that ran through her body had subsided, leaving her neck and shoulders with a dull, achy tension that added weight to her already troubled heart.

Though she found herself surrounded by a hundred villagers going about their daily work, she'd never felt so alone. Snatches of Khmer drifted to her, the unfamiliar cadence jumbling in her head. She spotted Pastor Barnes talking to a small group of women. Normally she'd have made a beeline for him, desperate to have someone to talk to, but Oliver, so in tune with the silence, had somehow given her a greater appreciation for spending time alone with her thoughts.

She headed toward the patch of fertile soil being cultivated for vegetables, calling up an image of Oliver in her mind. His face, with its sharp angles, had become so very dear to her. She missed his reassuring presence. What if he died trying to get to a radio? What if, right now, he was lying in the jungle somewhere in a pool of his blood, drawing his last breath? How would she ever find him? How could she go on, knowing he was lost to her?

There would be no letters, no evidence of their connection left to hold close. She'd always wonder what had happened to him, just like her dad. The not knowing would leave another gaping hole in her heart.

Be safe. Come back soon.

She sunk to her knees, plucking a jasmine from the ground. Twirling the blossom in her fingers, she let the velvety texture of the petals ground her. The scent filled her with strength and hope.

He would make it back.

A strand of hair blew into her eyes, and with the wind came a sound—like her name. She reached up to brush the hair away, scanning the green valley before her, and caught movement flickering in the trees.

A man emerged. *The* man she'd just been desperately hoping for.

She blinked, wondering if her longing had somehow conjured an apparition of him. But, no, it was him, solid and real, his jade eyes glittering with determination, his arms clutching…

A child?

"Oliver?" Her feet took flight in his direction before her thoughts had the chance to catch up. "Oliver!"

The exhaustion etched across his face softened when he saw her, but he veered away from her outstretched arms and headed in the direction of the huts. "Gotta… get…her to…Barnes's wife."

Jocelyn could see now the child was, indeed, a girl. Her hair was tangled and matted and her skin had a yellowish cast to it. Bruises and cuts covered her skin, stamping her with signs of abuse and neglect.

Jocelyn's stomach churned with disgust. She charged after Oliver. "What happened?"

The commotion caused a stir among the villagers. They filed out of their huts. Those in the field dropped their tools and followed in Oliver's wake. Some of the women reached out their hands, murmuring as they tried to touch the child.

"Please." Oliver turned away, his choppy breath straining his voice. "She's very sick. I don't know if—" He made a beeline for Mary Barnes. "Help her."

The missionary woman wiped her hands on her faded apron. "Bring her inside."

Jocelyn followed Oliver and Mary into the hut. He tried to lay the girl on the mattress, but her lashes fluttered, and she tightened her hold on him with a moan. Over the top of the girl's head, Oliver speared Jocelyn with a look of such torment and uncertainty that she stepped forward to lay her hand on the girl's arm. The child's small hand against Oliver's chest curled tightly into a fist, turning her knuckles white.

Jocelyn frowned. "What's in her hand?"

Oliver glanced down. "I think she must've hurt it, she refuses to open it."

"Let's see." She touched the girl's fingers and spoke calmly, hoping to convey trust and safety in her tone since the girl wouldn't understand her words. "You're okay now. You can let go of what's in your hand."

The girl flinched.

Oliver said something to her in Khmer and lowered her to the mattress. This time she went willingly. He slid a hand over the girl's hair. The gesture put a lump in Jocelyn's throat. Mary bustled to the other side of the bed and leaned down to pat the girl's hand, crooning to her in lilting Khmer.

The girl opened her unfocused eyes and darted her bright gaze around the room. "Brother Chann say…we in danger. Someone come to kill us all very soon. We die…for this." Her fingers slowly unfurled, revealing a dull, unrefined, red stone in the center of her palm, and her eyes rolled back and she lost consciousness, almost as if she'd been hanging on to it for the sake of the gem.

Jocelyn sucked in a breath. "Oh, my God. Is that what I think it is?"

Oliver plucked the stone from the girl's hand and held it up to the wash of sunlight spilling through the window. "Son of a bitch."

Even without all the grit polished from the red diamond, it held a certain sparkle, sending bursts of scarlet dancing off the bamboo walls of the hut. Somehow this girl had found a piece of Kala's Ashes.

"Where?" The whispered question crossed Jocelyn's lips before she knew she'd meant to voice it.

Oliver shook his head, a frown lodging between his brows. He leaned over the girl like he meant to demand answers from her but instead, he adjusted the cool cloth that Mary had put on her forehead, brushed his knuckles against her dirty cheek, and stood.

As he passed by Jocelyn, waves of tension rolled off him and hit her hard in the chest. He left the hut without a word, the red diamond clutched in his fist. She followed, snagging a flask of water off the low table on her way out. He had to be exhausted, both physically and mentally, a fact that twisted her inside out when she saw him sprawled in a patch of grass not ten feet from the hut, his hands over his face.

She knelt next to him and handed him the flask. "Here."

He dropped his hands away from his eyes, but it took him another few seconds before he registered the container she held out. He reached for it. His arm trembled as he gripped the flask and greedily drank, water spilling down his chin.

She watched his throat work convulsively with

each swallow and fought the urge to pepper him with questions. When the flask was empty, he tossed it to the ground, and angled his face up to catch the warm breeze. She turned away from the barren hunger that swept across his features, and stared at the villagers clustering around the Barnes's hut.

She hugged herself. "How did you find her?"

"She was huddled under a tree, near the bend in the river. She's—God, when I first saw her—she's just a child. Eleven years old."

"Did she tell you who did this to her?" She turned back to meet his hard gaze, his dark brows drawn into a sharp frown.

"Who do you think?"

The half-starved boy at The Trinity's compound flashed in her mind. Her stomach dropped. "No."

"She spoke of a mine. I had to promise her I wouldn't take her back there."

"The Trinity's using them, aren't they? As…slaves." An acrid taste filled her throat.

"Yeah." He pushed himself to his feet and would've collapsed back to the ground if she hadn't reached out to steady him.

Pastor Barnes strode over to them. "You've brought new hope to the village."

White lines appeared beside Oliver's tight mouth. "What are you talking about?"

"The girl." Barnes gestured to the villagers lining up outside the hut. "I told you, the Tom Puon listen heavily to the spirits that inhabit nature. These spirits speak of a ghost that snatches children from the hill tribes. Some of the families here have lost their sons and daughters to this ghost. Some say they've even seen him."

The nausea in Jocelyn's stomach returned. She

looked at Oliver and saw the same premonition darkening his eyes.

"Did they describe this…ghost?" He all but spat the question.

Barnes divided a look between them, his gaze narrowing with speculation. "Big, broad, pasty skin, colorless eyes, vile breath. Until now, they've always believed the gods were punishing them, but this girl—she's been returned to them. Maybe others will follow."

Blood thundered in Jocelyn's ears. Pasty skin…colorless eyes…oh, God. It couldn't be—but the description fit Leo. No matter how much these villagers believed in spirits and ghosts, she knew better. Ghosts didn't snatch children and beat them. People did that. Sick, evil people. Like The Trinity.

Barnes moved on to reassure a group of villagers who'd left their work in the field during the commotion.

She waited until he was out of earshot, then turned to Oliver. "It's not their gods at all, it's The Trinity, isn't it? They're ripping innocent children from their families and forcing them to work in their mine."

A range of emotions washed across his face, flooding into his tight jaw, rigid mouth and turbulent eyes, as if the dam he'd erected to hold it all back had suddenly crumbled. Anger, sadness, determination, anguish—it was all bared for her to see—but the moment was fleeting, and before she'd had a chance to decipher them all, he'd shoved the emotion back where it had come from.

He started to walk away. "I want to check on Maelea."

Maelea. So that was the girl's name. The way it rolled off his tongue brought on a fresh wave of conviction. How many other children like her were there? Mistreated, starved. Slaves to The Trinity. How many had been killed for their greed? If there were any who could be saved…she couldn't turn her back on them now that she knew.

She laid a hand on his arm, staying him. "She's in good hands with Mary. Resting. Like you should be. You're exhausted. Then we need to figure out what we're going to do."

"I know what I'm going to do. Head back to the river and follow it into town. And then I'm going to find that radio and get you the hell home."

She prodded her fingers into his arm, gripping him tighter. "But…what about the children? Someone needs to help them."

His muscles vibrated under her touch. He looked down at her hand and his jaw tightened. "No. This is not our fight. I swore I would get you out of here, and that's what I'm going to do."

"These children need us," she pleaded, dropping his arm in favor of putting her hands against his chest. "We can't just turn our back on them. They're being abused and mistreated. They deserve to have the chance to grow up and have a life."

He leaned down, got right into her face. The anger she saw stamped on his features might have scared her if she hadn't understood that it was directed more at himself than her. Still, when he spoke, fury bubbled into his words. "You cannot save everyone."

What did he mean by that? "I don't want to save everyone."

His eyes narrowed. "No, of course not. Just me, a mine full of innocent children, a bunch of grieving villagers who've lost their loved ones, and hundreds of years worth of dead people."

His voice was like a rough slap across her cheek. She reached up to touch her burning skin. "I'm not—"

"You can't take away their pain. It is theirs alone to bear."

"That's not what I'm doing." She wasn't stupid enough to think she could absolve anyone's grief. But closure…that was in her power to provide. Why shouldn't she give it?

His brows lifted in reproach. "Why did you go to work for JPAC? Out of all the places you could've secured a job, why there?"

She opened her mouth, found it dry, and had to swallow thickly before speaking. A job was a job. She had no need to defend her choice to him. "I'm a forensic anthropologist. Digging up old bones is what I do. Where better than at JPAC—"

"But you're not just digging up bones, are you? You're not spending your days uncovering ancient artifacts or exploring cultures."

"What difference does that make? There are plenty of others doing that kind of work. It's not where I'm needed."

"What's your favorite thing about your job?"

Her stomach sank then rose again on a wave of awareness. She clamped her mouth shut, scrambled for an answer. "I—"

"I'll tell you what it is—"

"Making a positive ID," she blurted. She meant to end it there, but the words just kept coming. "Knowing that I've found someone who'd been lost to their family for years and reuniting them. It doesn't matter that they're dead. Most of their families have waited a lifetime to know what happened to them. And I can do that. I can bring them home—"

"Saving them," he bit off. "It all comes down to saving them."

He was right. She'd spent her career trying to save others from their pain, because she couldn't save herself from her own. "Fine. Maybe I am trying to 'save' everyone, as you say. But it's better than doing nothing."

The barb found its mark. His head snapped up. He plowed a hand through his hair. "You can't save a pile of bones any more than you can save those children. They're as good as dead."

"What a horrible thing to say! What if someone felt that way about you?"

"They already have." The quiet force of his words drew her back a step.

They had, hadn't they? Everyone had already written him off as a dead man. Everyone had already forgotten him.

"Then you know what it feels like. Don't let it happen to someone else. Don't let these children live in fear and slavery. They deserve better." She held his gaze. "These children need you, Oliver. You're their only hope."

"No. I'm not. You don't know what you're saying. No matter how much I want to help those kids...I put them in jeopardy just by being there. If we fail—and face it, the odds are not in our favor—The Father would do everything in his power to use me to hurt them."

"The Trinity will kill them," she whispered. "You know they will."

"I know." He closed his eyes. The tendons in his throat went taut with his swallow. "But I can't—I won't—be the cause of their death. I've hurt enough people."

How could she convince him this time would be different? It wasn't just him against The Trinity anymore.

He had her. And maybe they could convince enough villagers to stand beside them to even the odds.

He leveled her with a hard stare that gentled when he pushed a lock of hair behind her ear. He ran a finger across her cheek. "I promise you, when I get to a radio, I'll do whatever it takes to ensure they send in a military rescue."

He dropped his hand and walked off toward the waterfall.

If they waited for military reinforcements, it would be too late. "Oliver, wait—"

He shook his head, holding up a hand in a silent plea to be left alone and kept on walking. She watched him until her heart twisted and she couldn't draw a full breath, then turned back toward the huts. Her thoughts tripped over each other in her brain.

Oliver was right, there was no guarantee that they'd succeed in saving the children. Odds were they'd risk their lives without changing the outcome. But how could she live with herself if they did nothing? No one else could reach the children in time.

She glanced back over her shoulder. Oliver was standing in the waterfall's rocky plateau, looking over the edge where the water tumbled down to the next step in the cliff ten feet below. His stiff posture and bowed head reminded her that he was, after all, just a man. A flawed, flesh and blood man, rife with demons, and in desperate need of his freedom.

He deserved to find happiness, to go home to his glass house on the beach, rediscover his love of painting, and have a normal life. What right did she have to demand that some things were worth the sacrifice?

Hadn't he already sacrificed enough?

MAELEA MADE IT through the night.

Oliver squinted against the morning sun that streamed through the window. Pain seared the muscles in his neck and he tried to stretch from his cramped position on the floor next to the girl. He squeezed her hand, which had somehow found its way under his last night, and stood. She was still breathing shallowly, and when he brushed his hand across her forehead, it was still hot to the touch.

No change. But for the moment she was alive.

He glanced at Jocelyn across the room, slumped in the hut's only chair, her eyes closed. Her hair fell across her cheek. Instead of obscuring the lines of strain on her face, the dark brown strands somehow accentuated them. She was worried for the children. How many of them were like Maelea? Sick, scared, devoid of hope and trust. Stripped of their innocence.

He wheezed at the pain. How could he just turn his back on them? He didn't want to, but every time he thought of charging to their rescue, he saw himself being used to hurt them. He saw his curse, his damn King Midas touch, the one that would hurt them even when he meant to help. Whether by The Father or his own darkness, the result would be the same—their pain, their death.

Wouldn't they be better off if he didn't try at all?

Better off.

He really needed to strike that phrase from his vocabulary. Because, like they had before, the words taunted him. Told him what he didn't want to know, what Jocelyn already knew. If they didn't do something, who would?

He glanced over at Jocelyn to see her now awake, staring at him with those gentle eyes that took in everything he was thinking with compassion instead of harsh recrimination. She was a woman like no other. Strong and brave and giving. There was no duality—what you saw was what you got—and once she'd decided to invest in someone, she never turned her back. There was a cold, lonely place inside him that leapt with joy at the thought.

She could save him, make him whole. If only he had the courage to reach for it.

The air seemed to suddenly grow stiff. He tried to answer, to assure her that Maelea was still holding on, but his sore chest constricted his breath. His heart pounded hard against his ribs.

Jocelyn tipped her head. "How is she?"

"Fine. I...I need some air."

He darted past her and staggered out of the hut. When his feet hit the dirt, he started running, from the truth, to the truth, he didn't know which, but his body pushed him faster, his legs carried him into the trees, farther and farther until the leafy canopy overhead blocked out the sunlight, engulfing him in the moist, pungent jungle. At last, he put his hands on his knees and drew in a full, damp breath.

Maybe he wasn't as far gone as he'd always believed. Maybe there was something left of the man he used to be still worth fighting for. If Jocelyn could see it—believe in it—why couldn't he?

He didn't know how long he stayed enveloped in the trees, soaking up strength from their sturdy branches, but he finally dusted off his pants, stood, and headed back to the hut. He climbed the steps, anxious to speak with Jocelyn. When he tried to step inside, she was there, blocking his entrance. Tears spilled over her lashes, her hands fisted in his shirt.

"Oliver…"

He flicked a glance past her. She tried to shift her body, but she wasn't fast enough. He saw the white of a sheet as Mary drew it over Maelea's body. Up over her face.

"No." He pushed to get in the door, but Jocelyn held him back with a strength he hadn't known she possessed.

"She's gone," she whispered.

"No," he repeated. What an inadequate word. "She was fine. I just stepped out—I needed a minute—that's all. She was okay. She…she was going to make it."

"I'm sorry." A sob escaped her lips.

He staggered, caught himself, and spun and fled the hut. He heard Jocelyn shout his name, but he couldn't stop. Once more that desperate feeling welled inside of him, overtaking control of his body.

This time it propelled him to the waterfall.

He stepped into the pond and watched the water tumble over the rocks and swirl around his feet. Squatting, he cupped his hands, letting the liquid completely fill the well his palms made before lifting his hands and sipping from the makeshift cup. Cool moisture slid down his throat, coating the ball of emotions that tangled in his stomach.

Wash it all away.

He doused his hair with the remaining water, trying to eradicate the grief burning beneath his skin. It didn't help.

Jocelyn splashed up behind him and laid her cheek against his back. He fought the urge to shake her off, to shut her out. His throat ached, corrosive anguish eating its way up his esophagus. "I thought I could—that if I saved her—maybe—hell, I wanted it to be true. I wanted to believe that I could do it."

"Do what?" Her lips moved against his shoulder.

"Be the man I want to be. The one who does what's right and succeeds."

"Oh, Oliver."

"She wasn't supposed to die." He stood. Before he could put space between them, Jocelyn wrapped her arms around his waist.

He'd done what he could, and it hadn't been enough. Anger mixed with sorrow in an explosive cocktail. Goddamn it, why couldn't it have been enough?

The waterfall roared in his ears. He shrugged her off and strode forward with mindless determination, until the frothy, tumbling water was less than an arm's length away. He plunged beneath the hard torrent. It pummeled his skin, soaking him. He pushed through to the other side where a rocky alcove provided shelter from the falls.

Leaning his forehead against the slick stones, he let the thin shadows wrap around him. He heard Jocelyn burst through the wall of water. It would do him no good to ignore her. She wouldn't be dissuaded. It was one of the things he liked best about her.

"I should've known," he whispered. "About the children. I should've paid attention. Should've done something."

"You don't have to carry this burden alone." Her voice was an alluring invitation. He couldn't mistake her meaning. She thought she could ease his pain.

"How can you possibly carry it with me?" As soon as he asked, felt her go pliant against him, he knew exactly how to cure the blaze inside of him.

He could lose himself—in her lips, her body. A body

that was as cold and soaked to the skin as his. He tugged her against him and she came willingly, her breasts brushing against his chest. The thin fabric of her shirt molded itself to her body, hiding nothing. He slid his hand up her spine, caressed her nape and tried to ignore the way the cold water had turned her nipples into hard pebbles.

He sought her mouth instead. Their lips collided. She opened for him almost immediately and he speared his tongue inside her warm mouth, taking from her, riding on the wave of desire and longing that coursed through him. He wanted to devour her, inhale her goodness. To obliterate the blackness in his soul and replace it with her light. He fanned his thumbs across her cheeks, intensifying the kiss even further, melding his tongue against hers.

"Josie," he murmured against her lips.

He kissed his way along her jaw line. Touched his tongue to the sweet curve of her ear.

She gasped and pressed her cold hands to his face. "Oliver…"

He continued his exploration of her ear, kissing the spot behind it, eliciting a shiver from her, and moving down her neck until he reached the hollow of her throat. She threw her head back giving him better access and he reached up to trail his fingers along the edge of her shirt. The contrast between the coarse, wet fabric and her smooth skin sent a delicious friction through his body.

Texture. Was there anything more erotic than the feel of this woman?

Desire burned through him, hot and hard. He backed her against the rocks, fitting her into the natural niche beneath the falls. A stream of water rained down on his head, but he shook the droplets out of his eyes and took her mouth again. She tasted clean and crisp and as their tongues melded something burst inside his chest.

Sunshine and strength, a renewed fire he'd thought he'd lost.

The need to get closer overwhelmed him. He leaned into her. She arched her back, rocking against his arousal.

"Touch me." Her simple words sent a shudder of pure pleasure coursing through him.

He fit his erection tighter against the apex of her thighs and skimmed his hands underneath her shirt. Her ribs were more pronounced than they'd most likely been a month earlier, and feeling them under his fingertips brought a wave of regret tugging at him. But then his palms touched the undersides of her breasts and he caressed his way upward until his thumb flicked against her nipple and all he could think about was touching her there, tasting her.

Lifting her sodden shirt out of the way, he bent and swirled his tongue over her, chasing away the goose bumps on her skin with his warm mouth. She moaned, a low purr that hummed in his veins and urged his hands lower. He caressed his way down her body until he met the elastic waistband of her loose pants, then drove his hand beneath the fabric, gliding his palm over her sweet mound of curls, to tease her with his fingers.

She writhed against his hand, her head thrown back in wild abandon as he delved deeper, stroking her intimately. Watching the desire play across her features, the way her eyes fluttered closed and her lips parted, mouthing his name, nearly had him going off like a rocket.

He started to pull back, but she reached for him, surprising him by sliding one cool, delicate hand inside the front of his pants. She gripped his arousal, caressed her thumb over him. His blood surged, a harsh breath shot up from him. He detonated, finding his release.

Heat flooded his face. He shoved at her and twisted away.

She'd understand. It had been a long time since he'd been with a woman. But, he should've had more restraint than that. He wasn't some randy teenager getting naked with a girl for the first time.

"I'm sorry." He had to raise his voice to be heard over the waterfall, which only made his humiliation all the greater. "That was…"

He trailed off when he felt her come up behind him. Somehow he couldn't confess his utter embarrassment with her so close. She wrapped her arms around him and leaned up to whisper in his ears.

"Beautiful," she said. "That was absolutely beautiful."

That should've brought forth a laugh, but instead, he felt a hot sting against his eyes. Beautiful? Not even close, except it was just the kind of thing he knew she'd say, not because she wanted to spare him, but because she actually meant it.

He turned, still fighting to keep his emotions in check, and wrapped her up in his embrace. "Thank you."

She smiled against his neck. "For what?"

Everything—her gentle caress, her smile, her fierce determination—but most of all for seeing the very best in him.

"I should've known what The Trinity was up to." He pressed his forehead to hers. "How could we at the CIA know about the sapphire mine and the money the bastards were funneling to terrorists, and not know a damn thing about the way they were exploiting and abusing children?"

She frowned, as if struggling to keep up with the sudden shift of topic. "No one could've predicted how far they would go."

"Maybe not at first. But I should've paid more attention. I had plenty of chances to uncover the truth. I turned a deaf ear."

She clutched at his shirt. "No. You tried—"

"But I stopped trying. It hurt too much" Spilling the truth was like taking an M-80 to the heart, but it needed to be said. They both needed to hear it. "How many others died because I just gave up?"

He didn't want to look her in the eye, but he refused to let himself off the hook. Jocelyn had been right. Those children deserved better than being overworked, mistreated and slowly starved to death. It was too late for Maelea, but maybe it wasn't too late for the others.

Jocelyn must've seen the resolution in his gaze, for her eyes widened and she reached up to smooth his brow. "What is it? What are you thinking?"

"I'm thinking," he said, and had to swallow the lump in his throat before continuing. He ran his thumb along her jaw, teased it over her soft mouth. "That it's time to rescue those children. Whatever it takes. I won't walk away from them."

He dropped his hold on her and dove into the chilly waterfall. As the surge pulled at him and poured over his head, he felt something tug at him—something elemental and familiar, something he'd thought lost to him forever.

His freedom.

EIGHTEEN

JOCELYN IGNORED THE impulse to go after Oliver as he dove past the curtain of water. She slumped back against the slick rocks. Her entire body still hummed with desire and her skin still tingled with the memory of Oliver's touch.

She hadn't meant to take things so far—he was hurting and she hadn't been able to bear it—she'd only thought to take away some of his pain, to wrap comfort in a single kiss. But once their mouths met, once he'd pressed his body into hers, all hot and hard, she'd wanted so much more. And when he'd touched her, she couldn't resist touching him back.

Had she stopped to think, she would have realized that it had been a very long time since he'd experienced such an intimate gesture. But then he was losing control, pushing her away, and she'd seen a glimpse of a raw vulnerability that went far beyond his eyes. It touched his soul, and he'd suddenly become different—freer. She'd loved seeing that transformation, knowing she was, in part, responsible for it.

Pushing away from the rocks, she stepped into the waterfall, letting the water cool off her skin before coming out the other side. Oliver was already halfway to the cluster of huts, his shoulders and back rigid with purpose. He looked every bit the commanding CIA agent he'd once been. His wet, overgrown black hair gleamed in the sun. Coupled with the dark beard against his jaw, he looked dangerous, reckless.

How far would he go to do right by the children?

She raced to catch up with him. "What are you going to do?"

He stalked past her and headed for the rice fields. "You and I can't do this on our own. If we want a chance in hell of succeeding, we'll need help."

"But where—" She broke off as he approached Barnes.

The two shared a moment of low conversation, then Barnes went back into the field. Oliver waited at the edge of a patch of mud, tension in his spine, his focus riveted on the shafts of green rice rippling in the breeze.

Barnes reappeared, picking his way through the rows of rice. He sent Oliver a single sharp nod. "They want to help. They're tired of living in fear. The girl—her death—brought home to them how much they have lost."

"What about the sapphire mine?" Oliver asked. "Do they know where it is?"

Barnes nodded. "Near the Laotian-Vietnam border. It's a spot they've avoided for many years. They claim evil spirits inhabit the land."

"Evil, yes. Spirits, no." Oliver's jaw clenched. "The men we're up against are merciless. They won't hesitate to kill any of us."

Barnes's attention strayed to the villagers. Jocelyn could see the love of the people etched in his face and knew the idea of losing any of them weighed heavily. "They are willing to take the risk. Some of them lost children to these monsters. If there's a chance any of them are still alive—"

"What about cemeteries," she blurted, remembering her father's code. "Or sacred burial grounds?"

Oliver frowned, probably wondering what her questions had to do with The Trinity's sapphire mines.

"Hang on." She dashed to the hut and snagged the leather messenger bag off the floor. When she returned, she spread the logbook out on a flat rock. "My dad's cipher. I was studying it while you were away and I—I remembered something. I was about six or seven when my dad carved me a set of blocks. Each one was exotic, containing pictograms of places he'd seen. They were my favorite toys, I don't know how I could have forgotten about them."

Maybe because she'd put them away when it became clear her dad wasn't coming back. Looking at them had been so painful. She'd wanted nothing to remind her of the hollow space his disappearance had left.

"We used to play this game when he was on leave," she continued. "While I was at school he'd lay out a series of blocks throughout the house like a treasure map. As soon as I stepped off the bus, I'd race inside and use the blocks to find him, or some treat he'd bought for me."

She tugged her dad's hidden letter from where she'd pressed it in the logbook and handed it to Oliver. "That's why my dad drew the symbols in precise blocks. He wanted me to remember. He put the map together for me. So I could find him." Fresh emotion clogged her throat. "He carved me a block for Halloween once, with all different masks—like skulls—and hid it in the fake cemetery we'd put up in the front yard. That's why I think he crashed near a burial site. Although I still can't figure out why he would've included the elephant block as well—"

"The forests are scattered with chunchiet cemeteries." Barnes leaned forward, scratching his brow.
"Chunchiet. Minority. Families bury their dead in burial
houses and carve large statues to place around the site
to guard the dead. I've heard of one that used elephant
tusks as well. The Tom Puon would know of it."

"Oh, my God. It has to be real, then." She hugged
the book to her chest. "My dad—he's—I can't believe
I'm so close to finally knowing the truth."

Oliver waved the letter. "What does all this have to
do with the children or the sapphire mine?"

She blinked up at him, realizing that for a moment
she'd almost let herself forget the bigger picture. "Kala's Ashes. When my dad's plane crashed…I think he
might have stumbled upon Kala's Ashes." She pointed
to a block in the top left-hand corner of the book de-
picting a serpent eating its own tail, his body in a perfect circle. "The circle is generally a symbol of eternity.
And the serpent…"

Now Barnes leaned in even closer. "Kala Sarpa," he
breathed. "Serpent of time."

"If we can use this as leverage, negotiate the release
of the children in exchange for its location…"

Oliver looked up, his eyes gleaming with purpose.
"Send one of the villagers to radio the mine's position
to JPAC for backup and instruct them to get in touch
with the head of the Special Activities Division. Once
the S.A.D. knows I'm alive and requesting assistance,
they'll cut through the red tape and get a chopper headed
our way. We leave for the mine as soon as we can gather
enough supplies."

JUDE SURVEYED THE pit, watching all the children scurry
around like ants as they sifted through the dirt and

rocks, searching for the tiniest slivers of crude sapphires to bring to his attention. He hadn't made a visit to the mine—Leo's domain—in years, but someone had to deal with the tedious oversight now that both Leo and Chann were…gone.

His hands tightened into fists, twisting the scar tissue across his right knuckles into an uncomfortable crease. He gritted his teeth against the pain, ignoring the answering pull that tugged at the corner of his mouth and bunched in his right cheek. Leo and Chann had chosen their path. He would not mourn them for their betrayal.

He pushed away thoughts of the both of them, locking the rank memory of their deeds away in the darkest corner of his mind. As he stalked down into the pit, he turned his attention to his newest problem. Thom and Veha had failed to bring Shaw and Hewitt to him. He didn't tolerate empty promises any more than he tolerated betrayal.

He'd given his mercenaries plenty of time and incentive, and still he waited. For all he knew, Shaw and Hewitt could be exposing The Trinity's location by now. It wouldn't be long before the sapphire mine came under scrutiny. He was operating on borrowed time. Better to cut his losses and disappear.

But he couldn't. Not while Kala's Ashes remained in his grasp. He could still salvage his kingdom.

He could feel the hum of its power, had spent years cultivating it, until what was once only a tiny root flourished into a full-blown living, breathing entity capable of sustaining him even during his darkest days. Nothing could entice or worry him into giving up that thrill. Nothing.

His foot slipped in a patch of reddish mud, and he had to set his hand down in the wet grass to right himself.

He scowled, swiping his palm across his slacks. Dirty, smelly, rotten piece of land. What good was it now that it had stopped yielding sapphires?

He found Thom and Veha on the far side of the pit and his hand went for his gun. Whipping the Sig Sauer into position, he flicked off the safety and pointed it at Thom's head.

"It seems we have a difference of opinion on the meaning of the words 'we've found them,'" Jude snarled. "I don't see Shaw or Miss Hewitt here. Do you?" He transferred his aim to Veha. "How about you?"

Veha raised his hands. "Our boys lost them. They've paid for their mistake. We underestimated Shaw and the woman."

"It won't happen again." Thom's low rasp drew Jude's attention.

He swung his gaze—and his pistol—in his direction. "You're right it won't happen again—" Movement caught his eye. A scrawny boy behind Thom, slipping something into his mouth. "What was that?"

Jude stalked past Thom and Veha, suspicion eating at his gut. He reset the safety on the Sig Sauer and shoved it back into his holster. "What do you have?" He reached for the boy's bony shoulder and squeezed. Hard. "What are you hiding?"

The boy shook his head.

Jude gripped the child's jaw and squeezed. "Open up."

Before the boy's mouth opened fully, Jude plunged his finger inside and pushed his way under the boy's tongue. Something hard and small shifted under the pad of Jude's finger. He dug it out, held it up to the sun.

A sapphire.

Another dirty, conniving thief.

Jude pocketed the small stone then slapped the boy across the cheek. He shoved the child at Veha. "Round up the children. I want to examine each and every one of them. Now!"

His blood boiled, flushing his skin with a prickly heat that made his scars itch. Damn these juveniles. Damn them all. Even they had resorted to betrayal.

Let the little children come to me.

Hadn't he sheltered and clothed them? Hadn't he given them his all? Didn't they realize how lucky they were that he'd chosen them?

In minutes, Thom and Veha had all the duplicitous kids lined up. Their dark eyes stared at him, wide and frightened, so huge in their pathetic faces. He would not be swayed by their act. Those caught stealing would reap their punishment.

One by one, he went down the line, forcing their mouths open. The amount of stones grew heavy in his pocket. By the time he reached the end of the line, only five children stood apart from the cluster of guilty brats.

He stopped in front of the last child and inclined his head. "Open your mouth."

She was smaller than the others, not in age, but in frame. Her delicate hands clutched at her ragged shirt, her limbs like weak toothpicks. She tightened her mouth, blinked her dark eyes at him and had the gall to shake her head.

"No?" He snagged her jaw between his thumb and forefinger and squeezed. "Open your mouth."

Again, a jerky denial.

He gripped her head in one hand and jammed a finger past her lips. Just as he'd suspected, he felt the familiar hard ridges of a gemstone buried beneath her tongue. He yanked it out of her mouth, held it up to the light.

The sun glinted off the unrefined stone, reflecting just a hint of color.

Not blue.

Red.

Jude gasped, staggered back a step. A wave of dizzy euphoria washed over him and he fought to temper the swirling current, squeezing the stone in his fist. It might be only a ruby—but no, it was hard—harder than either a ruby or a sapphire should be.

He took one of the larger sapphires from his pocket and dragged the stones across each other. The red gemstone remained unscratched, but the sapphire...the sapphire had a clear gouge across its surface.

Only a diamond could cut into a sapphire.

A diamond.

Kala's Ashes.

He shoved the gem into the girl's face. "Where did you get this? Where?"

Covering her face with her hands, she started to shake.

He clenched his fist. "Don't make me beat it out of you."

She turned and ran, skipping over holes in the earth until she came to the back of the mining camp. Jude followed her up a hill dotted with green grass and jasmine and down into another valley that resembled some kind of crater or sinkhole. There, in the middle of the depression was another cavity, like all the other mining shafts, but this one only big enough for a child to fit through.

The girl scrambled inside and disappeared beneath the earth. He knelt at the edge and ran his palm down along the muddy wall as far as he could reach. There was something beneath the tips of his fingers—a place where the dirt ended and something else began. Flattening himself to the ground, he plunged his hand further along the side. His palm met cool limestone.

A cave?

He sat up, his heart racing. The girl's grunts of exertion echoed up from the dark tunnel. Silence. For several, long, impatient minutes. Then the sound of scratching and scrambling met his ears once more. He reached down and connected with the girl's hand. Wrapping his grip around her wrist, he hauled her out of the hole.

She stared.

He narrowed his eyes. "Where is it?"

She stretched out one long, waifish brown arm and opened her fist, inch by slow inch. Two small red slivers winked up at him from her palm. He snatched them out of her hand. His body started to quake. He spun, stumbled out of the crater, to the top of the grassy hill.

Kala's Ashes—he'd found it—here, beneath the fucking sapphire mine. Here, where he'd trod all over the muddy, loamy earth for years, never once suspecting what was beneath his feet. He pumped his fists in the air and threw back his head, waiting for the energy to fill his veins and the rich taste of success to tingle on his tongue.

If only he'd known, what a difference he could've made, what power he could've achieved—

But the brats *had* known.

And they'd never said a word.

THE FOREST ENVELOPED the chunchiet cemetery in its lush green embrace. Vines crawled over the faded burial houses, and lifelike wooden effigies rose out of the ground on either side, standing guard.

Jocelyn paused to take a drink from her canteen, the

sudden silence prickling her skin beneath her sweat-dampened hair. Four days of trekking through the jungle had given her a healthy appreciation for the constant buzz of insects and the comforting murmur of Khmer from the six Tom Puon men who'd insisted on accompanying her and Oliver to The Trinity's mine. But here, on this sacred ground, it was as if all sound had fallen away and unease took its place.

She turned, throwing a glance over her shoulder to make sure she hadn't veered from the group, and caught Oliver's stare. They had no weapons save for his AK-47. Sotha and Kamol, two of the Khmer men, carried crudely fashioned bows and arrows. She didn't think they'd be of much help if they came under fire.

We're safe. There's no reason to think The Trinity is lurking around here.

She rubbed her arms. The quiet was making her jumpy.

Oliver made his way to her side. "Do you think this is it? The cemetery your dad wrote about?"

"I don't know. I thought I'd...feel it. Feel him." She spread her palm against her heart. "In here, you know?"

He covered her hand with his own and the warmth of his calloused palm jolted straight through her. "Maybe if we take a look around."

Jocelyn nodded, but couldn't tear her gaze away from his face. The shade of his eyes matched the carpet of moss winding its way against the bark of a nearby banyan tree. Then his eyes darkened, and his hand slid to her cheek. She let herself fall into his touch for a moment, before forcing herself to pull away.

She'd followed Oliver's lead and avoided all talk of what happened at the waterfall. It was easier that way, to forget about the future and the fear and the danger and just live for the moment. For the *more* that had quietly developed between them. Each time they touched something fisted in her heart, something heavy and... important. Something that both centered her and set her off balance at the same time.

But she couldn't let herself bask in the glow of its hope. Not now. Not when she needed to channel every ounce of her concentration and strength into saving the children. Those faceless boys and girls haunted her, day and night. Above all, she couldn't stop thinking about the one she *could* put a face to—Maelea. Her courage, her sacrifice...she had to make sure the girl's death wasn't in vain.

They'd already taken longer than anticipated to reach the cemetery by traveling mostly at night to avoid detection. If the entrance to Kala's Ashes was here, like her dad had indicated, they needed to find it quickly and move on to the mine.

She circled the first burial house. "How far are we from the mine?"

Oliver followed, his eyes trained on the intricately painted wall of the second cluster of graves. "Not far. Kiri assures me it's just over the rise."

The "rise" was in the form of a rolling hill, stretching out to the north—maybe a half-mile at most.

"Good." She sighed. "Do you see anything?"

He frowned up into the shadows of trees, looking at one of the taller statues, its brittle wood splintered and jagged at the top where the head should have been. "I wish I knew exactly what I was looking for."

"A sign, or symbol, anything that resembles the image of Kala Sarpa. It's got to be here somewhere."

If it wasn't they'd have to rethink their plan to negotiate. What other leverage did they have?

She spied a third burial house. Leaves obscured the walls and dripped from the faded roof. Two statues peeked out from their perches on either side of the site, vines wrapped around their thick bodies. A set of large markers blocked the entrance to the structure. Although carved out of wood, they resembled—

"Tusks." Her voice croaked on the word.

The elephant in her dad's cryptogram.

She took off running.

"Jocelyn, wait."

She heard Oliver's warning, but she couldn't stop.

She was close. So close. He was here.

Her oversized boots slapped at the ground as her legs ate up the distance. Her foot snagged on something that sent her careening forward. She threw out her arms, but the impact of the fall still jarred her body, reverberating in her teeth.

"I'm all right." She shook herself, swallowed the dryness in her throat and sat up to retrace the area on her hands and knees. Her boot had connected with a solid object, nothing like the gnarled roots or dense vines that fed off the humid climate. "I tripped over something, something hard and sharp. It—"

A dab of sunlight flickered through the trees. Metal glinted. Her breath caught. She scrambled over to the patch of uneven dirt and grass. The monsoons had a way of rearranging the landscape, tearing the wetlands asunder, churning up mud, and with it, buried artifacts. She located the corner and dug her fingers into the damp dirt to pry at the piece of serrated metal. Oliver knelt beside her, taking up the opposite side and together they dislodged the fragment.

She swiped her palms across the surface. Instead of the gray she'd expected to uncover, it was a swatch of pale yellow. She smeared more of the dirt away. Oliver joined in to help, his hands dancing around hers until the full impact of the painted image was revealed.

A sun.

"Oh, God." She reached out to touch the faded drawing, but her hand trembled too badly and she had to furl her fingers into a fist.

A section of the wing from her dad's plane. He'd hand-painted the sun in reference to his nickname, Sonny. She'd found him. After all these years, finally, here was the evidence of his fate.

"Daddy." Tears coursed down her cheeks, splashing onto the wing and splattering more of the dirt aside.

Oliver's hand slid over hers. "Josie."

"I know." She met his worried gaze. "We have to go. I just—it's not only a hunk of his plane—it's *him*. I've dreamed of this day and I…" she tipped her head back, blinking away the wetness, "…I didn't expect to feel—sad—happy—scared—it's all churning away inside me and I can't seem to stop it."

"Look." His gentle command urged her to follow where he pointed, to the tops of a handful of trees that were shorter than the rest. Stunted and damaged. As if by the sharp impact of a plane's wing. "He came down, right through there."

She jumped to her feet, swiping at her wet eyes to study the trees for more evidence of the Bronco's trajectory. "The tall statue, the one with its head broken off."

And then where? She crossed over to the effigy, studied the pattern of flight. There. Another carving with a large gouge taken out of its body.

"Here." She spun at the sound of Oliver's voice. He tapped a nearby tree, drawing her attention to a gash in the bark.

She closed her eyes, picturing her dad struggling to hold on to the OV-10 Bronco as he brought it down. "This way."

Pushing past Oliver, she went into the trees, piecing together the clues. More scarred bark and broken limbs, permanent damage that remained to this day. She heard Oliver shout something in Khmer to the other men and soon all of them were hurrying through the jungle. New perspiration gathered at her temples, trickling down past her ears. Her heart revved.

Another shout drew her attention and she veered in that direction. One of the men bent over a hunk of rusted metal. It was mangled and worse for the wear, but still recognizable. Her mouth went dry and she couldn't seem to pull her gaze away. The Bronco had dropped one of its engines here.

So keep going. If the plane's here, you'll find it.

She reeled from the group and started climbing the sloping terrain. Her choppy breath masked the sound of Oliver's footsteps until he had slipped his hand in hers.

"Let me come with you."

She looked at their joined hands, his larger one almost swallowing hers in a firm grip. Whatever she found—or didn't find—it would be okay. He squeezed her hand and she glanced up at his strong profile, but he wasn't looking at her, he was looking through a big break in the trees.

Her footsteps slowed. Her breath fled. If Oliver's arm hadn't suddenly found its way around her waist, her knees would've buckled.

The wreckage of her dad's plane sat, undisturbed, between two tall, gnarled trees. Foliage had continued to grow around the Bronco, obscuring a good portion of the metal. The horizontal tailplane between the two booms was crushed, and one of the propellers was completely sheared off, but the cockpit had miraculously stayed intact.

She walked to the plane, ran a finger over the cracked window hanging back on its hinges and peered inside. A lizard scurried across the crumbling seat, over the severed seat belt and disappeared between a jagged seam in the metal. A layer of dirt coated the instrument panels, and thick thorny vines crept over the rim of the cockpit like dozens of brownish-green snakes.

Oliver's hand settled on the back of her head. He ran his palm over her hair.

She met his worried gaze and gave in to the urge to reach up and smooth away the crease between his brows. "We found it."

"You did." He fanned his thumb over her cheeks, brushing at the tears.

A laugh bubbled up from her chest and found its voice. Oliver's mouth hitched at the corners, slowly transforming his lips into a small, beautiful smile. Even through the sting that clouded her vision, the force of that smile hit her in the stomach.

His lips settled over hers in an infinitely gentle kiss that found its way into the smallest corners of her heart.

NINETEEN

THAT SIMPLE, SWEET KISS turned Oliver inside out.

He leaned his forehead against Jocelyn's, threading his fingers into her hair. "The connection to your dad is strong here, isn't it? Every crumbling, twisted piece of his plane—I wish you had more time to look around—"

She shook her head. "No, it's okay. His spirit is here, but his heart…" her hand slid over his and guided it to her own heart, "will always be right here."

He tipped her chin and kissed her, hard and swift, one last time, just because she made him feel…yes, she made him feel so many things he'd never thought to feel again. He pulled away with reluctance, and forced his focus back to the reason they were here.

Kala's Ashes. The children.

It took them another hour of combing the jungle before they found what they were looking for—an unnatural dent in the hillside. The pattern of dirt and rocks was consistent with a forced collapse, like that of a grenade blast. With the help of Kiri, Sotha, Yim and the other three Tom Puon, they managed to clear away the majority of the rubble, exposing the entrance to a cave, the craggy hole just large enough to squeeze through.

"Look." Jocelyn held up one of the few intact stone blocks they'd pulled from the pile and tilted the face toward him. Intricate, interlocking designs covered the surface, and stamped in the center was the circular image of Kala Sarpa.

His jaw went slack. "Son of a bitch, we found it."

She grinned—just for a moment—and the sight stripped away the last of the darkness from his soul.

"Come on." He nudged her. "Let's get what we came for and get out of here."

Kiri lit a makeshift torch out of a fallen tree branch. One by one the eight of them slithered through the hole and tumbled into the cave. Oliver went last, his fingers plowing into the extra fine sand on the cave floor. The glow of the torch bounced off the limestone walls. Stalactites dripped down from the ceiling. Minerals shimmered all around them.

He pushed to his feet and took the torch Kiri passed to him. The sand shifted as he trudged into the cave. The echo of dripping water rang somewhere in the distance. The sound popped in his ears but he pushed forward through the ever-widening passageway. Jocelyn positioned herself at his back, matching his strides, and the Tom Puon brought up the rear.

After three hundred yards, the ground suddenly sloped. His foot slipped against stone. He reached out to steady himself and connected with Jocelyn. She stumbled into him. Together they careened down the slippery rock, coming to a stop at the bottom. They'd hit the belly of the cave. Water trickled in a stream over the ground, seeping through his pants. He stood, raising the torch higher. Firelight danced over the walls. Thousands of red stones shimmered in the contours.

"Wow."

He swiveled around at the sound of Jocelyn's breathy whisper. The fading glow of the nearly burned-out torch played over her awed features. She lifted her hand up to the light. A small red diamond glittered between her thumb and forefinger.

"Holy shi—" His throat seized.

The ricochet of footsteps.

He spun, washing the area in light. Kiri, Sann, Bora, Yim, Sotha and Kamol halted their slow descent into the cave. The hair on Oliver's arms and at the back of his neck prickled. Sweat beaded above his brow.

Someone was coming.

He motioned the Tom Puon back, out of sight. When they complied he plunged the torch into the water at his feet.

He snatched up the AK-47 slung over his shoulder. "Josie. Get back."

The beam of a flashlight hit him full in the face, blinding him. Jocelyn screamed.

A low chuckle slithered around the cave's interior. "Won't Jude be surprised when we tell him we've found more than diamonds in this moldy old cave. Hand over the gun."

Oliver gritted his teeth, wrapping his finger around the trigger. The mercenary shifted his stance, angling the flashlight aside. Oliver blinked Jocelyn into focus. The second mercenary had a gun to her head.

His stomach twisted. He had no choice but to surrender the AK-47. "Take it." He held out the gun. "Just don't hurt her."

The man grinned. "The Father expects you two intact. As much as I'd love to kill you two nice and slowly, I have my orders."

Oliver tried to catch Jocelyn's eyes. She looked at him, and he willed her to see the reassurance he tried so hard to reflect in his gaze. But they both knew the truth. Their plan to use Kala's Ashes as leverage had failed.

The Father had already found it.

There was no reason to keep any of them alive.

THE BARREL OF the pistol dug into Jocelyn's temple. Perspiration soaked through her shirt and clung to her face, but she still felt the chill of steel all the way to her bones.

She caught Oliver's gaze again for a split second before the oily man dragged her across the mining pit and over to a raised platform where The Father sat in a captain's chair under a wide blue-patterned umbrella. He was dressed in a white linen shirt and pants. A straw hat perched atop his head, shading his eyes. She didn't have to see his golden stare to know it would be narrowed and devoid of all warmth.

"You're just in time for my bonfire." He squeezed a large glob of sunblock into his palm and slathered it over his arms, leaving white streaks across his skin.

She tracked his nod across to the other side of the pit where a pulley system was used to haul buckets of dirt from the sapphire mine. Strung up on the wire were close to twenty children, their arms bound high above their heads by thick rope threaded between them.

Her heart twisted. She met each one of their dark, shiny eyes. Their gaunt faces crumpled. She wrenched her arms, trying to dislodge herself from the mercenary's grip. He forced the pistol harder against her temple.

"You bastard."

The Father descended from his platform and stalked toward her. His disfigured face was coated in a thick layer of white sunblock that cracked when his mouth twisted into a satisfied smile.

He reached out and touched her cheek. "Do you know how much trouble you've caused me?" Underneath the casual question, the threat simmered.

She flinched before she could catch herself. *Don't you dare cower in front of him!* She stuck out her chin.

"Hopefully enough to cost you a whole truckload of money and then some."

He slapped her.

Her head snapped back, a sweltering throb raced up her cheek. She glared at him. "Look, you've got me. Why not let the children go. They're of no use to you now."

He laughed. "The delinquents have been stealing from me. That kind of betrayal can't go unpunished."

"Haven't they been punished enough? You've ripped them from their homes, their families. They're starving and mistreated—"

"Enough!" He grabbed her shirt and hauled her close. "I do not answer to you."

"But you will answer to me if you lay another finger on her or any of those kids." Oliver's voice rang out, a calm rasp that sounded nothing like him.

The Father pushed away, and spun to face Oliver, giving her an unobstructed view of the rigid set of Oliver's shadowed jaw. There was something different about him...a strength that affected his stiff stance and his rock steady gaze.

He commanded authority despite the knife at his throat. The mercenary holding it tightened his grip on the blade and prodded it into Oliver's neck. He didn't even flinch. A bead of crimson trickled down his neck. She watched it slide to the hollow of his throat.

"The only one you'll have to answer to is yourself, Shaw." The Father's face broke into a volatile smirk. "They'll all die at your hands and no one else's."

The loud rumble of a truck broke into the tense silence. It backed up to the edge of the pit. Two fifty-five gallon drums of gasoline sat in the bed, along with an electrical pump. The driver shut off the engine and opened the door, emitting a creak. He stepped around to the back of the truck and motioned to one of the nearby mercenaries. The man tossed him a length of hose.

"Come along, dear," The Father taunted in her ear. "We don't want to miss the fireworks."

"No!" She recoiled then had to fight to retain her balance as the scumbag behind her dragged her up onto the platform after The Father. "You can't do this."

"Watch me."

"I can't." Her voice cracked.

God, it was just as Oliver had feared. The Father would force Oliver to do his dirty work. This time it wouldn't just break him, it would kill him.

The Father tugged the umbrella down to shade more of his face. "Then you'd better close your eyes."

The mercenary pushed her to her knees, plucked a coil of rope from his pocket and used it to bind her hands and feet, pulling the cord extra tight. A burn seared across her skin. She clenched her teeth, but she didn't close her eyes. She wouldn't give herself a pass. Just like Oliver hadn't forgotten the deaths of his friends, these kids would know they were more than disposable slaves.

A pug-nosed, beady-eyed mercenary led Oliver over to the truck and prodded him into the bed with the barrel of a machine gun. The truck driver had put one end of a hose into the drum of gasoline and connected the other to the pump. He handed Oliver a section of hose rigged to the other end of the pump and gestured at the nozzle.

"Pheakdei!" The Father bellowed. "Where the fuck is my tea? I can't be expected to watch the fireworks without refreshments. And it had damn well better be hot."

Fireworks? The Father's intent became crystal clear. He expected Oliver to spray the children with gasoline and set them on fire.

"No. No, no, no." She struggled to stand despite the rope holding her down, but then Oliver turned, hose gripped in his hands, and his eyes locked on hers, knocking the breath and the fight from her.

The Father had made a huge tactical error.

He was banking on the Oliver he knew, the broken, scarred man. But as she stared into the determined gaze of a fighter, she knew something The Father didn't.

Oliver was no longer that man.

OLIVER CURLED HIS fingers tighter around the hose. What he was planning would put Jocelyn in harm's way, but she would never forgive him if he chose her safety above the children's. They were his number one priority right now. As long as he remained focused, he'd find a way to get her away from The Father. Once upon a time he'd excelled at thinking on his feet. He'd accept nothing less now.

He yanked the pull chain on the pump's motor. It spluttered, coughed, fell silent. He gave it another vicious tug. All but one of The Father's mercenaries had lined up like a firing squad, their weapons trained on him. Far enough away from the children, yet still close enough to make a nice, big target. If he so much as tilted the hose in the wrong direction, they'd pepper him with bullets.

Good. He hoped they were feeling trigger-happy.

He clenched his jaw. Ripped the pump's cable again. "Come on, you piece of shit."

The motor chugged to life. Smoke billowed from the top of the pump. He flipped the switch and the machine went to work. The hose inflated in his hand, becoming nice and fat with fuel.

Oliver flicked a glance at the lone mercenary standing on The Father's platform behind Jocelyn. He held his AK-47 loosely, his flat eyes lazily sweeping the pit. Worry tightened Oliver's gut. Sweat pooled at the base of his spine. The man was too close to Jocelyn.

She sent him an almost imperceptible nod—there it was again, that overwhelming faith in him. She'd never once wavered in her belief that redemption wasn't beyond his grasp. And now, he believed it too. Enough to know there was nothing he wouldn't do for her, nothing he wouldn't sacrifice for her and the children cruelly strung up in front of him.

He reached for the valve on the hose's nozzle. Making sure to take his sweet time so there was no mistake that he was complying with The Father's orders, he deliberately aimed the hose at the children. Their collective whimpers and sobs ate at him.

Hang in there, kiddos. Just a few more minutes.

A flicker of movement caught his eye from the crest of the hill behind The Father. A flash of an arrow's tip. The Tom Puon had circled back through the cave and arrived at the mine from the opposite direction.

Pheakdei shuffled into view from one of the camp's outbuildings, carrying The Father's tea on a serving tray. Oliver was glad to see him alive and unharmed. Hopefully he could count on the old man as an ally.

"Get on with it," The Father snarled. "We're losing the light."

Oliver bared his teeth. "Yes, sir."

In one swift move, he swung the hose toward the line of mercenaries and spun the valve. Gasoline shot from the high-pressure hose. The mercenaries flailed. The sharp retort of their guns split the air, flash igniting the fuel. Flames burst to life. The men staggered around, their shrieks and screams rising about the roar of the fire.

Oliver jerked the valve closed and dropped the hose. Bright orange flames slithered against the ground, licking the trail of fuel back to the truck like a fast and furious snake bent on destroying everything in its path.

The heat hit him full in the face, robbing him of breath. He leapt off the truck. Before his feet had completely cleared the bed, the vehicle exploded. Something hot and sharp embedded itself in his leg. Agony shot through him. He hit the ground and rolled. His hands flailed for purchase in the dirt, but he couldn't catch himself. Couldn't stop his momentum. He careened into a hole. The jolt knocked the breath out of him.

From somewhere above, twenty children began screaming at the top of their lungs.

THE FORCE OF the explosion rocked beneath Pheakdei's feet.

He stumbled on the top step of the platform and wrenched around, barely managing to right himself in time to rescue the mug of steaming tea. Screams rang in his ears. The American sailed through the air and came down hard, rolling into one of the mining shafts.

Pheakdei felt the impact jar his stomach every bit as if he'd been the one to go plowing into the unforgiving crater of dirt.

Jude jumped to his feet in a blur of white linen. "Get out of my way."

The growled words snapped something inside Pheakdei, something fierce and burning. He couldn't control it. No—he didn't *want* to control it. He welcomed the fire, turning the fear that had consumed him for years to dust and leaving behind only an aching desire to do the right thing.

Here. Now. When it mattered most.

Well, there are some things a man just can't run away from.

He let John Wayne's famous line from the movie *Stagecoach* whisper in his head. Who said only Americans could be cowboys? He licked the bead of sweat from his lip, snatched the mug, clenching it tightly, and tossed the steaming contents onto Jude.

Jude clawed at his face and stumbled backward, raking his nails down his scarred cheek. "No! Get it off. Get it off of me!"

His guttural scream prickled up Pheakdei's spine. He shuddered and out of the corner of his eye caught sight of the mercenary standing behind the woman, his finger poised over the trigger.

Rage tore from Pheakdei's lips. He swung the tray in his hand at the man with all of his strength. The crude weapon found its target, striking the mercenary full in the face with a satisfying crunch.

He hadn't expected to disarm the man, but blood poured forth from his nose and he pinwheeled, loosening his grip on the gun. Pheakdei yanked it out of the man's grasp and pushed him, sending him crashing through the flimsy platform railing and tumbling the few feet to the ground below.

Pheakdei bent and gasped for breath. Six Khmer men suddenly spilled over the hill. They bellowed out a high-pitched war cry, bows and arrows raised. Pheakdei fumbled to get the gun in position, but the men split off and darted past, heading for the children. He slumped in relief.

Flames shot into the air. Stray sparks lit the sky in

an arc that landed on Jude's blue umbrella. The fabric sizzled and started on fire. Embers floated down and landed on Jude. He fell to the ground, writhing and screeching, still raking at his body as if some phantom blaze engulfed him.

The woman inched forward on her belly, making her way to the edge of the platform despite the bindings on her hands and feet. By sheer willpower, she tumbled down the stairs. Pheakdei leapt after her, tearing the knife at his belt out of its sheath.

He slashed the rope and pressed the blade into her free hands. "Go. Help the children. I cover you."

JOCELYN FLEXED HER fingers around the hilt of the knife. Her heart swelled. Pheakdei had come through for them, every time they'd needed him. "Pheakdei, I—" she wanted to tell him how much his help meant, but words seemed so inadequate.

He waved her off. "Go. Now."

She swallowed. "Thank you."

Kiri and Bora were already working to hack through one end of the pulley ropes. She raced over to them and took up the task at the other end, sawing at the threads with a shaky hand. The smell of charred flesh permeated the air. The truck continued to burn, belching black smoke into the purple sky. The children's cries drowned out the roaring of the fire. Her face grew warm. Sweat poured off her forehead and she tasted salt on her lips.

The rope started to fray. She slashed at it harder, the rhythm of her movements snagging to a stop when the pop of a gunshot burst into the air. She whipped her head around. Pheakdei crumpled to the ground.

"Pheakdei!"

The Father stood in the center of the platform, smoking pistol in his hand. His hat lay by his feet. With nothing to shield his eyes, the wild, piercing madness of his stare bored into her. He took one deliberate step. Then another. He kept on coming. Arrows went flying from Sotha and Sann's bows. The Father stopped and swayed. Blood bloomed on his sleeve.

Hurry.

She sliced at the last strings of the rope. Kiri and Bora's side snapped first, and with one last frantic cut, hers followed. The children fell to their knees. Some rested their hands on their thighs, exposing raw, pink skin. She swallowed the cry that rose in her throat.

There would be plenty of time for sympathy later.

"Come on! Get up!" The boys and girls looked at her with blank stares. "We've got to get you out of here!"

She lifted one of the smaller girls and pressed her into Bora's wide arms. "Take them. All of you. Take them and go."

Pheakdei staggered over to her. Blood seeped from his shoulder. His ashen face twisted into a grimace.

She reached out to steady him. "I can't make them understand. Go with them. Get everyone out of here."

"I—can't. Need to help you—"

"You've done enough. Help the children now." She flicked a glance at The Father. He had shrugged off his daze and thumped down the remaining stairs. She shook Pheakdei. "Go. Keep them safe. Please."

He snapped off a nod and spoke in rapid fire Khmer to the children. They scrambled to their feet. The Tom Puon circled the boys and girls like a human shield, and as one they ran for the safety of the cave.

Jocelyn waited until they'd disappeared inside then spun toward the fire.

Oliver.

He should've joined her by now. Where was he? He'd made it off the truck. She'd watched him fall. And then—

She didn't know. She'd lost sight of him while cutting the children free.

The wind changed direction and sent a cloud of black smoke into her face. "Oliver?"

"You are all guilty of betrayal!" The Father's feral roar hit the air half a second before another shot rang out.

She dropped to the ground. Crawled forward on her stomach. The smoke obscured her vision and stuck in her throat. She coughed. Her palm slipped in the dirt. A hand clamped over her wrist.

She screamed.

"Josie." Oliver's voice.

The wind picked up again, whipping the smoke back in the other direction. The last tendrils dissipated and she saw him, attempting to scale the side of a freshly dug mining hole.

"Here." She reached for his hand and dug her boots into the dirt for leverage.

He tightened his grip, hoisted himself out, giving her a good look at the mix of blood and mud that saturated his left pant leg.

"You're hurt." She reached for him.

"Vengeance is mine and mine alone!" More gunfire peppered The Father's tirade. "You will pay for all that you have destroyed!"

Oliver grabbed her hand and pulled her into a crouch. "Run!"

She barely had time to gain her footing before Oliver dashed over the uneven ground. Her sweaty hand slipped out of his and she fell to her knees behind a large metal cart with rusted wheels, used to haul dirt from the pit. Bullets pinged off the side.

She huddled closer to Oliver and tried to draw a breath around the furious pounding of her heart. "Your. Leg."

"Shrapnel. From the truck." Black soot streaked his face. His close brush with the fire had singed part of his eyebrows. A bead of perspiration ran down his nose. He leaned over to take her face in his hands. "I want you to get out of here. I'll create a diversion. Run straight for the bastard if I have to—"

"What?" She gripped his hands and felt the rapid throb of his pulse. "No way. That's insane. You'll die."

His eyes glittered. "Not until I make sure he'll never hurt anyone ever again."

"Oh, Miss Hewitt? Come out, come out wherever you are!"

She flinched. The Father sounded so close. Too close. How could Oliver ever hope to get the upper hand?

"You can't do this alone." There had to be another way.

"I have to. No arguments." He splayed his fingers across her mouth, ensuring she would be forced to comply. "I want you out of here. Unharmed. Alive."

"What about you?"

"I'll be right behind you." He let up on her mouth. "Give me the knife."

She placed it in his palm, gripped his fingers. "Don't do this. Don't sacrifice yourself for—"

Curling his free hand around her neck, he jerked her close, cutting off her breath and her words. He kissed her and she felt the hum of ruthless determination in the crush of his lips before he turned and buried his face in her hair. He shuddered and held her for a long, beautiful moment.

She didn't want to let go.

Burnt oil filled her nose as the breeze picked up once again and swirled thick, dark smoke back over them. She gagged on the acrid taste and tried to cling to him.

He set her away from him. "Go. Use the smoke as cover. Don't stop until you get far away from here."

She had no intention of leaving him to fight the sadistic bastard alone, but arguing with him would waste precious seconds. Working into a tight crouch, she crept to the edge of the cart and peeked around the corner. The smoke made visibility next to nothing. If she couldn't see The Father, did that mean that he couldn't see her either?

God, she hoped so. His last rant had come from the left. As long as she kept to the far right and followed the edge of the pit, hopefully she could avoid him. She plunged into the curtain of smoke. Her eyes started to sting and her throat burned, but she ignored the discomfort and ran like hell for the edge of the pit.

She heard the unmistakable cry of a child. Coming from the left.

She froze.

No. Keep going. You're hearing things.

The wail rose to a crescendo.

No she wasn't. There was a child out there. Alone. And he or she was about to walk right into The Father's clutches.

She changed directions.

OLIVER GAVE JOCELYN a second's worth of a head start, then he tore off from the opposite side of the cart, hoping to lure The Father's attention.

He waved away a pocket of black smoke, ignoring the way the smoldering tendrils clung to his nostrils and coiled in his throat. If he could get a bead on The Father's location, he could get behind him and—

"Oliver's dead."

Jocelyn's shout brought him up short.

What the hell was she trying to pull?

"You'll forgive me if I don't take your word for it."

The smoke thinned, revealing The Father, the pristine white of his clothes now marred with dark streaks of soot. With his back to Oliver, he squared off with Jocelyn, angling his body just enough to reveal the boy clutched in his grip.

"It's true. The explosion killed him. He—he's gone."

"Prove it." The barrel of a pistol flashed, just a glint. The Father's aim wavered between Jocelyn and the boy. "Bring me Shaw's body and I'll spare the boy."

Jocelyn raised her hands, palms out. Her tremors wrung Oliver's heart. He crept closer, trying to keep his focus on The Father. If he looked at Jocelyn—worried about her—he'd falter. He had one shot at taking The Father by surprise. He couldn't blow it.

He fixed his attention on the back of The Father's head, but then Jocelyn spoke again, and Oliver couldn't stop himself from glancing at her.

"Why not let the boy go right now?" Her gaze shifted to Oliver for the barest of fractions, just long enough to impart a silent message, then focused back on The Father. "He's of no use to you. The others—they're long gone. Soon everyone will know what The Trinity has done. You're finished here. You're selfish and evil, Jude. Just like your father."

Christ.

Oliver flinched and lost his grip on the knife. He

fumbled for the hilt before it hit the ground. His clammy fingers met warm metal and gripped the weapon once more.

She'd just gone and painted a bull's-eye on her chest. Now The Father would have no choice but to rise to the challenge.

"Don't ever mention the Reverend to me!" The Father's body vibrated with rage. He drew the boy against his chest. The pistol wavered before he brought it back under control and aimed it dead center at Jocelyn. "That man was a—a—fraud—a hypocrite, following God's Word on Sunday and shedding His teachings as soon as the sun rose Monday morning. I am nothing like him!"

"You killed my dad, didn't you? He tried to show you how to be an honorable man, but you turned against him—"

"Honor?" The Father threw back his head and barked out a laugh. "He was no better than the Reverend. Spewing meaningless words about kindness and principles while fucking my mother behind my father's back."

Oliver watched Jocelyn flinch as if slapped.

Stay calm, Shaw. Keep a clear head. Creep up slowly. Wait for the right opening.

"You know that's not true," she said, her voice breaking. "There was nothing between them. My dad loved my mother until the day he—until you—you killed him."

The Father spat. "If it weren't for the sanctimonious Donald Hewitt, she would still be alive."

"You loved her very much, didn't you?" She shifted closer, ever so slightly, but the movement was enough to tell Oliver he had to make his move now, before she tried to rescue the child herself.

"She—she was everything." The Father keened low and Oliver used the distraction to creep up behind him.

He caught Jocelyn's eye. *Keep him talking.*

She bit her lip, gave him an almost imperceptible nod. "How did you kill my dad? Did you burn him? Is that where you got the scars? You get too close to the fire?" She took another step. "You like fire, don't you?"

The Father covered his ravaged cheek with his hand and reeled back a step, losing his grip on the boy. "I—" He broke off, his gaze widening on Oliver. "What the hell—"

Shit. This was as close as he was going to get.

He lunged, closing the gap by sheer willpower. The Father raised his pistol and squeezed the trigger.

Jocelyn dove in front of the boy and knocked him to the ground. "No! Don't!"

Oliver grabbed The Father's arm and wrenched it upward, trying to deflect the shot.

The report of a bullet rang into the air.

Jocelyn cried out. Her body jerked and crumpled to the ground.

"God, no!" A strangled howl burst past Oliver's lips. *Josie was hit. Where? How bad?*

Fear and anger shot through his veins. Consuming him. Strengthening him. He wrapped his arm around The Father's throat and yanked the man to the ground. They tumbled over each other. He came out the loser, landing flat on his back with the bulk of The Father's weight on top of him, crushing him.

"End of the line, Shaw."

The butt of the pistol slammed into Oliver's temple. Stars swam in front of his vision. He parted his lips to tell The Father to go to hell, but the words wouldn't come.

He tamped down the nausea, blinked away the fuzz.

The Father's face loomed above, patches of twisted red flesh visible beneath the dirt and sweat that tracked his skin. He bared his teeth and his eyes glittered amber. "Pity I can't continue to let you paint for me, but I do believe Miss Hewitt has well and truly ruined you."

He jammed the pistol beneath Oliver's chin.

Oliver laughed. It started low in his gut and vibrated into his chest, surprising The Father into relaxing the pressure of the pistol. *No, Jocelyn hadn't ruined him. She'd released him.*

He skimmed his right hand across the dirt until the tips of his fingers connected with the knife he'd dropped in the scuffle. Pulling the hilt into his palm, he steadied the weapon in his tight grip. "Time to say your prayers, Jude."

With one swift move, Oliver brought the blade up, embedding it in The Father's neck. Sinew parted with the twist of the knife. Blood spewed, running down The Father's white shirt.

Oliver ignored the metallic taste of bile and shoved The Father off him. He crawled to his feet, turned in search of Jocelyn and found her sitting in a patch of grass, legs sprawled out in front of her to make room for the boy she'd wrapped in her embrace. The kid had buried his face in her chest. Her cheek rested atop his shaved head, blood soaked her thigh. Her eyes, though murky with pain, were fixed on Oliver.

He gave one last glance at The Father. Vacant, golden eyes stared back at him. Shouldn't he feel something other than cold numbness? He searched for more but felt nothing. Not remorse, nor satisfaction, nor anger for the power he'd given this man over his life for the better part of two years.

It's over.

Those two simple words filled his head in a restless chant.

It's over.

He hurried to Jocelyn and dropped to his knees. Thank God she was okay. But the blood…so much blood. His hands wouldn't stop shaking as he yanked at his shirt, tearing the fabric from his body.

"Damn it, that bastard shot you." He couldn't ease the burn that came from stating the obvious.

She wasn't supposed to get hurt. She should've been with the others by now, on her way to safety. He ripped at the leg of her pants, slitting the thin material up the middle and parting the fabric.

She hissed.

He stilled.

Her hand covered his and squeezed. "I'm okay."

He nodded, but didn't trust himself to speak. The bullet had gone clean through the fleshy part of her thigh, missing muscle, bone and major arteries by mere centimeters. A spasm of relief leapt to life in his jaw. Moisture stung his eyes. He cleared his throat and snatched up his tattered shirt, winding it around her thigh and tying it off tight to slow the bleeding.

She touched his cheek. "You did it. Because of you, all these children have a second chance at life."

He turned his head, blinking hard. "I just did what was right."

"I know."

Yes, she'd believed in the honor and goodness inside him even when he'd thought it gone. He leaned forward, seeking the kiss he knew would be waiting for him, but before he could claim it, the young boy in her arms squirmed to life and bolted away from her.

He pointed into the smoky sky and began to shout.

"What is he saying?" Jocelyn moved to stand.

He caught her arm, helping her to her feet. "Bird?" He frowned. "I think he's saying…bird…"

Bird. What the hell did that mean?

And then he heard it. The distinct thump-thump-thump of chopper blades slicing the air.

Jocelyn registered the sound at the same time as he. "Helicopter!"

The Huey soared into his line of sight, the sun catching the U.S. Army emblem on its tail.

"Come on, we've got to get to higher ground."

He grabbed the boy and settled him against his shoulder. They hobbled out of the pit, hurrying up the slope. The shrapnel lodged in his leg shot fire into his shin, but he disregarded the pain, squinting up into the sky so he didn't lose sight of the helicopter.

The chopper rose above the distant trees, but the direction was all wrong. If the pilot continued, he'd bypass them.

"No! Come back! Over here!" Jocelyn threw up her hands and waved, scrambling to the peak of the hill despite her injured leg. "Please! Look this way!"

He joined her. "We're here! Over here!"

The helicopter didn't change its course. His heart sank. The pilot hadn't seen them. In a minute, the chopper would be out of sight.

He filled his lungs, determined to give it one last try, and got a mouthful of pungent air. The wind picked up, shifting the last of the dark smoke over them. The helicopter dipped behind the trees.

So, that was it then. More trekking through the jungle in their future. He glanced at Jocelyn. Sweat coated her pale face. Blood had started to seep past the makeshift tourniquet. She wouldn't make it much farther. No matter how much she would insist otherwise.

Suddenly the copter rose out of the trees again. It banked in the air, and veered left. Turning around. Heading straight for them. Tendrils of dirt and smoke whipped around. He pressed the boy's face into his chest to shield him as the helicopter drew near, pelting their bodies with the backlash of the rotors churning the air.

The U.S. Army helicopter set down several yards in front of them. A soldier in fatigues rushed out of the plane and met them halfway.

"Are you Jocelyn Hewitt?"

She grinned at the man, her smile lighting up her dirt-streaked face. "Yes, I am."

The soldier matched her grin. "Commander Norris will sure be glad to hear that." He held out his hand. "Oliver Shaw? We got your message, Sir. Some high-level spooks are dying to talk to you."

Oliver shook hands with the man and followed his lead to the open bay of the helicopter. Jocelyn stopped the soldier before he could help her inside. "There's seven men and about twenty children hiking through the jungle west of here. We need to find them and call in reinforcements to get them out of here."

The man's smile faded. "I have express orders to get you back to Siem Riep on the double—"

"I'm not leaving without them."

Oliver raised his brows at her steely tone. "If I were you, I'd do what she says."

The soldier stiffened. "I take it I shouldn't tangle with her then?"

"Not if you know what's good for you."

"Get in the chopper. I'll radio in and let them know

we'll be delayed." He tapped two quick fingers to his temple and scrambled inside the cockpit.

Oliver helped Jocelyn into the helicopter, handed her the boy and climbed in beside her.

She leaned her cheek on his shoulder. "What do you say? Ready to go home?"

"Yeah."

He was more than ready to leave Cambodia behind for good.

TWENTY

It was supposed to have been nothing more than a simple dinner. They both had to eat, it made sense they would do so together, especially on their last night in Cambodia. But, as Oliver sat across the table from Jocelyn, the night tied him into knots.

With its graceful arches, subtle touches of pale yellow and burgundy, and muted lanterns strategically scattered around the tables, the hotel's open-air restaurant invited intimacy. Not the desperate kind, where basic survival stripped inhibitions and forced connections based on mutual dependence. No, this was different. This was…subtle.

A look, a touch, soft conversation.

Ceiling fans stirred the warm breeze overhead, lightly, like a lover's caress. A small pond rippled beside their table. He tore his gaze from a bright purple flower spinning in the water and looked at Jocelyn.

Candlelight flickered across her solemn face in a glow that glinted off her shiny dark hair and sparked in her hazel eyes. She wore a traditional wrap dress that wound around her in a colorful floral print and left her shoulders bare. It was a far cry from the tattered, shapeless fabrics she'd worn in the jungle. But, then again, Siem Riep seemed like a different world, so full of traffic and tourists and laughter.

And a whole new, beautiful, unattainable Josie.

Oliver swallowed, meeting resistance in the form of

a hard dry lump in his throat. He reached for his water. His fingers fumbled the small stem and knocked over the glass.

He jerked his napkin off his lap and tossed it on the growing puddle. "Shit."

"You look like a different person. Without the beard, the long hair." Jocelyn's hesitant voice immobilized his frantic attempts to sop up the mess.

He ran a hand over his cropped hair, scrubbed his palm over his crisp, new jeans. Three days ago when the helicopter had touched down in Siem Riep he hadn't wanted any reminders of the jungle and he'd went about shedding them as quickly as he could.

New clothes, new haircut.

He raised his eyes to Jocelyn's. "It's still me."

She slid her hand over his. "I know."

But even as he said it, he wasn't so sure.

He'd spent the last few days sequestered with the man he'd once called both boss and friend, undergoing a thorough debriefing. He'd recounted the events of the past two years over and over with a bittersweet ache in his heart until the CIA was satisfied they'd pried every minute detail from him.

And when it was done, he'd suddenly realized he didn't know who he was anymore. Surely not CIA agent. Not soldier, nor captive. Not artist. He'd ceased to exist in the normal world a long time ago and now he had to find a way to survive the life he was left with.

He blinked Jocelyn's hand back into focus, feeling awkward, out of his element, without a clue as to how to sit at a nice restaurant and eat a real meal or have a real conversation. Her mouth turned up into a reassuring smile, and he couldn't keep his gaze away from her lips. If he got through this dinner, would she reward him with a kiss when he walked her to her room? Or would she shy away from him now that they were out of the jungle?

He cleared his throat. "How's your leg?"

"Fine. Sore, but I know I got lucky. It could've been much worse." She tilted her head, squeezed his hand gently before returning her own to her lap. "You?"

"The same."

She nodded. "Well. That's good."

They'd had no time to talk once the hospital had treated and released them. She'd had her superiors at JPAC to contend with and children to worry over while they searched for their families. Tomorrow morning he and Jocelyn would hitch a ride on a military transport back to the States. After a brief stop in Langley, Virginia, he'd head to California. By that time, Jocelyn would be in Hawaii—an ocean away.

His stomach rolled. Screw it, he was no longer hungry. He couldn't sit through an entire meal making small talk, pretending they were a normal couple out for a romantic dinner. They'd shared far too many raw and honest moments for that.

Jocelyn deserved candlelit dates, holding hands in the moonlight, sweet seduction…all the things he didn't know how to give her. Not anymore. And, yeah, maybe there was a part of him that was too much of a coward to try. He wasn't ready. Didn't know if he could ever be ready.

Oliver pushed his chair back. "I'm sorry. I—I can't do this."

Once again, the simple touch of her hand stilled him. "What do you say we get out of here?"

He dug a wad of riel out of his pocket and tossed

the banknotes on the table. "That's the best offer I've had in days."

More lanterns dotted the cobblestone path that led around the waterfall pool and back to the guest rooms. Jocelyn's hand slipped inside his, and he tugged her closer, their hips brushing as they walked.

He didn't attempt to fill the comfortable silence with words. All too soon they were standing in front of her door and he was left with one of two choices—ask her to invite him in or say good-night. But saying good-night was the equivalent of saying goodbye and he wasn't ready for that.

She leaned back against the door. "This must all feel so very strange to you."

"Awkward." He fingered a lock of her hair, tucking it behind her ear. "I don't remember the rules."

Her brow wrinkled. "What rules?"

"Like how to let you know that I want to kiss you—"

She launched herself at him. He wrapped his arms around her, finding her inviting mouth. Her lips parted and he slipped his tongue inside, letting the honeyed taste of her sweep him away.

The kiss turned hungry. Desperate. God, he couldn't get enough of her. Arousal thickened his blood and turned him hard as a rock. Need buzzed in his ears doing its best to impair his judgment. He pressed against her, ran his palms down her back. The sleek fabric of her dress provided only a thin barrier between his hand and the warmth of her bare skin. He wanted to touch every inch of her, to lick and taste at will, to memorize the way she smelled, that unique cross between cherry blossoms and pomegranates.

He kissed a trail down her neck, nipped at her shoulder.

She threw her head back. "Come inside."

Her whispered command brought him back to his senses. He closed his eyes briefly then lifted his head to meet her gaze. "Are you sure?"

Instead of answering him, she pressed her key into his hand.

He opened the door and followed her in. A small light burned in the corner of the room, casting warmth over the rich chestnut plank floor and spilling its muted glow over the bed's mosquito netting.

Jocelyn reached for the light to chase the rest of the shadows from the room.

He let the door fall closed. "Leave it."

"Why?" She came to him and slid her hands up his chest.

His muscles jumped under her touch. He caught her hands and brought them to his mouth, saying nothing.

"What's wrong?"

"I…" How could he admit the root of his discomfort? Two years of torture and a steady diet of rice and vegetables had not kept his body in top form. He couldn't bear the thought of disappointing her.

Instead of telling her any of that, he placed a soft kiss on her mouth. He let his hands drift to her waist where he found the clasp that held her dress in place. Inch by agonizing inch he unwrapped her, taking his sweet time.

She was the most beautiful present he'd ever been offered and he wanted to savor her.

The fabric fell from his fingers. Oh, Lord, she wasn't wearing anything beneath the dress.

"Damn, you're perfect." He reached out and ran a knuckle over her breast. Her nipple pebbled under his touch.

"Oliver…" She shivered. Her eyes drifted closed and

the tender smile that tilted the corners of her lips sent something sweet and profound filling him.

He tried to clear it, but the sensation just moved upward, prickling in his eyes.

"Kiss me," she commanded.

He smiled.

She didn't have to ask twice.

JOCELYN'S FINGERS TANGLED in the buttons of his shirt. It wasn't fair that Oliver should be the only one allowed to touch. He ramped up their kiss, drawing her tongue into his mouth, robbing her of the ability to think. By sheer instinct, she managed to get his shirt off him.

Still kissing her, he caught her at the knees, carried her to the bed and laid her down beneath the canopy of mosquito netting. His warm, solid weight followed. He smelled of woodsy soap and she took a moment to just inhale before reaching out to run her hands over his chest. She slipped her palms around his back. Her fingers found the crisscross of scars there.

He flinched and broke the kiss, resting his forehead against hers. "Don't."

She forced him to look her in the eyes. "Your scars are not a turnoff to me. Your body is not a weakness. You are…beautiful. In every way. And I—I'm desperate to touch you—all of you. I want to feel you against me, inside of me—"

"Josie." He pressed his mouth to hers in swift, hard possession. "You make a believer out of me. How do you do that?"

The swell of his erection pressed against her thigh. He trailed kisses down her neck to the hollow of her throat where he opened his mouth on her, his tongue swirling against her flesh, then detouring down to her breasts. She cried out, tangling her hands in his hair, rocking against his hard length.

Without taking his mouth from her, he unsnapped his jeans. She helped pushed them down his legs and he kicked them free. The first touch of skin on skin had her sucking in a ragged breath. Oliver's hand trailed down between her breasts and continued lower, stopping just short of his target. She arched off the bed.

He lifted his head and stared into her eyes, his face tense. Rigid.

She ran a finger along his jaw. "So serious." She'd hoped to tease a smile out of him, but if anything he just grew more solemn, his eyes darkening.

"I want this to be good for you." He kissed her temple, her eyes, her mouth.

She swallowed back a groan. "Oliver, please…"

"Please, what?" Now one corner of his mouth hitched, so slight she would've missed it if she hadn't been focusing so intently on him.

She threaded her fingers through his hair. "Touch me."

He inched his hand down, his fingers barely grazing her. "Like this?"

"Yes." She parted her thighs further, throbbing with need. "More."

"How about this?" He fondled her, teasing every sensitive inch.

Her stomach quivered. Heat pooled through her. "Yes, God, yes."

She reached down and grabbed his wrist, trying to urge him to go faster. He rewarded her by slipping a finger inside her, plying her with slow, deliberate strokes and increasing the torture by adding another finger.

Jocelyn writhed beneath him, no longer content with

the gentle seduction. She wanted him now, hard, urgent, no holds barred. To make sure he understood, she brushed her hand against his erection, but when she went to wrap her fingers around his full length, he pushed her hand away.

He growled in her ear. "We're not doing that again." He rolled away from her. "Not this time."

She was lost without his warmth. "What—?"

He leapt off the bed and retrieved his pants from the floor, fishing around in the pocket. He yanked out a condom.

She smiled. "You knew we'd end up here tonight."

"I'd hoped." The confession was said with such sincerity, her heart turned inside out.

He joined her on the bed, so perfectly attuned to her that he leaned down and kissed away the wetness at the corners of her eyes.

She reached for him. "Hurry."

He tore the condom package open with his teeth and quickly sheathed himself. She welcomed his weight as he covered her with his body, nudged her thighs apart and drove inside. Clutching at his shoulders, she echoed his rhythm, arching against him. She soared higher and higher. As she erupted, he took her mouth, swallowing her cries and moans, letting her ride the wave of her climax until she started to come back down to earth.

She wound her arms around him, clutching him closer. He slowly pulled out, teasing her at her center for half a second before thrusting back into her. He repeated the movement, rough, then gentle, fast then slow.

She raked her hands down his back. "Oliver, oh, God, Oliver."

He gritted his teeth. A muscle leapt in his jaw, as if

he was trying to hold back his pleasure. But then, his face relaxed and he lost the battle.

"Josie, sweet, Josie." The endearment burst from him in a raw shout. He climaxed, clasping her to him. Shudders wracked his body so intensely they sent her right over the edge again.

He cupped her face in his hands and captured her lips in a tender kiss, before pulling out of her and slipping from the bed. The meeting of mouths, and the mingling of breath was a hello, not a goodbye.

She only hoped he would still feel that way when she told him she wouldn't be getting on that plane with him tomorrow.

THE BREEZE AWOKE Oliver, and he opened his eyes to find the first stirrings of dawn streaking into the room.

He touched the cool sheets beside him. The bed was empty.

Turning his head toward the open French doors he caught sight of Jocelyn standing on the balcony, her back to him, wrapped in a white robe that hit her mid-thigh. He swung out of bed, found his pants and threw them on before joining her. She turned at the sound of his approach. The sad tilt of her hazel eyes hit him square in the gut.

She'd changed her mind. About him. About them.

He shoved his hands in his pockets to keep from reaching for her. "Josie?"

She leaned into the railing, looked away. "I'm staying in Cambodia."

He frowned. "What? Did they put you on a different flight? Why would they—"

"No. Nothing like that. I…I just can't go home yet." She bit her lip. He could see her weighing her words.

"My friends—they died for me. Out there in the jungle. I'm the only one who knows where. Their families deserve answers. They deserve to be able to bury their loved ones. I can't deny them that."

"So draw a map." The curt words spewed out of his mouth. "Send someone else."

God, you're such a selfish bastard, Shaw.

He couldn't help it. Panic clawed through him. He needed her on that plane with him. This couldn't be the end. Not after last night.

She came to him and laid her palm against his cheek. "It's got to be me."

He stepped back. "You may not find them. After, what, forty-five days—"

"I know." She curled her arms across her body. "But I've got to try."

She did. He didn't want to admit it, but he knew. Her dedication was one of the things he admired most about her. Without it, she wouldn't be the woman he loved. But knowing she needed to stay didn't make it any easier.

He swallowed. "For how long?"

One shoulder lifted. "As long as it takes. I…was kinda hoping…you'd agree to stay with me."

"Here?" Was she crazy? "In Cambodia?"

"Last night was more than just sex. We both know it. But my emotions are all jumbled up." She ran a finger over his chest. "We need time to just be us."

He stilled her hand. "We could do that in California. Or, hell, even in Hawaii. You pick. I don't give a shit as long as it's somewhere on American soil."

"I'm needed here. Not only for my friends, but for the children as well. I can't leave without knowing they've been reunited with their families. I made a promise to them." She looked at him with those huge eyes that never failed to set him on fire. "Please, Oliver. Say you'll stay."

He wanted to say yes. He wanted to tell her nothing mattered more than being with her. But the words stuck in his throat. "You don't know what you're asking of me. If I never step foot in that jungle again, it will be too soon. Every leaf and tree and ruin is a reminder of the darkest days of my life."

She tilted her head. "They're a reminder of some of the brightest days of mine. Tragedy does not wipe out beauty. That's what I found in the jungle. That's what I found in you."

He squeezed his eyes shut. Could he really find a way to look at the jungle through her eyes? He let the whispers of the rainforest roll over him. The dampness, the noise, the pungent odor of leaves triggered memories that squeezed at his throat, suffocating him. "I need to go home," he choked out. "Where I can breathe again."

"Yes. You deserve that." Her mouth trembled and he reached for her, determined to assuage the hurt however he could, but her next words stopped him cold. "But don't just go home to your empty beach house and shut yourself away from the world, convinced that's all you need out of life because that's not living, Oliver. That's surviving."

He dropped his arms back to his sides. "I don't see the difference."

She bowed her head, fingering the sash on her robe. "Someday, I hope you do."

Someday. It sounded so final. So empty.

Desperation itched inside of his lungs, frantic to get out. "You could teach me."

"Maybe." Her gaze found his. "If you stayed."

And there it was. The line in the sand. She wouldn't come home with him. And he—

"I can't. I'm not ready."

"I know."

His admission had torn his heart out, but her quiet acceptance threw the still beating organ on the ground and stomped on it.

"Josie—"

Somehow she ended up in his arms. He slanted his lips over hers, pouring all of his pain and confusion and dread into one last wretched kiss that he hoped would clear his head and provide him with the solution to their standstill.

But when they came up for air, he was still as lost as ever.

He ran his thumb across her cheek swiping at the tears that leaked from the corners of her eyes. She sent him a wobbly smile.

"Goodbye, Oliver."

She pushed past him and disappeared into the bathroom, leaving him to retrieve his shirt and shoes to the sound of her sobs. He stared at the bed, where he'd spent the most magical night of his life, then he turned and left the room.

His flight home was in less than three hours.

LEANING AGAINST THE side of one of JPAC's Jeeps, Jocelyn squinted against the bright sun glinting off the tarmac and watched Oliver's familiar stride eat up the distance to the C-17 parked on the runway.

She didn't call out to him. And as cowardly as it was, she hoped he wouldn't turn around and find her staring. If she'd had any willpower at all, she wouldn't be here. Nothing good could come of watching him walk out of her life. She had to stay in Cambodia and in order for Oliver to heal he had to leave. It was the only way, but it didn't make it any easier.

He'll come back to you.

God, she wished she were sure of that.

She watched him stop to talk to one of the crew loading supplies into the cargo hold. He swung his duffel bag up on his shoulder. The gesture pulled at his shoulder blades, made her think of the scars across his back hidden by his gray T-shirt. Scars that defined his strength and courage and honor.

You should've told him you loved him.

No, she'd done the right thing. Her words might've swayed him, but they wouldn't have held him.

So you're just going to set him free?

She bit back the desolation. No, she was going to let him set himself free.

He clapped the crewman on the back and headed for the plane. Just steps from boarding, he looked over his shoulder. He swung fully around and his whole body went rigid.

Too late to cut and run. He'd seen her.

She met his eyes over the expanse of runway that separated them. She couldn't see them clearly, he was too far away for that, but they'd be a wash of green, like the jungle after a monsoon.

He lifted his hand and put it over his heart.

She did the same, trying to stop hers from breaking wide open.

But her heart still bled when he disappeared into the belly of the C-17.

TWENTY-ONE

OLIVER SET DOWN his paintbrush and stretched. The muscles in his neck and shoulders burned. His stomach rumbled and his mouth begged for a drink. He glanced around the studio. Sun spilled through the floor to ceiling windows from its position high in the sky.

He'd completely lost track of time. Again. He'd been at this all night.

The smell of oil and turpentine permeated the room, wrapping him in its familiar, comforting scent. Over the past two months he'd found his love of painting again. Amongst his dad's brushes and easels and framed pictures from the pages of Peg Digby, Oliver had buried himself in the world of color and shadow and texture.

Finished canvases sat all around the room. They leaned against every spare inch of the walls, filled the easels, both big and small, all containing a variation on the same theme.

Her.

No matter how many times he painted Jocelyn, he couldn't purge her from his system. He blew out a breath and touched the canvas in front of him. The line of her jaw smudged beneath his fingertip as the wet paint shifted.

He flattened his palm on the canvas and smeared the rest of the painting until it was no longer recognizable. It made no difference. Her face was imprinted on his brain. Her smell still lingered in his memory. The ghost of her touch still slid across his skin hundreds of times a day.

Turning his back on the canvas, he plucked a rag from the nearby table and began rubbing at his hands.

He was content here, damn it.

Who you kidding, Shaw? You miss her. Every minute of every day.

That's why he couldn't stop painting her. He wanted to keep her close. Needed to touch her, even if only on canvas.

Connections.

Jocelyn had been right. They were important.

Since returning home, he'd worked hard to reacquaint himself with his memories of his dad. He'd always believed his dad hadn't paid much attention to him. The man always seemed so wrapped up, immersed in an imaginary world where Oliver couldn't follow, but for the first time he understood that his dad had given him the most important piece of himself. His art. Now, every time he picked up a brush, his dad painted with him.

Connections.

Without them, what was life?

Feeling restless, he left the studio via the balcony, descending the wide steps to the beach. His bare feet sank into the sand, and the salty breeze blew into his face. He continued to the water's edge, letting the frothy tide wash over his toes and dampen the ragged hem of his paint-splattered jeans.

It was just after 6:00 a.m. in Cambodia right now. Jocelyn was probably just waking up, those gorgeous eyes unfocused from sleep, her hair mussed. Maybe she'd been dreaming about him. Instead of hitting the ground running for another day of trudging through the dirt, maybe she was snuggling beneath her sheet, reluctant to let go of that dream.

It's what he did. When he managed to sleep.

He picked up a discarded stick of driftwood and rolled it between his fingers as he looked back at his house. The two-story steel and glass structure dazzled in the sand and sun, a perfect place to live out his days. If occasionally he still jerked awake from a restless sleep with the weight of bars crushing him, well, he just needed more time. That was all. Sooner or later, he'd find his peace.

He squatted and sank the stick into the wet sand, pulling it across the ground like pen to paper. His hand idly moved, blindly sketching with broad, unhurried strokes.

Don't just go home to your empty beach house and shut yourself away from the world, convinced that's all you need out of life because that's not living, Oliver. That's surviving.

Jocelyn's words slashed through him.

She was right. God, she was so right. He was doing exactly what she'd warned him about. Hiding out, believing that surviving was enough. She'd freed him to make a life for himself, and here he was, setting up another prison. Sure, this one was infinitely more comfortable, but it was every bit as lonely and unsatisfying.

His hand stilled. He looked down at the sketch he'd drawn in the sand.

Josie.

Hell, even when he wasn't trying to draw her, he did.

She was his freedom. His everything.

The tide crept up the beach, washing away part of her beautiful face. But that was okay. He didn't need his memories anymore. Not when he could have the real thing.

He stood, chucked the driftwood into the churning waves, and sprinted for the house.

"IT'S TIME." Jocelyn gave the order to the half-dozen crewmembers milling around the excavation site. Her voice cracked on the words. After two months of searching and digging, JPAC was calling them home. "Break down the equipment and load it up in the truck."

They'd done all they could.

She'd found both Claire and Jason's remains. In the eyes of JPAC, the mission had been a success. But not to her. She hated the thought of leaving Matt behind. Maybe she should stay on in Cambodia herself. Keep looking. But if, like she suspected, predators scattered his bones, her chances of ever recovering his remains were slim.

Jocelyn excused herself from the group, passing the tents that housed the geological sieves and ignoring the stack of half-filled crates near the dig site in favor of the shade from the cluster of Moringa trees down by the stream. The breeze blew her hair into her face. She swiped it aside impatiently with a dirt-covered hand and inhaled the scent of damp earth.

She hadn't been wrong about Cambodia. The land possessed a serenity she'd barely begun to appreciate, and every new day she spent in its soil, she knew she'd made the right decision to stay.

Except that she missed Oliver.

Sometimes she'd take a break and his presence would come over her, so strongly it knocked the breath from her. She'd have to stop what she was doing and close her eyes to picture him taking long walks on the beach, clearing his head. Learning how to live again.

God, she hoped he was learning that.

She ached to do more. *You cannot save everyone.* Oliver was right. Sometimes people had to save themselves. He needed to choose what he wanted out of life. And whatever he decided…well, she hoped he was happy.

As for her, knowing Oliver had given her a new appreciation for being alone. Where once she never liked solitude, now she craved time spent walking alone. She could honor her friends with her thoughts. Talk to them, her dad, her mom, and take comfort in her memories. Oliver had given her that gift. His quiet strength had taught her the value of reflection.

Now, if only he were here to share it with her.

She knelt at the stream and trailed her fingers in the tepid water. No, he wouldn't come back to Cambodia. He viewed the land as another enemy.

You could go to him.

Maybe she could. Just a quick visit. To make sure he wasn't holed up in his house, keeping the world at arm's length.

Footsteps thumped behind her.

Jocelyn sighed. Time to return to crating up equipment. "I'm coming."

She swirled her hand through the water one last time and stood.

"Do you have to head back just yet?"

Oh, God. Her heart jumped. She knew that voice.

She braced herself and turned. Oliver leaned against the nearest tree, looking relaxed in a pair of faded jeans and a blue T-shirt that brought out the vibrant green of his eyes. Mud coated the bottoms of his black boots. She blinked. Was she dreaming? Hallucinating? But, no, he was smiling at her—really smiling. The Oliver in her dreams never smiled. He brooded.

She swallowed. "Hey."

"Hey."

She wanted to run to him, fling herself into his arms, but her feet were rooted in place. "I didn't expect to see you here."

He slowly uncrossed his ankles and pushed away from the tree. "That makes two of us. The first day I stepped back into the jungle I bawled like a baby. I'm surprised my guide didn't renege on his promise to bring me here."

Sympathy washed through her. God, how hard that must've been for him.

So say something. Tell him how glad you are to see him.

The words wouldn't come. They hadn't parted on bad terms, but neither had they parted on the best of terms. Where did that leave them? Friends? Lovers? She didn't know and the uncertainty was killing her.

"So." Nice. Any other brilliant words for him? "What are you doing here?"

He closed the gap, lifted a hand, and brushed her cheek. His gaze swept over her face. "I've missed you."

"I—I've missed you too." So much. She fought to swallow. Would the pain in her throat just go away already?

He dropped his hand, tucking it into the pocket of his jeans, leaving her bereft. "Looks like your crew is packing up. A few days more and I'd have missed you. Did you find your friends?"

"Claire and Jason. Not Matt." The admission caused fresh needles of emotion to jab at her.

"I'm sorry, Josie."

She dropped her gaze to her fisted hands. "Yeah, me too. It's been...hard."

He tipped her chin. Forced her to meet his eyes. "I should've been here with you."

"I wanted you to." All the pain she'd felt watching him walk away rushed back into her heart. "I asked and you—"

"Refused. I know."

HE WANTED TO pull her into his arms. Beg her forgiveness.

Oliver reached for Jocelyn's hand, and when she didn't resist his advance, he brushed his thumb over the skin at her wrist.

"Do you have any idea how much I wanted to stay with you?" They weren't the words he'd meant to say, but they came croaking out and he knew they were the right ones. "I wanted nothing more than to glom on to you and never let you go."

"Then why didn't you?"

The hurt in her voice punched him in the gut. "Because I was...broken. Being with you, I felt different, freer. Like you'd put the pieces of me back together. You asked me to stay in Cambodia and I just...splintered. Again." He shoved his hands through his hair and pulled away. How could he make her understand the panic he'd felt? "I realized I wasn't fixed. Not even close. I thought if I went home, I could make myself whole again. But nothing was the same as I'd left it. Nothing felt right."

She came up behind him, laid her hands on his back. The gesture reminded him of their time in solitary confinement, but this time, he didn't want to shy away from her touch. He wanted to drown in it.

"It takes time," she said. "You can't be expected to—"

He smiled. "And there you go again…"

"What? I was just trying—"

"To make everything okay. I know." He turned. Her eyes shone with moisture, bringing out the muted golden-gray hues. He touched her jaw. "That's how you're made. And I love that about you. I love the way you see the good in every situation. The way that you don't let anything get in the way of what you want. I went home and I tried to be like that. I tried to find the good in the fact that I was free. But all I felt was alone. I didn't want to go out. I stayed in my studio and painted."

She fisted her hand in his shirt. "Did you love it?"

"I did." His pulse raced, he leaned his forehead against hers. "I filled every canvas with images of you."

"Oh, Oliver."

He closed his eyes briefly. Here came the hard part. "I'm not the same man I was, Josie. I can't view life like—like it's mine for the taking, anymore. Most days it still feels very much a prison."

"But—"

He pressed a finger to her lips, and nearly abandoned the rest of his speech to devour that sweet mouth. But he had to make her understand. Had to tell her how he felt. "The minute I saw you standing there, the breeze teasing your hair, I felt…like I could fly. Looking at you just now, for the first time in my life, I feel true freedom."

"Love is freedom," she whispered.

He caressed her cheeks with his thumbs. "Love is freedom," he echoed. "Home was a prison. Cambodia was a prison. But you…you're my freedom, Josie."

She wrapped her arms around his neck and tugged him closer. "If you don't kiss me, Oliver—"

He covered her mouth with his, sipping at her lips, letting the feel of her in his arms assault his senses, and little by little, he felt the rest of his darkened soul fall away. He wanted to drown in her forever, but after a while he came up for air, brushed the hair out of her eyes so he could look into her smiling face.

"I'm still learning how to live," he told her. "Some days, I get this feeling, like I'm going to suffocate. But with you—with you—as long as you're by my side I can find my way out again."

She leaned back to look at him. "So…you're staying?"

He shook his head, ignoring the frown that turned down her sexy mouth. "I'm going. Wherever you are. Wherever you want to take me. I'm asking you to be my guide, Josie. My guide for the rest of this life and even into the next, even though I know I'm bound to be a pain in the ass." He brought her hands to his mouth and kissed her knuckles. "But, will you have me?"

Tears sparkled on her lashes. Big, fat, happy ones that teased a wide grin from her mouth. "Yes."

The simple word hit him, more eloquent and more potent than he'd ever expected. He bowed his head and welcomed the sudden sting that filled his eyes.

The touch of her fingers on his jaw grounded him. "I love you, Oliver."

"I love you too. God, Josie. So much."

He spun her around and crushed his mouth to hers, sealing their promises. Branding her. She was his. When the kiss was done, he threaded his fingers through hers, not willing to give up touching her just yet.

"I should get back," she said. "I need to help the crew get all the supplies loaded. You want to help?"

"Just show me what you need me to do."

He threaded his arm around Josie's waist and started the trek back to the base camp.

Life beckoned.

And he was so damn ready to answer the call.

* * * * *